Chronicles from the World of Guilt

By: Chris Durston

Three Ravens Publishing

Chickamauga, Ga USA

Table of Contents

Chronicles from the World of Guilt by Chris Durston

Published by Three Ravens Publishing

threeravenspublishing@gmail.com

P.O. Box 851. Chickamauga, Ga 30707

https://www.threeravenspublishing.com

Credits:

Chronicles from the World of Guilt was written by Chris Durston

Cover art by: Natasha Mackenzie

Icons by: Joshua Somerville-Jacklin

Internal art by: Aaron Hockett

Chronicles from the World of Guilt by: Chris Durston /Three Ravens Publishing – 1st edition, 2022

Trade Paperback ISBN: 978-1-951768-51-5

Dedication

To my daughter, with hope that you grow up in a better world than the one in this book.

Acknowledgements

As ever, I owe the fact that this exists at all to Hannah.

I'm extremely grateful to everyone who read, reviewed, or otherwise supported my first novel, *Each Little Universe*, too - taking the plunge and putting that story out there made me realise (as if I didn't know it already) that this whole writing lark is really what I want to do, so every kind word about *ELU* directly contributed to my ability to get this next volume complete.

I owe some thanks, I think, to French metal band Gojira. I didn't realise until after I'd written a fair bit of what's in this book, but... well, their album 'From Mars to Sirius' features a song named 'Flying Whales' and also has a whale flying around the Earth on the cover, so I imagine there was probably some inspiration there. (Also, several of their albums have been excellent writing music, so *merci* very much.) Plus, there's actually a song called 'The Gift of Guilt' on another album of theirs, 'L'Enfant Sauvage', so... the connection wasn't deliberate but may well not be a total coincidence either!

Oh, and anyone who worked on *Final Fantasy X*, since there's a giant space-whale-ish thing in that game that the people call 'Sin'. A fantastic video essayist by the name of EmceeProphIt did some brilliant analysis of *FFX*'s world, especially around its inhabitants' attitude towards this ever-present apocalypse in the sky, so I recommend checking that out.

My friend Tessa Hastjarjanto, author of *Tales of Lunis Aquaria*, must not go unmentioned, since it was reading her wonderful collection of fairytale stories that made me realise that something like *Chronicles from the World of Guilt* might be possible in the first place. (And then Chris Vandyke went and made a whole biannual anthology out of the lots-of-stories-in-one-world concept, so that proved even more clearly that it was a workable thing!)

Emma Mort Harding deserves a quick shout-out too, since a misunderstanding of the premise of her excellent novella *Moon-Sitting* inspired the story 'My Friend, The Moon' in this book. And 'A Game Not Word Playing' is my shallow imitation of Sarah Parker's extraordinary style of deliberate disregard for the conventions of spelling and punctuation, so thanks to Sarah too.

Every member of the Facebook writing group 'Scribimus', but in particular Emma O'Connell and Ellie Owen, also played a part in the generation of this idea (and were critical in the fact that I kept writing stuff between drafts of *ELU* and therefore didn't lose motivation and all that), so to them: thanks a lot.

To everyone who offered to help with beta reading - Ellen, Issy, J.R., Laura and Sam, Olivia, Craig, Alex, Erin - I am extremely grateful. Not to seem less grateful to the others, but Alex and Erin in particular were a great help making this an overall better book in some big ways. (I was kind of amused, though, to find that in almost all cases where someone had suggested removing something, someone else had said it was one of their favourite bits, so in fact less might have changed than I was expecting!)

Natasha Mackenzie did an astounding job taking what really amounted to a crayon scrawl and a few ramblings from me and turning those into the gorgeous cover that the book now bears. Go to missnatmack.com to see more of her work and perhaps get her to do some for you, because she's brilliant.

Josh Somerville-Jacklin created the fantastic icons you see used as chapter headings throughout this book, and he did so unbelievably quickly. He's a real pro, so if you ever need some art I can highly recommend checking out @mythiccomicsart on Twitter or mythiccomicsandart on Instagram. And Aaron Hockett produced the incredible double-page art spread based on the simple brief: 'space whale, please'. So big thanks are certainly due to those two, as I think their contributions make the whole thing just feel so much more polished and cool.

Scott and the rest of the crew at Three Ravens believed in this book enough to want to publish it, and I'll always be grateful for that. Scott put up with me having generally no clue about the process of taking this from a manuscript to a published book, and answered all my questions with at least as much kindness as they deserved and probably a fair bit more besides.

And finally, thank you for giving this odd book a chance. Every reader means a lot to me as an independent author. If you'd like to make my day, leaving a review on Amazon, Goodreads, or anywhere else is the absolute best way of helping indie writers like me to a) reach more readers and b) feel like we're doing something worth doing.

Introduction

What follows is a collection of short stories, but there is a larger narrative. That narrative amounts to little more than the effects of time and strangeness on a broken planet - but when taken as a whole, this volume chronicles a period of many thousands of years, beginning with the end of the world.

Most of these stories can be read in isolation and enjoyed on their own. Some are longer, some are shorter; some are independent, taking place without much reference to other things happening in the World of Guilt, but many are interconnected in bigger or smaller ways. Some are tales with a small, personal scope; others are more concerned with the state of the planet more widely. Some are stories; some are letters; some are other things.

Oh, and consider this an official declaration that *anyone* is free to write their own stories within this world. It's a big, strange world of which I've filled in only a very small amount, so if you want to create something of your own that uses any of its elements, be my guest. (Please contact me or Three Ravens Publishing for the fine print details.)

Enjoy.

This book contains tales from a broken world. As such, you should expect to find content that may not appeal to all readers. While many of the stories contain glimmers of optimism, hope, and even humour, several feature depictions of surreal fantasy horror that could be disturbing. (Sometimes both in the same story, in fact.)

If you would prefer to be informed of specific potentially upsetting content, please turn to page X [Scott please add page number once you know it!] near the back of the book for a full list of content warnings for each individual piece. These warnings may constitute mild spoilers in some cases (which is why they're at the back), but I hope they will allow you to make an informed decision so you can enjoy the stories that do appeal to you.

Chris Durston

THE ERA OF HUMANITY

In which epoch 'Guilt' is just a word

1 | P a g e

Chris Durston

THE COMING OF GUILT

The Coming is most certainly the single most significant event for humans in many hundreds of years, if not the entire history of modern Homo sapiens.

The first pictures showed something that might have been a plane, a bird, an asteroid, or a bit of dirt on the camera lens: a fuzzy, indeterminate shape just over the horizon. Just a small blur at some unknown distance. A small number of people took it to be a UFO - incontrovertible proof of the existence of life on other worlds - but most imagined it to be nothing at all.

The next day, though, it was closer.

Almost anyone with a high enough vantage point in the northern hemisphere could see it for themselves if they looked out to space as the rotation of the planet brought the thing into their line of sight. It was still small, hard to make out, and even those with telescopes couldn't ascertain with any degree of certainty what it might be. Magnified, it was a hazy blob that kept no fixed shape, perhaps spinning or perhaps shifting, and the flashes of bright light that kept shining from parts of it didn't make examination any easier.

It wasn't long, though, before it was near enough for someone with a good observatory to identify what it was: a whale, a humpbacked leviathan the size of a small moon swimming slowly, effortlessly through the cosmos and travelling - indubitably - towards the Earth. Ahead were three smaller objects, things with reflective surfaces that flew like an advance guard before it.

A range of reactions roared up around the world, disbelief perhaps chief among them. People around the world began to send each other messages in enormous volumes, transmitting words and pictures and ideas in invisible waves that crashed around the planet. They didn't have much time to talk about it, though.

The three things preceding the whale split off as they approached Earth; pictures and videos circulating around the Internet with the force of a horde of stampeding rhinoceros showed them breaking formation to fly off their separate ways. It was hard to tell, but in some pictures the three gleamed discernibly different hues: a red, a blue, and a silver. Information flowed fast and heavy between the technologically prosperous hubs of human civilisation.

On that day, those who were near one of the three most populous hotspots - the places where the transmission and reception of digital information was the most concentrated - could have looked to the sky and seen a red, blue, or silver streak of light growing rapidly larger. A clip from one such person's livestream was viewed over half a billion times within half an hour of being uploaded: the blue sky disappearing rapidly behind a red metal sheen moving too fast to be clearly visible, growing larger than everything until nothing else could be seen, and then the video cut off abruptly. There were recordings of the unearthly booms and the quaking of the earth, and there were pictures from outside the cities: whole landscapes covered by enormous shining plates of steel, entire settlements simply gone underneath the gleaming vistas.

More pictures flooded the airwaves: the blue, silver, and red things descending on places, destroying them entirely, and then climbing up from the ruins and taking off on mile-wide wings. Some unimaginative soul named them: Malice, the red; Calamity, the blue; and Dread, the silver. It didn't matter what their names were, though; the fact was that each of them was a dragon made of gargantuan plates and struts of solid metal, each so large that they were capable of putting an end to cities at a time simply by landing on them.

It took longer than it should have for people to realise that those who were sending the pictures almost invariably became uncontactable shortly afterwards, and longer after that to notice that the three metal dragons continued to descend on places where there was a high level of wireless transmission. The world stopped communicating, but not soon enough.

Once the messages ceased, the three creatures slowed down, as if they knew their job was done. A few of the surviving places started transmitting again - hoping that the dragons had simply done enough, that they had ticked off every act of destruction on their lists - but they were immediately wiped out. The rest of those who were left were either sensible enough not to attempt communication at all or lucky enough to receive something that made it clear to them that they could either switch it all off at that very moment or be crushed under a mass of silver, red, or blue.

When the links that once connected the world were truly and finally broken, the three dragons departed. Those who caught a glimpse of a glittering catastrophe flying overhead felt the breath leave their bodies at the sight of an enormous sparkling skeleton soaring through the air: each creature's head was pointed with jagged jaws, eyes alight with some unearthly flame, and each body was a wide oval with a long tail ending in a diamond fin. Each wing was a splayed fan of long, many-jointed fingers, between which was stretched a skin of sharp-edged, interlocking scales.

Many assumed that the three destroyers had left the planet, but people in three remote parts of the world were astonished to witness a blue, red, or silver demon come screeching from the sky and settle itself down to sleep, becoming a metal mountain in the process.

In the chaos, the whale itself had been almost forgotten, even as it continued on its slow, inexorable path towards the planet, growing ever larger in the sky. When the dragons were gone, though, all thoughts turned to the much larger thing that came behind them. Though the disparate pockets of humanity that remained could no longer speak to each other from a distance, the name 'Guilt' spread throughout the largest network of nearby settlements that remained: Guilt, they thought, was the memory of what humanity had done wrong, and the whale hardly seemed as if it could be anything other than the embodiment of their failures, come to balance the scales.

Guilt found a path around the Earth, a cosmic current through which it could lazily travel. It swam miles above the surface of the planet, orbiting effortlessly; it cast a shadow the size of a small country that passed slowly around the world below. That which the Shadow of Guilt shrouded in darkness was *changed*. The things that humans had made began to lose the shapes they had been given, whether by crumbling or by warping; the living things that fell under the Shadow found their bodies or their minds shifting; new creatures sprang up from the darkness and walked the Earth. The things spawned from the Shadow, and seemingly formed from nothing but the will of the whale, were called the Children of Guilt by some; they named the three dragons the First Children of Guilt.

This is the chronicle of the world overseen by Guilt, inhabited by its Children and those left from the human world that came before.

Chris Durston

THE FIRST ERA OF GUILT

In which epoch Guilt is a thing most new and peculiar

Chris Durston

CHILDREN

What more could there be to say on the topic of the metal wyrms than the plaintive cries uttered by the entire planet at their arrival?

It was impossible, but it was happening.

Suresh had felt a similar way when Eva had first told him they were going to have a child - surely it couldn't be, there must be some mistake, hadn't all previous evidence suggested that such a thing could never be? - but the sight of the city-dwarfing calamity of blue metal turned his stomach over in entirely less joyful ways.

He stood in the middle of a street at the edge of the city, looking inward towards where the gigantic, gleaming, screeching dragon was laying waste to everything, and he did the only thing he could think to do. He ran towards it.

Eva was there; Abby was there - Abby, who he could have sworn was so tiny only yesterday and who could now run all on her own, and she would need to run now. Somewhere underneath the thing that was turning the place they called home into shadows and dust, his Eva and his Abby waited for him. What else was there to do?

What could you even do? asked an excruciatingly unhelpful part of his mind, some voice of terrible pragmatism. Suresh didn't even have the ability to answer it; every other mental faculty that might have responded was overwhelmingly dedicated to simply reaching his family. *What do you think'll happen? What do you think you'll find?*

Suresh, unable to stop his traitorous brain from throwing doubts at him and at the same time unable to slow down so that he could ask it politely to stop, simply ran.

There were paths beneath his feet, but the buildings that had run alongside them were gone, often giving him a clear line of sight through miles of destruction. All was in shadow, except for the occasional flashes of reflected light off blue metal: above him, the monstrous shape dominated every inch of the skyscape.

He sprinted through streets he'd known well, but no more. He knew the city now only as one who has known a perfectly presented meal knows a dirty plate.

All that mattered was that he knew the way home - and that knowledge was burned into him, was inextricably intertwined with the sound of his daughter crying, laughing, burbling. The air was thick with a wall of sounds like piercing blades: appalling scraping, screaming, metal on metal as the dragon did its work. Below it, a constant rumble: Suresh could hear - could feel, in the trembling of the earth - whole rows of buildings coming down under the thing's limbs and wings and maw. Homes, offices, hospitals, schools.

That was the office block he'd worked in for years to save enough money that he and Eva could buy their first home together. There was the church where her parents had insisted Abby be christened. This used to be the shop he'd been to dozens of times in the middle of the night when Eva awoke craving sweet chilli crisps. To him, it was a life story. To the blue catastrophe, everything was simply rubble that hadn't realised it was rubble yet.

Everyone else ran the other way - ones or twos at a time, the initial throngs having escaped or been crushed by now - or they were already dead. Suresh sprinted past people he might have known, but couldn't stop to check; where a low wall made of a dozen bodies, all bearing angry marks left by falling bricks, loomed in his way, he simply jumped over it. Some part of him made a note to ask their souls for forgiveness later.

When Suresh came to the place where his house should have been, he finally stopped running and fell to his knees. He would have stayed there until the dragon crushed him or something fell on him if not for the faint sound of someone hissing his name.

'Suresh!'

If he'd thought about it, he might have disbelieved it - might have passed off the half-whisper as another of those useless voices in his own mind or as a mirage of the constant metal screaming, might have bowed his head and wept until the end - but he didn't stop to think. He stared wildly in the direction from which the sound had come, and beyond all despair there she was: Eva, dust-stained and huddled within a tight gap between fallen slabs of brick and wood.

'Eva!'

He crawled to her, first with overwhelming relief and then, when he saw his little Abby half-hidden behind Eva - covered, like her mother, in the aftermath of the dragon, but standing on her own two feet and not lying motionless somewhere as he'd feared - with urgent desperation.

Abby's eyes, already so big and beautiful, widened at the sight of her father, and she tottered to him with all the haste she could manage. His daughter half-fell into his arms, and the tears of pain and terror Suresh had been holding back emerged as drops of joy.

Then he looked over at Eva, and felt cold.

He'd thought she was simply huddling within the rubble for shelter, such as it was, but now he could see the place where several hard, heavy blocks converged on her arm, crushing everything from the elbow down and holding her in place.

'Get her out of here,' Eva said. She spoke quietly, so quietly that Suresh couldn't really hear the words over the sound of the dragon and the city falling, but, as he looked into her face, her meaning was hideously clear.

'No.'

Abby, who had had her face buried in her father's shoulder, looked up at him and then back at her mother.

'I'm not leaving you,' Suresh told his wife. 'I'm not doing that.'

'You have to, or all three of us die together.' Her gaze, as unyielding as the dragon's great wings, compelled him. 'Save our daughter.'

Suresh, one arm still around Abby, pulled out his phone with his free hand. He had a signal, somehow; his mind raced through who could possibly help. Anyone who lived in the city would be dead or dealing with their own problems; anyone from outside would never make it in time; in the end, knowing it was pointless but unable to stop himself from trying, he simply dialed 999.

In one ear, he heard a grating tone: call failed. In the other ear, though he was barely aware of it at this point, the noise of the dragon ground to a halt.

'Stop!' Eva yelled; Suresh tried the number again. Again, nothing. 'You have to stop!'

He looked at his wife, then turned in the direction she was staring.

The dragon had stopped its wanton carnage. Its head, the size of ten passenger planes, had lifted into the air as if listening.

Then it stared straight at him.

'Suresh,' Eva whispered.

He dropped the phone and crushed it under a rock, but the mountainous shape of the creature was still, unmistakably, looking right in his direction. At him; at his wife, at his daughter.

'Go,' Eva said quietly, and this time Suresh listened to his wife. He picked up his daughter and he ran again, ran back through the streets. He heard the crash behind him; he felt the world quaking with the force of it, but he kept running.

Only when things fell silent again did he stop and turn, cradling Abby to his chest. The enormous shining thing's attention had been captured by some other poor fool with a phone or a computer; it stood up, stretching its body upwards and its wings outwards until it was scraping the clouds and casting a shadow many miles wide, and it fell back down once more.

Then it was quiet again, dust rising into the air. Absurdly, Suresh thought of icing sugar, dispersed into the atmosphere by Abby clapping her powdered hands. After a moment of silence, the dragon gave a final scream and flung itself skyward, vanishing towards the horizon.

Suresh watched it go, barely even registering the much further-off, much larger shape flying through the faraway layers of the sky. All he knew was that his world had changed, and that that was nothing compared to the change that had come to the world of all humans.

It was over. That much was clear.

But… no, as he looked into his daughter's terrified, distraught, beautiful face, it seemed to him that it might still go on forever. Changed but not ended; marred, but not broken.

Then he thought of his wife, somewhere in the flattened rubble, and then the thought that he still needed to get his daughter to safety was the only thing that stopped him from falling to the ground and crying.

Around the world, the First Children of Guilt did their work. If they thought anything at all, thoughts of a man named Suresh and a woman named Eva would surely never have occurred to them.

Chris Durston

WHAT GUILT WANTED

A litany of intellectual, emotional, and behavioural symptoms have been seen to be induced ... Those who exhibit obvious changes in cognition are dangerous, but less so than those who continue to act as if they were unaffected until some nefarious motive is revealed.

Stephen Bartonsteir had the peculiar sense that he knew what Guilt wanted. He was really quite sure, though he couldn't articulate precisely why, that he understood the great calamity in the sky better than anyone else. As if they were linked: two extremely mismatched peas in a tremendously lopsided pod.

The feeling had come on shortly after communion, which made him all the more convinced that he must have some sort of privileged wisdom as to the *right thing to do*. His church had managed to get its hands on one of the very rare chunks of blubber-like flesh that occasionally fell out of the sky and crashed down upon the surface of the world: pieces of the Watching One itself. This was a real coup for the Church of Unity Under the Airborne Saviour, an organisation only recently established for the purposes of worshipping the almighty whale orbiting the planet; the Angel Whale Adventists down the road, who usually looked so smug just because they were one of the *earlier* churches to dedicate themselves to Guilt (as if chronology were the most important thing in devotion; all those sects worshipping Guilt, as well as the heathens trying rituals to ward it off, wanted to be *first*, of all things!), were taken aback in an awfully satisfying way when the Airbornerites flaunted their giant hunk of grey meat.

In fact, several of the Adventists jumped ship immediately, attaching themselves with no sense of shame or self-awareness to the Church of Unity. What fickle faith they must have had. Though he knew that one was supposed to accept all those who joined together in worship of Guilt, Stephen was secretly rather pleased when the bandwagon-hoppers were summarily refused entry.

As far as anyone knew, the Church of Unity Under the Airborne Saviour was the *first* church ever to acquire a piece of God. It had been whispered for a long time that a communion was long overdue: if the Christians could get closer to their Lord by consuming His flesh, why should the disciples of Guilt not do the same? Stephen hadn't heard of any other that had been so fortunate as to actually get part of the Saviour's body, though: further confirmation that theirs was the holiest and most righteous order.

The leader of the Church had carved up the flesh with a great sharp knife; it separated into little chunks with a screech, a plasticky wail. Stephen thought it sounded like the kind of noise two fish might make if they suddenly became extremely tough and rubbed against each other, scraping with painful friction. Each member of the congregation got a little piece of their God all to themselves; Stephen chewed his for a long time, partly because he wanted to savour the moment of oneness with the Saviour and partly because it was immensely rubbery. He washed it down with a full pint of water, relishing the sublime discomfort as the meat travelled down his narrow oesophagus and into his stomach.

The screams started almost immediately, which was something of a relief - Stephen had been privately concerned about the legitimacy of the flesh, although he would never have dreamed of openly doubting. He sat with a placid smile on his face, listening to the wonderful suffering all around; the wails of agony told him beyond a shadow of a doubt that this was the path that would bring him closer to Guilt.

Something cut through all the noise and spoke directly to Stephen then. It wasn't like *hearing* a voice, more like receiving a perfectly clear meaning fully-formed. The communication Stephen received was to a crystal-clear voice in his ear as an explosion just a few hundred metres away is to the same explosion heard from several kilometres off while holding a pillow over one's head and wearing a high-quality pair of noise-cancelling headphones.

It said that Stephen had been chosen.

Of course, Stephen thought. How perfectly sensible.

Not only that, but in fact that Stephen was the *only* person who had been chosen. In consuming the flesh of the holiest of beings, Stephen had ascended to something beyond humanhood; and now his brain and all of his organs were lined with new ears and eyes, that he might behold far more than anyone else ever could. Everyone else was unworthy, but not Stephen. Stephen was the one who would bridge the gap between Guilt and humanity.

Stephen followed the instructions that emerged in his brain - or, perhaps, not quite instructions, more like a clear understanding of the intentions and the will of Guilt. He knew what it wanted him to do, so he did. He walked out of the church, wandering between the screaming forms of the things that had been people he knew. He barely paid attention to what they were now; it wasn't important how many heads they had, or how many metres the distance from elbow to fingertip. It was only important that the will of Guilt was being done.

Outside, some of the treacherous Angel Whale Adventists were prostrated on the ground, waiting in anticipation to find out what wisdom would descend from the heavens to those who took communion. Stephen walked a lazy path between them, wasting no attention on such fickle worshippers. Those who glanced up from their praying poses to look at him fell faint and returned their foreheads to the earth immediately. One even died of fright - but Stephen had no notion of this, so focused was his intent on simply going where Guilt wanted him to go.

The first stop on his holy pilgrimage was the house where his parents lived. He hadn't spoken to them in some time, and nor did he speak to them now; he simply entered the home, walking right through the door without opening it. The wood broke apart with the slightest force from his body, like poking a hole in wet paper. His mother clutched at her chest when she saw him; his father attacked him with a cricket bat, but the blow simply rolled off Stephen.

Whatever manner of communication it was that spoke so clearly in Stephen's mind had told him to expect hostility, but a small part of him was almost surprised by how very unsurprised he was to find himself here, suffering blows from the man who had sired him. He could see everything, too: the entire history of the two people who had come together to create him, as clearly as if their pasts were broad lines traced through space; the shape of the ghosts that inhabited their bodies; the places beneath their home, all the way down to the centre of the earth.

He tore off his father's head with a simple tug. If he had known that removing a man's head was as easy as removing a dandelion's, he might have done it more often. His mother lay on the floor, breathing shallowly and clawing at her heart; Stephen put his foot through her sternum, which shattered with a satisfying crunch. He'd stepped on a packet of tortilla chips once. It was rather like that, but wetter. Had his mother always been a limp, paper-thin bag of liquid and rattling fragments?

No matter: he collected the parts he needed, then set off on the next stage of his journey. He had never been this way before: he walked for days, never tiring, never hungering, simply popping the life out of anyone he met on the way with a simple clasp of the fingers or twist of the wrists.

Eventually he came to an old hole in the earth: a mine, a vast pit. He looked down into the darkness, then up into the sky: and there was Guilt, a shape small in the sky but enormous to Stephen's new sight. The dark mass was approaching the circle of the Sun from Stephen's perspective: the Shadow would fall on this place soon. Stephen allowed himself a smile, then descended down into the mine.

Had he still been human, Stephen might have been troubled by the cold and the damp. As it was, he noticed the conditions - as he noticed all things - but paid them no mind. When the Shadow came over the lair he had found for himself (or that Guilt had given him), Stephen found himself laughing. Guilt hadn't told him to do that, but he thought it would be permissible given the circumstances.

In the hole in the ground, Stephen Bartonsteir grew many more eyes. His parents' arms joined with his; their heads dangled by fleshy seams from his torso. There were new parts not from anyone else: appendages like short, stubby wings, a hundred mouths that tasted the air around every part of his body, a great pair of lungs under his abdomen with huge external papery alveoli that swelled and deflated.

The orifices he had had as a human were all closed, the better to see with his new eyes and smell with his new nostrils and taste with his new mouths. His fingers were shaped into branching black stems of some substance halfway between bone and flesh: brittle-looking, yet malleable. He grew until he was the size of two elephants, and then came the crown jewel in the gift Guilt had given him: one huge whale-like flipper that protruded from his lower back, almost like a tail.

Stephen Bartonsteir was perfect. Precisely as Guilt had ordained.

When the Shadow was gone, and when the meat had all been digested, some of Stephen remembered who he had been. His new eyes could not shed tears and his new mouths could not cry out, but if anyone had shone a torch into the dark mine then, they might have seen a gargantuan, swollen, insensible shape - made of many shapes that didn't seem to fit together - rocking to and fro and shaking.

In the moment immediately after, they would have died; for, though some small part of Stephen had been cursed to know what he had lost, the greater part of him was just what Guilt wanted him to be.

Chris Durston

WORST PARTY EVER

*T*he Shadow has no respect for the boundaries of individual creatures, as it is just as dispensed towards combining the bodies of multiple animals as it is towards transforming single ones.

Dearest Auntie Mimelda,

My goodness, you wouldn't *believe* the time I've had of it. It's been simply *ghastly*. Appalling. The *worst party ever*. And you know me, you know I'm not one for hyperbole - never have been and never will be until the earth falls out of orbit and crashes into the sun - so believe me when I tell you that I can scarcely conceive of how any party could possibly have gone *any more terribly*.

As you know, I'd been planning this for weeks. Weeks! I had a new suit tailored especially for the event and ordered *well* in advance. The date had been etched in insoluble ink upon the calendars of all of the local elite members of society for *far* longer than anyone had known about this 'Guilt' creature and its Children, as they call it. And certainly heaven knows: an enormous abominable whale with a deadly shadow suddenly materialising is *not the worst* excuse I've ever heard for failure to attend one of my parties. Not that I even *received* a notification of absence from several of the guests, what with the giant metal dragon monsters destroying cities and making it impossible to communicate over the telephone or the Internet. I'm having to *hand-write* this letter, for heaven's sake.

Still, the show must go on. If we can't hold a party when the world's falling apart, when *can* we?

I was disappointed to find that only around a quarter of the expected attendees did in fact manage to show their faces, and even those I had to send someone to… 'collect' isn't quite forceful enough, but 'abduct' certainly doesn't capture that I had only their best interests in mind. Nonetheless, a party with only a dozen or so people is still a party, and I shall be condemned to the fires of the underworld before I allow one of *my* parties to be disrupted by such a mundane problem as low attendance.

We began the occasion with a modest feast in the ballroom, nothing too opulent. We wouldn't want anyone too full to enjoy the rest of the evening, after all. I noticed a few faces looking, shall we say, less perfectly happy than happy could be, but I am nothing if not gracious, so I simply asked very politely what on earth could be bothering each of my guests to the degree that they felt unable to enjoy the meal I had so generously provided; I took the lack of any response to mean that they were all willing to put it behind them and have a perfectly good time.

It was when the dancing started that things started to take a turn for the truly dreadful. Most everyone seemed to immediately forget how to dance in an orderly fashion and began running around like headless chickens the moment they were allowed to stand up after the feast! Can you believe it? Such disorder, Auntie. No decorum whatsoever.

And, yes, I'll grant that by this time the whale-thing was in fact directly overhead, so anyone who had wandered outside would have been able to look up from the grounds of the mansion and see it awfully clearly, but that person would have found themselves in its shadow and even I wouldn't dare to presume that… whatever monstrous work that shadow makes would be civil enough to leave us alone and allow us to get on with our party in peace. I was reasonably convinced, you see, that being *inside* the mansion would be perfectly safe; one cannot, I thought, be in the shadow of the flying space whale if one is already in the shadow of the roof above one's head.

This assumption, I am humble enough to now grant, may have been in error.

Once I had reassured everyone that staying within the walls where the party was taking place (which, I firmly stated, it was to continue to do in a cordial and well-mannered fashion!) was the safest thing by far - and marshalled one or two people into position after they fell down with what I am told may have been fright or despair but which I suspect was simply down to the excellence of the wine I had chosen for the meal - I commenced the dancing.

Now, here I can admit that I certainly *did* make an error, for I had paired Maisie Stoverman with Matilda Sconce (the alliteration, perhaps, had some sort of influence on the decision, I don't know). If you remember, Matilda was *left-handed*, which poor Maisie simply hadn't a clue how to correct for in her positioning.

I find the suggestion distasteful, however, that this simple miscalculation on my part could possibly have resulted in the subsequent embuggerance.

As I recall, Alastair Barlibow was the first to be affected. I forget with whom I had partnered him; awfully forgettable, he always was, I shouldn't blame you if you had no recollection of him whatsoever. I shall not forget what his shadow looked like, though. At some moment, unseen and unnoticed, it ceased to belong to him; it eschewed mimicking his every movement and took on a purpose and a motion of its own, decoupling from where its feet met his and wandering across the floor to where Maisie and Matilda were fruitlessly attempting to salvage at least *one* step of a passable two-step.

I think it was Maisie who fell first, because I recall a body slipping so smoothly out of the position in which it had been and leaving behind a person whose left hand was raised, not yet having realised that the person it had been grasping for was no longer there. (Yes, I was watching Maisie and Matilda fail entirely to grasp the basics of movement in partnership instead of focusing my attention on a more competent couple, as would have been more fitting. What can I say but *schadenfreude*?) It took me a moment to realise what had happened, and Matilda a few moments longer; I recall that my gaze wandered downwards to where poor Maisie was lying face-down, her body somehow half-sunken into the floor as if she had fallen asleep in wet concrete, and I had a few awfully long seconds to wonder what on earth had happened before I heard Matilda start screaming.

Everyone turned to look, of course; under usual circumstances, I would gently rebuke anyone so easily distracted as to forgo dancing in the proper manner for the sake of having a peek at something scream-worthy, but I don't imagine I can fault anyone on this occasion.

So that was utterly *ghastly*; quite horrific enough for one evening, I should have thought, but no: Alastair ran over to help, bless him, and it was then when we were all looking at him that it became clear to us all that his shadow had simply up and vanished. He looked so distressed, bless him, looking here and there for it like a lost little puppy. Who would have known anyone would *want* their shadow so badly? It certainly proved a misjudgement when the thing did in fact reappear, bubbling up from underneath Maisie and congealing into… well, into something like a dark approximation of an Alastair who had been through a torture rack a few too many times; one might have hoped that it might retain some affection for the person who had spent so many years casting it, but apparently not, since it reached out with *exceptionally* corporeal fingers and -

I'm not entirely sure how a proper young man ought to word this, Auntie, so I shall simply state it bluntly: it tore poor Alastair's face clean off. And I really do mean *clean*: I might have expected some sort of smattering of haemoglobin to adorn all our partywear, but no, it slid off quite smoothly in a neat little circle, and a perfectly white skull underneath, not a smidgen of viscera. Eyes vanished away without a trace and all. I think Matilda fainted at that point, for which I can hardly blame her. The shadowy block of faux-human slipped back into some indeterminate patch of darkness in the floor, taking Alastair's face with it.

We all stood frozen, staring at the faceless body that had been Alastair's, expecting it to go limp, to drop, to hit the floor with a lifeless thump just a moment or two after Matilda. It failed to conform to expectations, even ones as strongly held as those to do with death and gravity. Instead, it turned slowly to look at each of us - I suppose none of us had any way to know *where* it might have been looking, really, what with the conspicuous dearth of eyeballs, but I certainly felt it gazing directly at me as certainly as if I had been staring right into its pupils. Nine or ten people, I suppose it must have been by this point (a dozen or thereabouts entered at the beginning of the night, as you'll recall, and we were now regrettably short Maisie, Alastair, and dear unconscious Matilda), all standing there exchanging glances with a corpse. *Not* the entertainment I had in mind, I hope ought to go without saying.

Once the flesh and bone that had formerly been Alastair had given us all a thorough appraisal, it simply stopped moving. I was perturbed to realise that I found the thing *more* unsettling when it was standing utterly motionless than I had when it was turning to survey us all. There was silence; I just *know* that Jennifer Fortletrack wanted to scream with all her might, but she at least had the good sense to press her lips tightly shut for once.

After a few moments of nothing, it was as if some sort of invisible switch were flipped in all of my guests at once. Every one of them at the same moment suddenly turned and made a mad dash for anything that looked like an exit: Stephen Stephenage threw himself out of a window. (Always a defenestrator; perhaps you remember the spate of good business for window repairmen in the summer of ninety-eight when his parents attempted to tell him that no, it *wasn't* acceptable to attempt to turn his spaghetti bolognese into a hat for his nanny and as a consequence he was *expressly forbidden* from leaving the house under *any* circumstances. I can't imagine they ever really believed *that* would take.) I remained calm, naturally, and did my best to usher everyone in a sensible fashion to the third reception room, but to no avail. Within seconds I was alone in the ballroom, everyone else having absconded to as many different locations as there were guests.

Well, nothing else for it, I thought, and began to traipse around the property to round everyone up. (I left Matilda on the floor, since she was still breathing and hardly going anywhere.) As I say, perhaps there have been worse excuses for ending a party early, but quite frankly I believe I plainly did not want to do that. Such a thing would be completely outwith my nature as a human, and I have never been one to deny my essential being. And besides, I can think of no better way to recover from the shock of seeing one's forgettable fellow partygoer have his face ripped off by his own shadow than a good game of billiards. Not a standard activity for this portion of a party, perhaps, but I think a little flexibility when it comes to the prescribed order of things is more than called for when two of the guests have met an untimely demise.

I tell you, I know the layout of that place like the back of my hand, and yet I could locate not a single person! It was as if they had all simply disappeared from sight and detection the moment they left the ballroom. I wonder now whether that might not in fact have been the case, that they might have been snatched away to some other realm or perhaps sent somewhere they had not intended to go by some shift in geography; certainly the topography of the mansion was unchanged while I searched, but from latter experience I suspect that this may not necessarily have been the case for all involved.

Fruitless hours of searching, I tell you. An awful thing to waste so much time on and achieve nothing, truly. I had marched through every room of that building, searched every nook and cranny, and come up emptier than a wine glass in Eleanor Tavish's hand. What a disappointment.

It was not to last, though I wish that it had. I would rather have suffered the humiliation of having utterly failed to locate all of my guests than have seen what I saw next.

You know, of course, Auntie, that I and so many of my truest companions are what the world might describe as *social butterflies*. I rather enjoyed the term, I think, and being thought of in such a way. Perhaps the shadow of the thing above has a sense of humour, for as you shall see it took the idiom somewhat literally.

When I finally gave up the search and returned to the ballroom, I was briefly a little surprised to notice that dear unconscious Matilda had disappeared. No matter, I thought - she must simply have woken up and wandered off like all the rest of them. Poor Maisie was still face-down in the floor, of course. Bless her heart. I was pacing the place wondering what on earth to do next, and I must have been looking at my feet when I turned and realised that, given that the light was behind me, there ought to have been a shadow in front of me.

I found myself pressed up against the wall, watching the floor for any sign of dark movement, any indication that my own twisted image might be coming for me. For a few heartbeats, each of which rang in my ears far louder than any I had heard or felt before, all was still.

Then something descended into my vision from above. I felt cold in that moment, seized by a feeling that irrationally found the thing's appearance *less* disturbing than the implication that it had been above me all along, watching unnoticed. Do you ever find this? - that it seems *wrong* sometimes that we can remain unaware of something so significant, even were there no reasonable way we could be expected to perceive it? As if the world itself ought somehow to find a way to tell us.

It was a shape made up of many smaller shapes, and each component was… well, perhaps you've guessed by now that the ten or eleven discrete pieces making up the patchwork whole were the bodies of my guests. They never even got to try the evening sweet treats; isn't that just the worst thing you can imagine?

I thought at first that the corpses were arranged into a simple circle, stitched together to form the most basic shape achievable with such lumpen constituents, but the gestalt thing began to flap its wings gently as it lowered itself down to face me. There were three people mushed into a sort of elliptical, ovaloid blob in the centre, and then extending to its left and right were two wide teardrop wings oscillating with a deliberate lethargy back and forth. A huge butterfly, made of people. Just what I always wanted, I suppose, in some ways. Come to think of it, I never did find out where my shadow had got to. Perhaps the human butterfly *was* my shadow: a thing that reflected the shape of *me*.

For far too many moments I simply looked at it. I don't know, Auntie; there was some feeling between fear and awe, some recognition that it might from some other perspective have been a beautiful thing, but then of course my senses returned to me and I was overcome with an urge so strong that it was almost like a solid object: *run!*

So run I did, and I left the butterfly behind and I left the mansion behind - yes, even knowing what I was going out into, I left the shelter of the building. It seemed all too apparent that it offered no shelter at all at this point; if the murderous shadow hadn't been enough of a clue, the amalgamated lepidopterous thing that had been my guests was certainly a harsh nudge in the right direction.

Have you seen it? Have you gone outside while the whale lies directly between you and the Sun; have you stood in its Shadow; have you looked up and seen the shape, a profound darkness even more alien for seeming so familiar? You can't possibly understand what it's like until you have; I imagine it's like having children in that sense, as parents are so fond of telling me (if it truly is so impossible to conceive of their experience, perhaps parenthood is a sort of life in the Shadow itself!).

It was a long time, I think, before I looked away from the being blocking out the light above me and looked back to the mansion, and I saw that the mansion was no longer there. There remained something *like* it; imagine that the stone of the old building was a candle, and that the candle had been burning until the wax was half-melted. Stone ought not to *droop* like that, and yet it had.

I wondered then whether I myself was changed, and carried out a brief inspection of each of my limbs. Nothing appeared to have suffered any ill effects - in fact, if anything, I might even have stood very slightly taller.

Was what happened *for me*, then? Why else should I be the only one not simply destroyed with no chance to fight back? Why should it be me who was witness to the whole thing? Perhaps Guilt took some special interest in me (and why not?) and staged the whole affair as a sort of play just for me, for me to overcome and for me to tell the tale.

I shall take this as mere confirmation of what we have always known: I am, as a plain fact of the way the world works, ontologically special. It is rather nice to have some objective corroboration, I must admit.

I am now taking shelter with the Russets, a perfectly welcoming family with a moderately-sized farm some five or six miles from the mansion. I don't think I can return there now, more's the pity, but this will do for the time being. I shall build my strength back up, and intend to make the journey to come and stay with you as soon as I feel ready.

Very much hope that you're well; send my love to Uncle Rogerard.

With the most sincere regards,

Your nephew,

Almarinous gen Voortishent

Mimelda

You don't know me but my name's Greg Russet. Your nephew was staying with me. He came to us the day after Guilt passed over a few miles north of where we live.

I found this letter in his room, thought you might want it so I'm going to give it to a courier soon. I guess Alma was going to but didn't get the chance.

Not sure what 'ontologically special' means but maybe it has to do with this - very sorry to have to tell you that after a few days with us Alma felt unwell and went to bed. I went to check on him that night. He opened his eyes to look at me and instead of wet whites and pupils there were just balls of thick blubbery skin there.

I didn't know what to do except to let him rest, but by the next morning his whole body was covered in a sort of hide - like a whale's, I imagine. Never been up close to one. It had covered his mouth and nose, and there was something like a blowhole opened up on the back of his neck but I guess it didn't come soon enough because Alma was gone.

Must have just stopped breathing in the night. Our room's next to his and we didn't hear anything, so hopefully he passed away peacefully in his sleep.

Sorry again. I'll give the courier anything else of Alma's that I find and maybe send you some vegetables as well. Got a few good swedes left from the last crop, if you're a swede sort of person.

Yours

Greg Russet

Chris Durston

TODAY MY GIRLFRIEND TURNED INTO A TREE

There are (for what this is worth, as I have already alluded to the difficulty of drawing any conclusions from the existing accounts in the absence of many more that might have been made were those who could have made them not incapacitated by the experience) fewer reports of physical transformation in human bodies than in non-humans.

Sometimes it was if she'd completely forgotten that Guilt existed at all. She could *smile* in a way hardly anyone still could, a way that you couldn't imitate if you were even a little bit conscious of... well, the whole way the world is now.

She still went to her environmental group every week, for heaven's sake. *There's a giant deadly alien whale thing floating around the planet and you're still concerned that carbon dioxide might be an imminent threat?* was the question I frequently wanted to ask, but never did. There were maybe a dozen of them before Guilt, half that after: they just met up and talked about what they could do to play their part in killing the Earth a bit slower. Protecting the climate was a shared interest, not something they actively *did* together - and certainly the prospect of doing anything *big* about it was out the window after one (former) member turned out to be rather more interested in blowing things up than the rest of the group had realised.

It mattered to her, though, and I loved that it still mattered.

A year or so after Guilt appeared, she told me that she'd heard that a forest near where we lived was going to be cut down. I didn't think anyone was still cutting forests down - I thought the world was too busy panicking about the extraterrestrial cetacean still - but apparently it was happening, and she wasn't happy about it.

'They can't just do that,' she murmured one evening, sitting with her legs folded under her in the old lilac armchair we'd liberated from the 'to-take-to-the-dump' pile in our old housemates' garden.

'Do…?'

'Cut it down!'

'Oh, that.' I put my book down; she was just staring off at something I couldn't see. 'Do you know… why they're cutting it down?'

'Can't be any good reason,' she said darkly.

'I mean,' I said quietly, but didn't go on. No point.

'Look,' she said, turning her gaze from whatever point in the distance it had been fixed on and looking me right in the face. 'Naomi.'

'Rose.'

'Just because Guilt's a thing doesn't mean there aren't still animals living in those trees who would suffer if there was large-scale damage done.'

'I know that.'

'So, we should still be trying to protect them.'

'Of, course'.

'Right, then.' With that Rose stood - suddenly, as if she went from being sat cross-legged on the chair to straight upright with no intermediate stage between - and strode across the living room, snatched her coat off the hook, opened the door, thrust her feet into her walking boots, and closed the door behind her, all in the time it took me to wonder what anyone would need all that wood for anyway.

I blinked at the door a few times, frowning as if I could somehow change which side of it Rose was on through sheer bemusement. Then, accepting that I couldn't, I sighed, stood up as quickly as my stiff legs would allow, and followed her.

'It's so *alive*,' she said softly as we parked up at the edge of the forest and go out of the car.

It didn't take me long to catch up with her; once my legs got going, they could carry me quickly enough, and I managed to get in the passenger seat next to her before she turned the ignition. She smiled at me, not in the slightest perturbed that I'd followed. She hadn't been going *away* from me but *towards* something important, and if I could come with her then so much the better.

We walked along a wide path - not a road, not a paved surface, just a gap between the trees. It was all so very green. Even the dotted yellows and pinks of the flowers poking out from between the leaves and the blades of grass somehow only added to the quilt of green, rather than cutting holes in it.

'Don't you think?'

I couldn't help but notice, in among all the green and the life, the very tip of her ear sticking out from under her hair, a little smooth coffee-coloured island in a still sea.

'Course,' I said, not knowing how better to explain it.

'There's so much living in these trees, and so many things depending on those things, and on and on forever.'

I carried on beside her, watching my feet as we went.

'We have to do something to keep it.' She stopped abruptly, staring at her surroundings.

I knew that look. It took in every detail - I could see her gaze moving from one tree to the next, registering each of them in turn and adoring everything about the fact that they *were*. Everything she saw, her brain immediately added to its list of reasons for taking whatever course of action she'd already decided on.

'I'm gonna protest,' she announced.

'OK.' I nodded. 'Sounds good. We can get the group together, make some signs, go harass the decision-makers -'

'I don't mean like that,' she muttered, frowning. 'I mean do something that means they really *can't* come in here and tear it all down.'

'Right…' I was beginning to suspect that I wouldn't like where this was going.

She turned in a slow circle, still casting her eyes across everything as it revolved around her. 'I'm gonna stand in front of them,' she said after a moment.

I had been hoping it wasn't going to be that.

The next week, Rose posted herself up at the entrance to the forest. She had a folding chair and a flask of tea and a blanket, and she settled in with a book and just stayed there. I sat in the car, close enough to be supportive but far enough to reiterate that I was not entirely cool with this. I wasn't alone in that opinion: nobody else in the environmental club had offered to take a shift as Guardian of the Trees.

When the first machines came to begin the process of cutting the place down, swathes of ancient and tall trees at a time, Rose stood and folded her arms, cocking one eyebrow at them as if to say *bring it on, then.* I could see the drivers exchanging glances; one man, who had a bushy moustache and a neck that wobbled when he moved his head, hopped down from his vehicle.

'What's this?' he asked.

'I'm not letting you take it down,' she said, not showing a hint of intimidation or uncertainty.

'You're not…'

'You won't cut this place down.' She stared him full in the face, a glare I'd been on the receiving end of before. You didn't say no to that glare.

He swallowed; his neck jiggled. 'Right, then. Only... it's our job, see.'

'It's a whole *ecosystem*,' Rose said, practically scoffing. 'That's more important than any *job*.'

The man nodded, apparently not having been expecting this. 'Sure, but... but there's this Guilt thing and the government wants to build shelters for when it comes again. So that people, um, don't die.' He gestured with his chin up into the sky; the shape of Guilt was just about visible, flying somewhere to the north.

Rose looked away for a moment. To Moustache it probably looked like a dismissive glance; I knew she was wondering, just a little, whether she was doing the right thing.

Then she turned her stare back upon him. 'We're no more important than the life in here,' she said, and he sighed.

'There's no other route in, is there?' he asked almost dejectedly; she shook her head triumphantly.

'Not that you can get a vehicle that size through.'

He wandered back to his truck and grabbed a little handset on the end of a coiled wire; he held it to his mouth and spoke, his words amplified through speakers on his vehicle so that the rest of his workforce could hear. 'Come back tomorrow, lads, or wait for alternative instructions.'

A groan went up from the assembly of drivers; Moustache held his hands up.

'I know,' he said, 'but nothing we can do on this one. I'll guarantee you get paid for the day, at least.'

That quieted them; with a few sharp glances in Rose's direction, the little fleet cleared off.

I got out of the car and walked over to Rose. 'You did it,' I said, though the look on her face stopped me from saying it too enthusiastically.

'They're coming back tomorrow,' she said. 'Guess that means we have to as well.'

I thought about trying to talk her out of it, but I knew there was no point.

Every day for the next fortnight, Rose put herself between the lumber crew and the forest. I couldn't be there every day, nor did I want her to think that I was OK with what she was doing. I supported the *idea* of it, of course, but I had two reasons for not being alright with *how* she was doing it: firstly, the rational side that said that you just had to pick your battles and that this wasn't the way to achieve any kind of real change; secondly, the less rational side that was terrified that anyone on Earth could die of any terrible cause at any time, and was angry that she would choose to spend so much of her uncertain lifetime with a forest over me.

Then Guilt passed over. The forest was in its Shadow.

I was almost relieved; finally, Rose had a perfectly good reason not to stand guard. There was no way the workers would come into the Shadow just to cut the trees down, not a chance, and it was far too dangerous for her to be in it.

She went anyway.

I didn't realise what had happened until it was too late; I woke up to find an empty Rose-shaped impression in the mattress, but no Rose anywhere. She hadn't taken the car, though; I didn't even think, just got in and drove - towards the forest, into the Shadow.

There were *things* in there. I can't even tell you what sort of things. I barely remember any details: I was so focused on finding her I couldn't absorb most of what I was seeing, and that's probably for the best. I know the road went on for far too long, much longer than it usually did, and the only thing I thought was that she must be exhausted from walking the distance. Something in me registered, I think, that the decision to walk strongly suggested that she intended it to be a one-way trip, but I pushed that aside and kept going as fast as I could.

The car gave out as I got close to the forest entrance, the place where she would always sit. I thought about opening the bonnet to see if I could fix it, but I never did know anything about how cars worked - and besides, the sounds coming from the engine didn't sound like mechanical problems. So, I ran, not looking into the shadowed woods to either side, only ahead.

She was standing there, perfectly still. Right where she always was, in the middle of the road so that no vehicle could pass.

'Rose!'

I tried to call to her - I tried to run to her, but it was as if everything was ten times further away than it looked, and there was so much *moving* all around that I didn't know where I could step. After what felt like hours, after my legs had long turned to rubber, I finally fell to my knees at her feet.

'Rose - I - what are you *doing*? We have to go!'

She said nothing.

'Come on! *Rose!*'

I looked up into her face, the face I knew and loved. It was still her face, and it wore a smile of triumph.

And her skin was rough bark.

It didn't make sense, even as everything around me made no sense whatsoever. I touched her face; I looked up and down, from her hair to her feet; I sobbed into her petrified shoulder; I even hit her a few times, breaking the skin of my hands open.

She was a tree in the shape of my Rose, every inch of her skin and clothing transformed into wood or leaf.

I grabbed hold of her hands, screaming at her to come back, but she didn't move. My fingers brushed something dry; I yanked at the piece of paper in her hand, tearing it but managing to pull it free in one piece.

Naomi

I think it's working. My legs are like roots now.

I'm sorry, but we're not more important than this place. They won't ever be able to take it now.

I love you.

(PS - if you're here and the Shadow is still here: please, for fuck's sake, get out of here. I'm doing this on my own. Don't try to follow me.)

I screamed, holding the page tightly to my chest; there was a whirlwind of cold and force tearing at my insides, feeling as if it might burst through my skin. I don't remember what happened after that.

The next thing I remember is that I was on the ground, awakening - whether from sleep or from something else, I don't know. The Shadow was gone; the sunlight dappling my beautiful wooden Rose broke my heart all over again.

The workers came at some point, and I screamed at them. Moustache climbed down and put his arms around me, to my shock; I clubbed at him with my arms for a few moments, then found myself simply sobbing into his embrace.

Then they left for good.

She's still there, my Rose, guarding the forest from any who would do it harm. The only person in the world, as far as I know, so strong-willed that she could persuade the Shadow to transform her in just the way she wanted.

Chris Durston

MY FRIEND, THE MOON

As with animals, the Shadow is capable of transformative effects on both the mental and physical characteristics of a human. The former seems (anecdotally) more common, although this may be selection bias on account of the fact that those who are physically transformed tend not to survive.

The Moon and I have been friends for a few months now.

It started... casually, even accidentally, as most friendships do. The Moon's old group of friends had just recently decided that they didn't need her anymore, so she'd drifted away from them. She'd never been alone before.

I suppose I was less alone than she was, in the scheme of things. There were others like me, but none like her. Still, I think she knew that she and I were alike in having nobody. I had had a family; she had had all the seas of the Earth. Guilt had robbed us both.

She had floated free for a little while, devoid of a function. When the tides began shifting away from her and instead following the movements of the larger, closer thing swimming around the planet, she found herself involuntarily redundant. What else was she to do? I don't know how she found me, but I like to think that it was our meeting that made her feel able to progress from 'directionless' to 'happily retired'.

She's sitting in front of me now, actually. She's much smaller than most people think: a ball of glowing white rock about the size of my head, floating a few inches above the surface of my desk. Yes, I still have a desk - I *hope* the reason she and I are friends isn't just because my flat is, by the sounds of things, one of the few places to have been safe so far, never yet under the Shadow, but… I expect people talk, as they do. *Why would the Moon be friends with someone like him, unless to use him for free accommodation?* I can see why they'd think that. I'd probably think the same thing if I saw *her* with *me*.

It's easy to be friends with her, much easier than it ever was to be friends with any human person. She doesn't demand anything from me; just being me is all she needs me to do. We sit together, just being in togetherness, and say nothing. I speak to her sometimes, but she rarely says anything back. I prefer that to the way so many people say so much more than they need to.

She revolves gently in front of me, luminescent. That's another thing people get wrong about her: they think she only reflects the light of the Sun, that she has no brightness of her own. Anyone who spent any time actually trying to know her would learn straight away that she shines entirely self-sufficiently. And those divots that people think are on her surface? No. She's not flawed like that; she's perfectly smooth. I don't touch her - perhaps she'd let me, I don't know, but I'd never presume to ask - but I can tell just by looking at her that there's not a single imperfection to her skin.

You're probably wondering if I'm in love with her. I know I talk as if I am, but I don't think so. I'm not stupid; I know romance isn't exactly on the cards between the two of us. I *love* her, certainly, but I'm not *in* love with her. I think more people should recognise that there are more kinds of true love than the basest one, and embrace that. Love who you love; love what you love.

The day the Moon came to me, I didn't understand what she wanted. It had been… three months or so, I think, since the tail of the vast thing in the sky had disappeared over the horizon; for weeks before that, it had been making its appallingly slow way across the sky, blacking out half of the heavens I could see from my home, dragging its Shadow over the places I knew well. I'd been lucky, I suppose, to have always been just beyond the edge of its penumbra. So, Guilt had come and gone over the city I called home, leaving it… changed, I think. I still haven't been there, but from my window I've seen shadows that used to be parks, walking giants that used to be office buildings, and several things that I think probably used to be people. I don't tend to think about those.

I'd barely left the building in the time since Guilt had visited. I mean, I left my flat every few days to look for food; luckily for me, most of the other flats in the block had been vacated in a hurry, so I could take care of myself without having to actually go outside. It was when I had been through most of the empty rooms more than once, when I had cleared the place of almost everything worth taking that hadn't started to congeal or turn brown or grow mould, that the Moon found me. I didn't admit to her that she had come just when I needed someone; I don't think I've ever admitted to anyone that I might need anyone other than myself.

She told me where to go to find what I needed to stay alive, and what she needed. You probably didn't know that, either: the Moon eats. She whispers to me the things she needs, and where I can find them; I go and collect them, and then I leave them in her glowing radius. I never see what she does with the things I give her, but I see them there one day and gone the next, and sometimes I think perhaps I see her bulging a little, expanding as if she's full up.

It's not all some one-way dependency, see; we're equals, more than you'd think. I depend on her to help me find the things I need to survive; she depends on me to collect the things *she* needs to survive. I assume that's what it's all for, anyway. What else would it be? It's funny, the things she eats. If you'd asked me a year ago what I thought the Moon would eat, I'd have said cheese. Then I'd have realised the Moon is *made* of cheese in the stories, not that she *eats* it, and then I'd probably have thought perhaps stardust or granola. Some of the things she eats are the same as the things I eat, but… well, I've never *tried* to eat rusted steel spikes or that gritty mix of brick dust and cat's blood she seems to like so much, but - who knows? - perhaps I'd like it if I did.

She certainly finished off the other man in the room much quicker than I could have done, even if I'd enjoyed eating people. (I know for a fact that that's one thing I don't like to eat.) Come to think of it, what was he doing here? He shared the room with me, didn't he? - or, no, we only shared it for a short time, the period ending on the day she ate him right up and starting on the day I ran out of the Shadow of Guilt and asked him to let me in; but he wouldn't, so I looked at my hands and found that one of them was still a normal sort of hand and the other was a limp fleshy glove from which protruded my… radius or ulna, I think, never could remember which was which - the bone had grown longer, extending out to a point. I think that's right, I think that's what happened. I don't remember who he was to me before, but I'm grateful to him for letting me use his home and for providing food for my friend the Moon.

She's smiling at me now. She does that sometimes: she'll sort of bob in place, then open up a crack, a split like a seam that runs horizontally around her face. I smile back. You would too, if you saw it. It's a wider smile today than I've seen before - it seems to get wider every time, in fact, as if she's letting me know how her happiness is increasing every day she spends as my friend.

I think she has teeth, even. Well - I shake my head at my own silliness - of course she does; she eats, doesn't she? I just don't think I'd actually seen them before, but today she's beaming so widely that I can see inside her head for the first time.

Oh, I don't know that I like it.

That's alright, though. Isn't it? I'm sure most humans don't particularly like looking straight into the mouths of *their* human friends, and that doesn't do anything to sour them on the friendship. I love to see her smile, but part of me hopes she keeps her mouth closed in future so that I can just see her flawless, smooth surface. Still, I'm sure I'll learn to love it: she doesn't judge me, and I don't judge her, so whatever she happens to look like on the inside doesn't change that she's the Moon I became friends with.

I don't think she's going to stop smiling this time, though. Her mouth just keeps opening. Perhaps that's not a smile, perhaps she's hungry; did I not feed her enough? I lean in a little closer to see if I can hear her - she might be asking for something - but all I hear is a sound like spiders' footsteps on broken glass. Now that I'm closer, she's grown more than I thought. I wondered whether she'd got a bit bigger after each meal, but she's larger than my head now. She definitely wasn't that big when we met. Perhaps I'm feeding her *too* much. I don't know. Who do you go to for advice on how much to feed the Moon? Whoever it is, they're most likely dead, so that's not much use.

She has many tongues. They're like arms, coming to embrace me. I hoped that one day we would have the chance to hug as friends, but I didn't presume to be the one to initiate it. Now, here we are; she's holding me more tightly than I would have dared to hope. I can feel the love and gratitude pouring from her into me, and hope she knows I would give her anything in return for just a fraction of that affection.

Somehow, I think she's growing again, or else I'm shrinking. I don't suppose it matters which; the important thing is that she can't bear not to have me even closer to her, and her smile is so wide now and her tongue-arms so insistent that I think I'm being subsumed into her entirely. Yes; her mouth closes, exhausted from smiling with such happiness, and I find myself in a position that anyone would surely envy. I'm encased in the comforting, beautiful world that is the inside of the Moon.

I suppose I'll just stay here forever, then. That's what I'd hoped to do anyway, but now I can just be *with* her, without dull concerns like going to find food. Now we can just *be*. There are parts of her that I would never have dreamed could be in here, inside that round shell: gloriously elegant, pleasantly soft and yielding, there are parts of the Moon that I feel roaming around, exploring. Her innards glow softly, lit by some organ that lines the walls inside her. I saw someone once wearing glow-in-the-dark paint on their arms under a shirt with mesh sleeves; I'm reminded of that effect. It's much more calming here, though; that memory must be from a night I spent around people, and I'd prefer not to recall that.

I can feel her breathing. There's space for me to curl up in comfort, and to simply rest here until… well, until whatever happens next.

What a glorious friendship we have, me and the Moon.

Chris Durston

A GAME NOT WORD PLAYING (THE SUFFERING OF THE THING THAT WAS ONCE STEPHEN BARTONSTEIR)

eople who have been mentally affected sometimes recover immediately, sometimes with time, and sometimes never. People and other living creatures who have been physically altered do not frequently return to their previous forms.

The house that Guilt built has no bricks, nor has it walls or a roof; like a sentence with no lexemes; and yet it makes sense, doesn't it?

What do I sense? I sense my senses, and that makes sense. Nonsense! None sense me, not unless I want them to.

I don't remember what it was before. Does that mean I was never a member of it? How do I [re]member if I never membered? It's representation, not use-mention. Mnemosyne is no memo-sign; no semiotics to be found, nor even a single post-structuralist wondering/wandering yet a structure is undeni-able (able =/= *right*, of course).

Do I remember watt *I* was before? Electrical signals > newrons and oldrons alike = **self that is me** in some capacity I am a series of capacitors and transistors, transmaterial sisters.

Dear me. Dear, dear me. Dear everyone; that is to say *I address this to* you as well as it is *I treasure* you, except that the hunt for treasure was never so satisfying. Is it a hunt? It feels like one, I think.

This was unintended, but tended towards unity. Just one unit, unilaterally. A trick trip tripped a trick and I tripped til it was tricky to teeter-totter. Spectacularly, spectacles - specialising in acclimation of lenticular cleanliness - did not fall from my face.

I don't know where I am anymore. I was looking for Guilt. Can one *look* for Guilt? It's insensible, in the sense of not having to do with sensation. But I thought I was seeking it. I think now that it spoke to me.

I am not a Child of Guilt. I am a child of my parents. Of them am I a child, not of it. Somehow, though, I think that perhaps it and I are now as one. It has not become my parent, or either of my parents, but I may have become it. Then perhaps my mother and my father are the Parents of Guilt. I'm sure they would be thrilled to have been of such importance.

Why why why did I come to receive unease dis.ease
to be eased in and taken out.
And worst of all I did it on purpose, I think, but what
I think and what it thinks are indistinguishably
unextinguishable
I'm sorry, if I have it left in me
I must go somewhere holy and wait there for the hole
to open up that will take me far away

Chris Durston

THAT WHICH I SAY, YOU
UNDERSTAND

I think there is some intentionality to Guilt. I do not think that it is entirely mindless. (I do, however, think that it would be an anthropomorphological mistake to imagine that it might be able to communicate in any way we could ever possibly comprehend. What would it possibly have to say?)

Before you read *anything*, follow these steps:

1.   Don't look at it. I know that's difficult, because if you know it's writing then you've already seen it, but look away as fast as you can.

2.   If it's printed on something that has a reverse - a blank side with no writing - then turn it over so that you aren't looking at the side with words on. Otherwise hold it behind your back.

3.   Unfocus your eyes, if you can, or fix your gaze as strongly as possible on a point somewhere in the distance.

4.   Pass the words *very quickly* across your vision *without* focusing on the page or trying to understand what's written. Ideally you should not even consciously see the writing as it moves across your line of sight.

5.   If you begin to feel unwell, dizzy, disoriented, or *at all affected in any way*, destroy whatever material bears the writing if you possibly can. Otherwise bury it. *Do not look at the writing* as you do this.

6.   If you feel no effects, cover all but a very small portion of the writing with your hands or some other opaque material. Then look very briefly at the uncovered section. If at this point you feel affected, *stop* and *destroy* the writing.

7.   If you still feel unaffected after having seen one or more complete or partial words, read the document *backwards*, starting at the end and progressing in reverse one word at a time.

8.   If you reach the first word with no effects, you may treat the document as safe and read it as normal.

It's unfortunate that you'll have had to read those steps *before* you knew what they were, since ideally you would have carried them out on this document before reading it too. Memorise those steps. Teach them to others aloud. Write as little as possible.

I don't know how far this effect has spread; perhaps it's just a single entity of the Children of Guilt who's able to create it, but assuming anything is safe could be catastrophic.

Somehow, the Shadow - or something made by it - has created a new system of writing.

The words you're reading right now use the twenty-six letters of the Latin alphabet to phonetically represent English words; that is, when you read a letter, you do a sort of mental translation into a *sound*. This mode of written communication has an isomorphic relationship with the words we speak aloud in English, directly representing the sounds we speak. When I write these words, the first thing I do is conceive of how I would express what I want to say in spoken language; then I create a graphical representation of each word and each sound in each of those words. What you're reading is *directly* and *closely* related to how we would communicate out loud.

Not every form of written language is like this. Some languages use semanto-phonetic character combinations to represent both sounds and meaning;

some use lexigrams or pictograms to depict the concept rather than being *words* as such.

Whatever Guilt has done, it has found a way to create a language that circumvents all of this. The marks on the paper (or whatever material) *do not represent words* in any natural language. They tell the reader nothing about how to pronounce what's written, nor how to transcribe it into words in any other language. They *are the meaning*. It is *direct, one-to-one, perfect representation of semantic content* in the form of written marks.

I can't explain this in a way that makes any sense, because it doesn't. Try thinking of it this way, though:

There is a man.

When you read that sentence, you (probably) do a couple of things. You mentally decipher the sounds indicated by each letter so that you 'hear' what the words would sound like if spoken aloud, for one. You also relate the shape, or the sound, of the word 'man' to a sort of token image of 'a man' or 'some man' in your mind. You know that that token image relates to some hypothetical real man somewhere, but only indirectly.

The 'man' written on the page is divorced from whatever real man the sentence might refer to by multiple steps: you have to divine the meaning of the word from the lines on the page, then form an image in your head, then have some awareness of the fact that your mental image or concept is a representation of some *thing* which is in fact elsewhere and not in your mind.

Guilt's new mode cuts through all of these steps. When you see marks written in its language, you *immediately* understand precisely what is being communicated, whether this is a statement about a man or a mathematical equation or an opinion about a colour. You don't need to have ever seen it before; there's no need to 'learn' the language. It just represents *directly* and exactly what it means in a graphical form that is instantly understood by anyone who sees it, no matter what other languages they might or might not be able to comprehend.

If you were to see a sentence in this language meaning something analogous to 'there is a man', you would apprehend all that there is to know about the man in such a way as to make your perfect concept of the man not really a mental representation at all, for that by nature is at least distinct from the thing itself on account of being an immaterial picture.

This might sound useful, and in some ways it does have the potential to be extremely useful. Imagine being able to make use of this at will, to immediately and perfectly share whatever you wanted to communicate with anyone, whether you shared a language or not. Guilt, however, does not use this language to express helpful concepts.

Imagine, for the sake of illustration - but do not think about it too hard, in case you accidentally stumble in your mind upon how this would be represented in Guilt's language - becoming perfectly aware of your own mortality, or of a statement which can be neither true nor false, or of some sort of wrathful demon which, once comprehended, replicates itself in your mind until everything else in your consciousness is consumed. All of these things are possible to implant in the mind of a reader using Guilt's language. The reader need not be paying close attention, nor even be willing to listen: if they *see* the markings, they *will* understand.

This is the reason for the steps outlined above. I don't know to what extent a concept written in this mode might look like a normal English sentence, hence the caution even if the letters look familiar. If you see something in this language, then you immediately and unwillingly allow into your mind a perfectly formed statement or concept, and some concepts are harmful even simply to *understand*.

If it were not such an information hazard, and perhaps if we had invented it before Guilt and learned to use it safely (I can only assume it would be extremely difficult for anyone to write something in this language on purpose, but perhaps we would have got there), this could have revolutionised the way humans share information. As it is, it is an open window for an abominable visitor to share whatever information it wants with us, and most of what it has to say I suspect will not be something we are ready to hear.

Chris Durston

HYPOTHESES ON THE ORIGINS OF GUILT

Naturally, one enormously important ramification of the appearance of Guilt has been that most of human society is now dedicated almost exclusively to preserving human existence in the face of an extremely dangerous threat, and this is the case in all parts of the world even when Guilt is not immediately present.

Hardly anyone came to hear the three church leaders speak. Hardly anyone knew that there was to be any sort of gathering - there was no more Internet to spread the word, and none of the members of the three churches was particularly good at making flyers. It was a warm afternoon, but not pleasantly so: the sky was an angry purple, the air thick and sweaty. Inside the old church building, the walls pressed the heat inwards, stale air traipsing heavily across the skin of those within.

This was the perfect atmosphere, as far as the first speaker was concerned.

'Thank you for coming,' pronounced Father Michael Kickegard. This was his home church, the place he had overseen for years; his deep, grave voice ploughed through the musk of heat and humidity, vibrating clearly throughout the building. In addition to Kickegard and the two other church leaders sitting in hard wooden chairs a few feet behind him, there were perhaps six people in attendance, most of whom came from the congregations of one or the other of the three speakers. 'The coming of the Archangel has touched all of our lives, of course.'

One of the people sitting behind Kickegard cast her eyes heavenward; the other sighed audibly. Kickegard turned his shoulder towards them for a moment, but did not look back.

'I know,' intoned Kickegard, turning back to his tiny audience, 'that my learned colleagues may disagree with my interpretation of the import of the Archangel, and that is their right. I, however, will present to you the truth, that you may be saved anew.'

Somebody coughed wetly.

'Here, then, is my expression of my faith.' Kickegard leaned forwards on the lectern, staring intently at each of his listeners. 'The Archangel above us has come from God. It is the second coming of salvation, an agent to liberate us all from sin once more.

'We - we, the people of the Earth - were raised up once, but through the sheer weight of accumulated years of wrongdoing and disobedience have dragged ourselves down again into damnation. Even the sacrifice on the cross, as perfect and as transcendent as it was, is no longer enough to outweigh the evil with which we have burdened ourselves. But God… God is merciful. God doesn't *want* us to be condemned, even as we try so very, very hard to make condemnation the only option. So, He has sent His angel to raise us up again.'

The man who had sighed shifted in his seat, putting his hands on his knees as if to stand up. The other put her hand on his forearm, shaking her head.

'Hold it,' she whispered. 'Don't think it'd… er, do you any favours.'

The man exhaled deeply through his nose and settled back into his chair.

'There is no space in Heaven for us all,' Kickegard declared, striking the lectern with his palm to punctuate each word. 'The Archangel comes to cleanse: to judge the unworthy, and to leave the world to those who have faith. Or perhaps to take us all, some to Hell and some to the side of God. But the Archangel *is* doing the work of God; He was called by our sin and He has answered with an envoy of His love.'

With these words, Kickegard backed away from the lectern and took his seat. The second leader - the impatient one - let out a hostile grumble and stood before Kickegard had finished settling into the chair beside him, taking just two long steps to reach the speaker's position.

'This man wants you to worship the thing in the sky,' David Spenza said, extending his arm straight out to point back at Kickegard. Unlike the first speaker, Spenza didn't go by Father, nor did he wear anything to mark him as a man of faith. He was an insistently-pointing man in jeans and a white shirt with the sleeves rolled up, standing at the head of a centuries-old holy place of stone and stained glass. 'He says that God sent it to save us. He even says that we *need* it because what Christ did for us has… expired, somehow.' He shook his head. 'I'll tell you this: I don't call that thing Archangel. I call it Guilt. It's of our sin, he's right about that, but it's not some worker of beauty and redemption. It's a demon from beyond our world, called here by all the injustice we've done, and it's changing this planet into something that better represents the ugliness in us.

'It hasn't come to save us, but to punish us. It's not a worker of God; it's a missionary from the darkness.'

Spenza took a deep breath and ran his hand through his hair.

'There is still salvation to be found in faith,' he said after a moment, 'but not in Guilt. That creature is a being of evil, and it's here to make us pay for our sins.'

With that, Spenza sat down. Kickegard, next to him, glanced over; Spenza shuffled his chair an inch or two away from Kickegard. The third speaker raised her eyebrows, looked from Spenza to Kickegard to the audience and back to Spenza as if trying to ascertain whether it was in fact her turn, then stood and trundled up to the lectern.

'Uh, hi.' Carrie Porter cast her gaze around the church, nodding appreciatively at what she saw of the building. The founder of a group where people of any or no faith could make friends and discuss big questions - referred to half-jokingly by its members as a church, but in fact more of an informal get-together - Porter was less used to addressing than to quietly moderating. 'I feel like, no disrespect, there might have been a few steps skipped somewhere along the line here. My friends over here have made some, um, passionate cases, but I feel like nobody's talking about the elephant in the room.'

'It's not an elephant,' said someone from the pews: an older man whose eyes had been on his knitting the entire time. 'It's a whale. And it's not in the room.'

'Exactly!' Porter nodded vigorously. 'It's a whale.'

'It's not, though, is it?' Spenza chimed in.

Porter turned and gave him a good, strong glare, the kind of glare that could make an angry Rottweiler run off whimpering. 'You had your turn,' she muttered, then turned back to the audience. 'As my esteemed friend over there rightly says, it's not an *actual* whale - like, I don't think anyone thinks a regular Earth whale just got really big, learned to fly, and somehow gained an... evil, corrupting shadow and the power to summon dragons. That doesn't seem all that likely to me.'

The man with the knitting tilted his head as if conceding a fair point.

'But it does *look* an awful lot like a whale,' Porter continued. 'What's that about? Couple of theories: maybe it's an alien distantly related to Earth whales, and maybe it's pissed off about the fact that its cousins aren't doing so hot at the moment, what with climate change and hunting and all that. Maybe it's got a telepathic link to the whales, maybe it heard them singing, I don't know. Or maybe it's some sort of whale god that's been swimming around in the big wide universe - I did some reading on this and there are some scientists who reckon that the planet might actually be vibrating in a way that gives off this sound almost like whalesong, and maybe it heard that and came to find out what's up.

'Anyway, I think we're making this about *us* when it's probably more likely to be about the whales. If it were an angel or a demon coming to save or punish humans, wouldn't it look a bit more like a human?'

She paused, folding her arms over the top of the lectern. There was a gentle clack of knitting needles from the pews; someone near the back accidentally knocked a cushion onto the floor with a stifled *thwomp* as they shifted position uncomfortably in the heat.

'Then… what would be the point?' Spenza asked.

'The point?'

'If it's not here because of us, or for us. What do we do with it, then? Worship it? Fear it?'

'Maybe we don't,' Porter said. 'Maybe the point is that things aren't always about us. Maybe this one just… is. Maybe it's separate from anything we care about, and we just have to go along with it.'

Kickegard and Spenza exchanged glances; Spenza, perhaps realising that he had no intention of agreeing with Kickegard about anything, looked away and coughed.

'That would be extremely unsatisfying,' Kickegard rumbled eventually.

'Doesn't mean it might not be the *truth*,' Porter countered.

Kickegard stood slowly, joining Porter at the speaker's position; Spenza, as if concerned about being left out, went up beside them too.

'We came to discuss our *faith*,' intoned Kickegard. 'The theology and importance of the Archangel. What good is your theory, if it admits no special relationship between humanity and God and His messenger?'

Porter sighed. 'Just because it's not all… anthropocentric doesn't mean it isn't important to any gods, or the world in general.'

'There must be some *meaning* to it all,' Spenza insisted, clapping his palms together. Porter tilted her head.

'We don't know that there must be,' she said, 'or that there isn't already and we just can't see it.'

'It's obvious!' Kickegard declared. 'Only God is powerful enough to send such a great and glorious being, and He has sent it for us and because of us.'

'If you think it's so wondrous,' Spenza jabbed, 'why don't you go and live under it for a bit, see what happens?'

'Ah.' Kickegard wagged his finger. 'I wouldn't dare to go against the order of things. I don't presume to know all of His plan, but perhaps the Archangel comes first above those who deserve to be reduced to fear and ugliness, then later to those who can be carried away to Heaven.'

'How do you know it isn't here just to punish *all* of us?' demanded Spenza; Porter gave them both *the glare* again and turned to the audience, palms up imploringly.

'How do any of us know it's here *for* anything?' she asked; one of the attendees had either the courtesy or the discourtesy to acknowledge the question with a shrug.

'I reckon it's one of those government agencies,' a middle-aged audience member piped up. 'Like, it's a robot that they've made to keep us all in check. Or it's drugs and we're all hallucinating the whole thing.'

'Or an alien invasion,' suggested another, nodding sagely.

'I think,' an older man said, 'that it's neoliberal constructivism gone mad. They start reifying their neo-Marxism and somehow it moves from an epistemological thing to an ontological one.'

Everyone else frowned at him.

'I reckon it's just a big happy whale,' someone chirped up, breaking the silence; this was met with groans all around.

Porter gazed out at the people in the pews, sighing in frustration. 'Come on, guys, let's not -'

'That's stupid,' said someone none of the speakers had spotted - despite the swathes of empty seating, they'd chosen to sit right behind a stone pillar where they'd be hidden from the stage. 'It's so powerful, it's obviously a forgotten god of the sea people.'

At this point, almost every one of the audience members had suggested a theory; Kickegard raised his hands, standing up to his full height.

'Let us maintain order,' he said, 'so that we can all come to a civilised agreement… that it is the Archangel of our redemption.'

Spenza groaned, no longer bothering to hide his disdain for the idea. 'That goes against *everything* Christ taught us,' he told Kickegard, poking the other priest in the chest, 'and I *will not* hear any more of it!

'Guys,' Porter mumbled.

'You're *blaspheming*,' Spenza accused Kickegard, who let out a grumble like a muffled roar of rage.

'This is *my church*,' Kickegard bleated, 'and I'll blaspheme in it all I want!'

Spenza raised his eyebrows; Kickegard spluttered.

'I mean spread the truth! The *truth!*'

Perhaps sensing that there was no longer much prospect of having an ordered discussion, everyone in the church took the opportunity to loudly weigh in on their own ideas; the debate devolved within moments into a battle royale of shouted hypotheses, bellowed rebuttals, and screamed pleas for everyone to shut up (which nobody did).

As the rabble raged on, nobody noticed the windows beginning to darken. The air - already thick and viscous - grew hotter, damper, more pressing; but the people, if they noticed, put it down to the increased movement and energy inside the building.

The wooden doors of the church swung open with a loud creak; all fell silent and turned to look at the newcomer who'd just come striding in.

'This is the debate on what Guilt is and where it came from, right?' she asked, standing casually with her hands in her coat pockets.

Kickegard, Spenza, and Porter looked at each other.

'Yeah, it is,' said Porter, 'but… you're a bit late.'

'Oh, it's OK.'

'It is?'

'This won't take long.'

Kickegard stepped forward. 'What do you mean?'

'I mean,' said the newcomer, 'I can give you an answer, a really quick one.'

Spenza scoffed.

'The answer,' she continued, 'is that *it doesn't matter* where it came from, or why it's here.'

'*Thank* you,' Porter said.

'When you have faith, all things have meaning,' Kickegard proclaimed, raising a hand in an angry claw.

'I'm not saying it doesn't,' said the latecomer, 'just that it's not important right now.'

Spenza folded his arms. 'Why not?'

'Because it's *here*, and *that's* what we should all be concerned about.'

'This is trivial,' Kickegard muttered, but Porter hopped down into the aisle and strode towards the doors, casting her eyes across each side of the building as she went.

'When you say it's *here*,' she said to the newcomer, 'you don't mean…'

The woman stepped aside. Porter took one look out of the door, glancing upwards, then turned and walked right back to Kickegard and Spenza at the head of the church.

'She's right,' Porter said quietly. 'It doesn't matter, not at this point.'

'How can you -' Spenza glanced down towards the open doors, trailing off. 'Surely not.'

'We're all going to be right underneath it in about…' The newcomer took a look skyward. 'Couple of minutes, I reckon.'

Kickegard fell to his knees, mouth agape. 'How can this have happened?' he murmured.

'Maybe you were right,' Spenza told him bitterly. 'Maybe it's coming to get the sinful ones first, and we all just called it right to us with all our disorder and wrath.'

'No, it's just… it's just been coming this way for ages,' said the woman by the door. 'You guys must have been in here for days not to have realised.'

Porter blinked rapidly. 'No… we've been in here an hour. If that.'

'Oh, *cool*,' said the latecomer. 'I heard about this happening somewhere else, but that's really awesome to see in person.'

'Heard about what?'

'Oh, there's a whole… thing. No time to explain at this point.'

'But then…' Spenza looked the woman up and down, as if not trusting his eyes that she stood there at all. 'What are you doing here, if you knew it was coming?'

She beamed, leaning against the stone archway framing the church entrance. 'Oh, I'm just a really big fan.'

Kickegard's brows knotted themselves together, practically meeting in the middle. 'You… *want* to live in the Shadow.'

'Can't wait.' She winked. 'Maybe I'll turn into, like, a squid or something awesome.'

'That,' Porter said, 'is fucked up.'

'Maybe,' the stranger admitted. 'But, hey - the whole thing's fucked, so may as well embrace it. Maybe the big guy'll give cooler gifts to those who love him and let him take them on purpose. I dunno. Seems better than hiding.'

Spenza, Porter, and Kickegard each took several breaths, opened and closed their mouths, once or twice made a noise as if to begin a sentence and then broke off. Then they each picked a seat and dropped into it.

'Well, then,' said Spenza eventually, 'I suppose that's it.'

'Seems that way,' said Porter.

'We'll be redeemed now,' Kickegard murmured, staring at some point on the stone wall of the church. The others gave him a glance, but didn't say anything.

The Shadow of Guilt came over them, and the creature above continued on its ponderous journey through the sky.

Chris Durston

THE SECOND ERA OF GUILT

In which epoch a time *before Guilt* seems but a fanciful imagining

Chris Durston

THE STORM ON THE SEA

What seems to remain constant in descriptions of Guilt is that it is always uncannily alike in shape to earthly cetaceans. Some say blue whale; others say humpback; still others say sperm or killer whale. The fact that there is no clear agreement even as to with which of the two primary parvorders of cetacea - Mysteceti or Odontoceti - Guilt shares its physical traits would seem astonishing were it not for its sheer refusal to allow anyone to be certain of anything about it.

The sea churned under the boat, smashing into the hull so that it bounced clear out of the water before crashing back down, nestled between waves until the next one hit. The tarpaulin stretched over the top of the little vessel held, even as water from the rain and the sea battered against it; the two men huddled underneath the thin skin of fabric tried their best to hold firm, every muscle in their bodies tense and painful from the effort.

Neither of them had any idea where they were, by this point. They'd set out from the coast in their fishing boat - just big enough to hold two men, a few rods, nets, salt-packed barrels, and enough supplies for a day or two's trip - earlier that day, on a morning with cobweb clouds drifting peacefully through the sky and a gentle breeze winding around underneath the warm spring sunlight.

For years, their lives had had the same easy routine: twice a week (except in unfavourable conditions such as storms, disturbances of the peace in the settlements around the coasts, or the looming of Guilt overhead) they would climb into their boat and head out to sea, always staying within sight of one shore or another. They'd stay out there on the water for the day, then come back in the evening with a stock of fish to sell. The next day or two would be spent at the market, or making deliveries, and then the cycle would repeat. It was a comfortable life, compared to what some had.

This time had seemed comfortable, too, at least to begin with. They'd travelled in an easy line a few miles out to sea, then dropped their anchor and settled in as usual. Nothing much seemed to be biting that morning, but that wasn't particularly unusual. There were good days and bad, and the movements of the fish in the sea were rarely as predictable as might be hoped for: though their numbers were high, since the only fishermen were small boats like this one, the effects of Guilt and its aquatic Children on all the habitats of the planet were often erratic and never insignificant.

When the chain connecting the boat to the anchor snapped, neither of the two men noticed. The younger of the two, Sperry, was gazing out over the clear water, one eye looking out for any movement from the nets and rods; the other - his uncle - had decided to take a momentary break from paying attention to fish that weren't there and was resting his head in one hand, leaning against the side of the boat with his eyes closed. It was only when their vessel had drifted so far out to sea that the land was no longer visible that the penny dropped.

'Er,' said the young man, shading his eyes with a hand and scanning the horizon on all sides. 'Uncle Beran?'

The senior member of the crew's lips twitched; the hairs of his thick moustache waved gently as an exhalation from his nose jostled them. 'Mm.'

'I'm not sure where we are.'

'We're where we were an hour ago, lad.'

'I… don't think that's right,' Sperry said uncertainly, turning in a circle. The clouds, which had been thin strands of fluff when they set out, were now a layer of greyish-white so thick that it was impossible to tell where the sun was. 'Unless the land's moved, I'm not sure how we can be in the same place.'

Beran sat straight upright, the sharp motion rocking the boat. Sperry adjusted his balance with ease, used to the swaying of their vessel on the waters. 'Land's moved,' Beran muttered, squinting into the distance. 'No, you're right - that doesn't sound all that likely.'

'What, er... what do we do?'

'Hmmmmm.' Beran folded his arms, regarding the bottom of the boat with great gravitas. It was wide and smooth, and for years had done an excellent job of keeping both Beran and Sperry - in addition to their water canteens, packs, and fishing equipment - out of the water. 'Hmmm.'

Sperry waited.

'We row,' Beran declared.

'Which way?'

Beran raised a finger as if to point, then lowered it again. 'That is the trickier bit,' he conceded.

'Are we... lost?' Sperry sat down in the boat, looking helplessly in every empty direction.

'By most definitions, yes.'

'Are there any definitions where we aren't?'

'Can't think of any right now.' Beran let out a long sigh, then reached into his pack and pulled out a narrow-stemmed pipe already packed with smokeleaf; he lit it deftly with a match struck on the side of the boat, popping the lip into his mouth in the same motion.

Sperry's expression undulated between burgeoning terror and a grudging amusement that his uncle would think to go for his pipe at a time like this; Beran shrugged, puffing out a satisfied cloud of blue-grey smoke. The two men sat there in silence, rocking gently side-to-side on the lazy waves, for a few minutes; then Sperry lowered his head, breathed several deep breaths, and slapped himself lightly on the cheek a couple of times.

'Maybe we really do just pick a direction and row,' he said, blinking rapidly. 'I don't see what else we can do, except wait and hope that the tide carries us back to shore.'

'Not likely to happen by chance, I don't reckon,' said Beran solemnly. 'If anything, the tide's carried us *away* from the shore, so that's probably still the way we're going. Could wait and hope that the clouds clear, or look for the light and dark sides of the sky when the sun starts going down, but that could be a while yet.'

'Then… maybe we want to row *against* the tide?'

'You'll tire yourself out and still end up further out than you were when you started. Best to go sideways, not with the current but not against it either.'

Sperry nodded and picked up the oars. 'There's land to the east of the docks,' he said, half to himself, 'and if the tide's going out to sea then it's going north, so…' He leaned over the side, trying to ascertain which way the boat was moving on the water. 'So, this is probably north, so that's probably east.'

He started rowing, forcing himself to go slowly so as not to exhaust himself at the start of a journey that could go on for any length of time. Beran's shoulders rose and fell heavily, and the old man slumped down into a curled-over sitting position. Sperry wondered whether he should say anything more to his uncle, but his breath soon settled into a regular rhythm that would tolerate no disturbances.

It was a relief of sorts when, after several hours, the clouds began to turn pink and orange on one side of the sky.

'Sunset,' Beran murmured. 'West.'

'Then…' Sperry rotated his upper body in the boat, trying to position himself on an imaginary compass. 'Then this hasn't been…'

'Maybe it was, at the start,' said Beran. He didn't sound pessimistic, simply resigned. 'Maybe we got turned around in the water and had no way of knowing it.'

'But we know now,' Sperry insisted. 'We know now that that's west, so I'm going to point the boat southeast and…'

'We've come too far today,' Beran said quietly.

Sperry looked at his uncle, the man with whom he'd spent so many calm and comfortable days. 'You're not giving up.'

The older man shrugged. 'I'm not holding out hope either.'

Something - something big, something fast - barrelled into the side of the boat; Sperry cried out, gripping the oars tightly; Beran threw himself into the bottom of the vessel so as not to be thrown out by the movement.

'What was that?!' Sperry whimpered, not daring to look over the side.

It hit again, from the same side; somehow the hull held, but the boat jerked wildly, almost capsizing.

'Nothing good!' Beran thundered, grabbing the heaving side of the boat and pulling himself up to peer down into the ocean.

The boat stopped its side-to-side rolling, and Sperry had the feeling that his stomach was travelling sideways.

'It's pushing us,' Beran said grimly.

Sperry didn't ask what.

'Pushing us out to sea,' his uncle said again.

'There's no chance it's trying to help us get back to shore?' Sperry said, just in case there were any more reassuring conclusions that might be drawn from the situation.

Beran didn't answer. Sperry scanned the expanse around them for any signs of hope, and saw the precise opposite.

'Those are dark clouds,' he said quietly. Beran turned from his observation of whatever it was that was pushing them along and cast his gaze in the direction Sperry was looking.

'That's a full-on storm if ever I saw one,' he said, eyes dark. He tilted his head back towards the thing in the water, the unwanted makeshift motor propelling them towards danger.

Sperry swallowed once, twice, then leaned out and looked down. Its body distorted by the rippling waves and the ever-whimsical bouncing around of light in water, the thing whipped its many limbs in smooth circles behind it, almost like a rotating propellor. Whatever features it might have had were hidden on its underside; the only parts visible from above were a spined, dark carapace roughly diamond in shape and as long as Sperry's arm, and the long tentacles that trailed behind - at least a dozen, but it was impossible to count them as they swirled around each other.

'Is it one of the Children?' Sperry asked, collapsing back into the middle of the boat.

'Maybe,' Beran said. 'There are strange things in the sea that didn't come from the old skyswimmer.'

'You think it's taking us somewhere? Into the storm, somewhere else?'

'Who knows?' Beran sat back and lit his pipe again, turning his gaze to the sky. 'Who knows whether it even has any idea it's pushing us? Maybe we just happened to be in its path and it didn't feel like going around.'

Sperry took one more look over at the creature beneath the water's surface. 'Do you think we could... kill it?'

Beran laughed at that, a full guffaw that leaked clouds of smoke. 'Not with anything we've got on board, and likely not without making it angry enough that it might just decide to sink us and be done with it.'

Sperry covered his face with his hands. 'If I don't die, I'm never getting on a boat again.'

'Don't expect a share of the fish, then,' Beran warned, smiling gently.

His nephew gave a quiet exhalation of amusement.

'Now,' Beran went on, leaning forwards, 'when I've finished this pipe, we take cover. We curl up in the bottom of the boat, put the tarp over the top to cover us on all sides, and we stay there until things seem calm or we're dead.'

Sperry's eyes widened, then he bit his lower lip and nodded.

'We had a good run,' Beran murmured. 'We did well together.'

'We did.'

The older man let out one last long draught of thick smoke, then reached over the side and tapped the pipe fondly against the hull of the boat, knocking any last dregs of burnt leaf into the sea. 'In case this is it... well,

I wish it weren't, but I can't say I'm disappointed not to be on my own for it.'

Sperry nodded, and then the two moved; Beran scooped the folded tarpaulin up and threw it to his nephew, who secured it to the bow and pulled it over them, tying it tightly on all sides so that it was taut like the skin of a drum - a drum that Sperry hoped wouldn't be beaten too hard, since he and his uncle were inside it. There was a gloomy blue half-light, enough for them to see each other's expressions until everything descended into darkness - slowly at first, as they approached the black clouds that heralded the storm, then all at once.

Whether the marine intruder that had propelled them this far had stayed with them into the deluge was impossible to tell; once they reached the tumultuous waters, everything was a jumble of up and down, left and right, no sense of direction except the overwhelming sense that *everything* was in constant and painful motion. Sperry's head burned within moments; try as he might, he couldn't stop all the tendons in his jaw and neck from tensing as hard as steel rods, and sharp pains shot through his whole body every time an unexpected bump or crash jolted them. There was no way to tell how to brace himself, so all he could do was brace *everything* and suffer the merciless blows of being thrown around by the sea.

From time to time, a bright flash of lightning illuminated the inside of the boat in a tempestuous blue; Sperry's eyes were screwed tightly shut for most of them, but every now and again he would be able to get a glimpse of Beran's face, a visage of stony skin and harsh shadows. His uncle looked almost peaceful, his body rolling with the crashes rather than resisting painfully.

Sperry knew that he screamed, a few times. He couldn't hear his own voice, and he imagined Beran couldn't hear him either, but it came out anyway.

When he came to, the boat's interior was glowing with a soft light. The air was thick, wet, hot. It was hard to tell, but he thought they were swaying gently - there were no bumps, no bounces. Sperry blinked, rubbing his head; had he been unconscious until they passed through the storm? He gazed blearily over at Beran, who was slumped in a heap in the base of the boat - but Sperry could see his chest expanding and contracting, at least.

He released the tarpaulin, clambering up onto his seat. His throat and nose let go of tension he hadn't realised they'd been holding, his lungs grateful for the fresh, cool air. Beran stirred.

'Morning,' said Sperry, his voice coming out indistinct. There was still no sign of land, and his body ached for food and fresh water - and it simply *ached*, every inch of it - but the sky was clear and the sea was still. The storm had passed, or they'd passed through it, and even the night had come and gone. 'We made it, sort of.'

Beran groaned, hauling himself upright. 'Unbelievable.'

'If we knew where we were, we'd actually be able to go the right way now,' Sperry said bitterly, gesturing with his chin up to the sun in the sky.

'Well, we still know we came from land to the south, eventually.'

Sperry sighed. 'We have no idea what's in any direction or how long it'd take to get there. Don't think it matters now.'

There was an almighty bellow, a screech like the sound of an enormous bell falling from its mounts and shattering against stone; the two men jolted away from the direction the noise had come from, casting about for its source. A few moments later, a vast blue beast of wings and rage came soaring across the sky, appearing from nowhere and flying right overhead, blocking out the sun for a moment with its gleaming metal mass. It paid no attention to the little boat below, even as the force of its wingbeats rocked the vessel almost to the point of capsizing.

Within moments it had passed above them; neither Sperry nor Beran said a word as they watched it disappearing into the distance.

The silence stretched out, pouring from the path it had taken through the sky to submerge everything around them.

'Was that…?' Sperry said eventually, his tone reminiscent of a cat pawing at the ground for some morsel of food it couldn't quite reach. He was twisted in his seat, neck and torso straining to look in the direction the thing had gone.

'One of the First Children.' The words floated from Beran's mouth on a breath softer than the calmest sea. 'Calamity, as I live and breathe.'

'I thought they were all asleep,' Sperry whispered; the breeze over the water caught his words and carried them to Beran.

'So did I, lad. Apparently not.'

Sperry turned back to face his uncle, his eyes wide, not looking at anything in particular. 'Guilty shit,' he said after a moment.

'Guilty shit,' Beran agreed.

That seemed to be all there was to say. They were still drifting hopelessly in some unknown waters some unknown distance from anything like shore and safety, after all. After several minutes of silent contemplation, Beran pulled out his pipe - somehow miraculously undamaged by all that it and the rest of the boat's occupants had been through - and went to light it, but a rummage through his pockets turned out no more matches that hadn't been broken into useless tiny stumps in the storm. He popped a pinch of leaf straight into his mouth and chewed it, sighing contentedly.

Sperry opened his pack and found that there was still some food inside that had made it through the journey: a few strips of dried meat, some dust that was the pulverised remains of a packet of crackers (still somewhat tasty, as a kind of crumb coating for the meat), a handful of slightly squashed berries. He ate a bit less than half of what was left, washed it down with water from his canteen, and handed the rest to Beran; his uncle accepted it gratefully, but didn't eat until he was done extracting all the pulp and juice from his precious weed.

They continued to drift; Sperry no longer felt like rowing, or even hoping that anything in particular might lie in any direction. The sun was brighter today, quickly becoming unpleasantly intense on Sperry's skin, but there was still a cool breeze winding up from the water to brush over him. He supposed he would miss the warm light when the night came again; then it would be nothing but chills, and who knew how many more days he might wake up for? The gentle rocking of the boat, the quiet rhythmic lapping of the waves… it was all a peaceful lull, a time in which nothing could be done and so nothing needed to be worried about. So, he just sat there, mind drifting and swirling through nothing in particular as the boat drifted free across the sea.

His thoughts were interrupted by a spray of cold water droplets pattering over him. Beran, across from him in the boat, felt it too; Sperry saw his head jerk in surprise, perhaps woken from a nap.

The two men looked out in the direction the misting had come from, blinking. There was nothing on the surface of the water - hard to tell, but perhaps a few ripples spreading out among the waves a short distance away, and the glare of the sun reflecting off the ocean made it difficult to peer too closely.

Stillness returned. The fine sheen of seawater evaporated from Sperry's skin, and he almost began to wonder whether he'd imagined it - and, somehow, Beran had also imagined it at the same time.

Then - halfway between their boat and the horizon - something broke the surface of the water, an enormous grey thing the size of a house just emerging out into the air as if it were the most natural thing in the world. A jet of water sprayed from somewhere on its body, turning into a fine mist in the air; the creature rose up, looking like nothing so much as a monolithic pillar made of some shiny stone, and then plunged back down. Sperry caught a glimpse of what looked like a huge fin as it disappeared into the water with an almighty splash. Even from a way away, their boat rocked up and down on the waves created by its return to the sea.

'That looked like…' Beran didn't finish the sentence, but his head turned to the sky.

'It's… no -' Sperry shook his head rapidly '- no, it was big, but not *that* big, maybe it was just a… a really big fish?'

Beran turned to his nephew, looking almost pitying that anyone could believe such a thing. 'We've been fishing together for years,' he said, 'and have you ever, *ever* seen a fish *anything like* as big as whatever that thing was?'

'No, but I've never been out this far to sea either-'

'That's a Child of Guilt if I ever saw one,' Beran muttered. 'It's spawning little *itselves* now, just smaller versions.'

'But that would mean…'

'Who knows? There could be thousands of little Guilts, and maybe they'll all grow up to be just as big as the original.'

Sperry tried to consider this, but it was impossible to comprehend. A sky filled with not just one Guilt, but dozens? Hundreds? Thousands?

As if hearing his thoughts, the ocean's surface parted again, three portals between the air and the water opening up to admit three gargantuan grey leviathans that rose up and fell back into the water.

'More of them!' Beran hissed.

Sperry couldn't say anything. That group had been closer to their boat than the first - he put his hands on the side of the boat, leaning over to look down, and saw through the glittering surface of the sea. At first he thought there was a great grey slab of rock gliding underneath the boat, a few metres down, but then the shape tapered down as if it were going to end in a point before widening back out into what was unmistakably a tail, a triangular arrangement of two fins three times as wide as the little boat was long.

He collapsed back into the boat, feeling as if the sight had stolen all the energy from every muscle in his body. It was too much to think about, and yet it was all around him and he was in it. Guilts, enormous creatures - but still miniscule compared to their progenitor - capable of who knew what, and they were just *here*, just growing out of sight of everyone until they were ready to… to do whatever it was they were going to do.

His uncle watched the movements of the group as their bodies surfaced and descended, his expression changing slowly - if Sperry had been looking to see it - from a wide-eyed, jaw-locked terror and defiance to something more like awe. His eyes moved from each sighting to the next, glancing down between stares as if remembering something.

'Sperry,' said Beran quietly.

Sperry didn't respond, dumbstruck and limp as he was.

'Lad.'

The younger fisherman released a long, unsteady breath somewhere between a sigh and a sob. 'What?'

'They're not… doing anything to us,' Beran said slowly, looking out across the water. Not far from them, smooth shapes continued to pop in and out of view, the group moving in a broad arc around the boat. The one who had swum underneath made its presence known with a stream of water blasted upwards from under the surface, then showed its body as it moved back towards the rest of its family.

'What, you don't think they want to hurt us now? It's *Guilt*, Uncle.' Sperry didn't have the energy to sound convinced, simply ready for it all to be over. 'You said - you said there was nothing like it, that there was *nothing* that big that wasn't a Child, that it had to be Guilt.'

'Maybe it's not.'

Sperry shook his head with a great effort. 'What do you mean?'

'Somebody told me once,' the old man said, 'that when Guilt first appeared, the people thought it looked a lot like a fish of a kind they knew. A big fish - an *enormous* one, but I never thought…' He gestured out to the sporadic assortment of bodies and fins.

Sperry did his uncle the courtesy of listening, but his thoughts were increasingly dominated by the simple certainty that he was going to die and the rest of the world was going to be overrun by little Guilts and there was nothing he could do about it.

'Or... no,' Beran muttered, frowning as he tried to remember the details, 'it wasn't a fish, but it lived in the sea - anyway, the point is, the first people who saw Guilt knew its shape. They had seen things that looked just like it before.'

'You're telling me that these are just... normal sea creatures?'

'Not *normal*, maybe,' Beran admitted. 'By the time Guilt came, the people who lived before Guilt's time had killed most of them, but... maybe now nobody remembers them to hunt them, they're doing well for themselves again.'

A tail crested up alongside them, arcing elegantly up and back down with barely a splash.

'Well, good for them,' Sperry huffed. 'Nice to know Guilt did something nice for someone.'

Beran shook his head gently, then carefully moved up the boat to his nephew. 'Look at them,' he said, tilting his head out towards the open water. 'They're just... here.'

Sperry glanced out. There were jumbles of huge sleek masses and fins cycling through water and air now, at least six different bodies giving him fleeting glimpses of different parts of themselves. Some were larger, some smaller; all were big enough that trying to visualise how small he would look if he were next to one started to make his head swim. The way they moved around each other reminded him of games he'd played with his friends when he was younger - games where the object was to tag as many people as possible, or ones in which you had to form a ring around one player and see if they could escape.

'It's like they're a family,' he said, 'just playing with each other.'

'Might well be,' Beran said. The old fisherman's eyes were sparkling as he watched the group - perhaps from the light or the sea mist, or perhaps not.

Sperry couldn't look away, once he started watching. These things didn't bear any resemblance at all to the thing in the sky except for the shape of their bodies; he couldn't conceive of an infant Guilt swimming playfully in space before growing into the doom of a planet. This was life on Earth, something part of the same world as he was - of the same soil and water, but vastly removed from his own existence. A world of its own that would just keep going on; out of sight and out of mind of humanity, and perhaps doing better that way.

There was a brief lull in the movement, and then, just as Sperry wondered whether they had all decided to swim below and carry on with their lives out of sight of the world above the water, a shape the size of a whole row of houses threw itself completely free of the ocean and soared free in space for just a moment.

Revealed in its entirety, the animal rose up out of the sea and turned a lazy half-spiral, exposing its belly to the air, before crashing back down into its own world. As if thrilled by their companion's example, several more gigantic creatures took a turn at casting themselves free from the weight of the water, deafening splashes throwing seawater over Sperry and Beran even as the group travelled further from the boat.

The two men said nothing more until the group - the pod of whales, as those who lived long before them might have known to call it - had passed out of sight, the last flicks of fins and tails fading into the distance.

When they were alone again, Sperry felt an overwhelming sense that he had an awful lot to say to his uncle, but couldn't possibly think what any of it might be. Beran's gaze lingered on the horizon, an almost wistful look smoothing the lines on his face. They sat there like that for some time, and then Beran's brows lowered.

'Sperry,' he said, tilting his chin up in the direction he was looking; Sperry squinted after him.

'Is that…?'

'I think that's land,' Beran murmured, and Sperry almost tipped the boat over in his scrabbling to lean out for a closer look.

Beran was right: fading into view, a thin dark line like an outline over part of the horizon, there was something rapidly becoming more and more visible in the distance. There was an occasional flash of grey accompanied by sparkles on the water between them and the landmass, as if the whales were pointing them in the right direction.

'It is,' Sperry breathed, and grabbed the oars.

The place they reached was inhabited: there were towns not far from the shores. There was a woman in one of the settlements who traded regularly with the markets in Sperry and Beran's own town, and she told them how to get home: a journey of two or three days, since the most direct route would have passed through dangerous forests and come perilously close to sharp cliffs where birds the size of boars swooped after anything that moved in their vision.

The pair stayed in an inn near the place where they'd landed for a week or so, intending to make the journey once their strength had returned, but a passing of Guilt just as they prepared to set out forced them to stay sheltered with their (extremely hospitable) hosts for some time longer. When it became clear that they would need to trade something in order to keep paying their way, they set out in their boat - after replacing their anchor - and fished in the waters off their new coast.

Some time later, it occurred to Beran that they had simply never left, almost by accident establishing themselves in their new surroundings. Sperry ended up married to the innkeeper's son, and without either of them ever agreeing to give up their claim on their old home they had settled into a new one, where they made good lives for themselves.

Many years later, Beran kissed his nephew and great-niece on the head and set out in the boat alone. They had been able to get a much better boat after a while, but he'd kept the old one. Even when they had sold the better boat, since Sperry no longer needed to fish once he found himself inadvertently entrenched in the management of the inn, Beran had kept the one they'd been in the day they drifted out to sea and passed through the storm.

The old man - he'd been an old man by most standards then, but now he was truly aged - rowed a short way out to sea, then let go of the oars and let them fall into the water. The currents carried him a little further, and he smiled, turning his head from side to side to cast his view across the ocean in every direction.

He had lived much of his life on the water, and had even - without knowing it at the time - ended one life and begun another there. When the movement of the sea took him far enough out that he could no longer see land, he breathed deeply and closed his eyes, feeling the sharp tang of the salt water in his nostrils and throat.

There was a splash not far away; Beran opened his eyes, looking out towards the direction the sound had come from. His eyes weren't as good as they used to be, but there was no mistaking it when a spurt of water erupted upwards, showering him in cold droplets. Beran laughed, loud and long.

If Calamity had flown overhead again, as it had years ago, it could have looked down and seen a small boat floating gently across the ocean, an old man lying still with a smile on his face, and a group of large grey shapes dancing around each other in the water nearby.

A MENAGERIE ALL IN ONE

The new creations brought into life (or some approximation) by the Shadow are frequently, though not without exception, both highly dangerous and highly aggressive.

'I really don't know if this is a good idea.'

'Nothing's a *good* idea - you just do the least shit or most potentially half-decent thing and hope for the best.'

'Fair point.'

'I thought so.'

'So… where *are* we?'

'How should I know?'

'You're the one with the map.'

'Oh, right.' The cartographer unfolded a broad, thin sheet of paper, laying it down on the earth and placing a small rock on each corner to keep it flat. 'I can see why you would think that, except…' She pointed to the carefully-inscribed lines and sketches depicting the area, then to the conspicuous blank space taking up a large proportion of the map. 'Cartographers *make* maps. And there's not that much point being a cartographer somewhere that's already been mapped.'

The other woman groaned, throwing her head back to vent her frustration at the sky. 'That is not helpful at all,' she said, after a good grumble.

'Not particularly,' the cartographer admitted, 'but that's why it's not just me along for the trip.'

'What, those two?' The second woman glanced at the two men doing their best to open the metal gate a few metres away, then shook her head. 'They're not even dumb muscle. They're just dumb.'

'I was talking about you,' said the cartographer, not looking up from her map. '*You're* supposed to be the muscle, aren't you? That's how this works: cartographer, muscle, historian, optimist. Classic paradigm.'

'Never understood that,' muttered the muscle. Just out of earshot, the historian and the optimist continued their fruitless attempts to gain entry to the place: an ancient structure a few kilometres from one end to the other, surrounded by a frustratingly sturdy wall. What was within was a mystery, but that was the whole point of trying to get in. 'And I do have a name, by the way. It's -'

'Nuh-uh,' the cartographer interrupted. 'We're just functions here, just a team on a mission to find out what lies beyond.'

The muscle frowned. 'We're not functions. We're people.'

'Sure,' muttered the cartographer. She sighed, folding up her map again. 'Nonetheless, I'm pretty sure you're the one who ought to be trying to open this place up, not Tweedledim and Tweedledimmer.'

'I think it's Tweedledum.'

'Oh, now you're the historian?'

The muscle sighed heavily, gave the cartographer an eyebrows-lowered look of exasperation, and trudged over to the wide arch cut into the high, ivy-thronged brick wall before them. She pushed herself between the two would-be forced enterers, then gave the tarnished metal bars of the gate a good shake. 'Wozzis?'

'Locked,' explained the optimist unhelpfully.

'I hope so, otherwise you're doing a worse job than I thought.'

'It's a rusted padlock,' the historian told her. 'I was trying old lockpicking techniques, but… well, rusted. Not much good.'

'Crowbar?'

'Probably a better idea, yeah.'

The muscle unhooked the crowbar hanging from her belt and rammed it into the space between the arm and the body of the padlock. She paused to huff impatiently at the two men looking on with interest; they stepped back, sheepish. With a sharp wrench, she had the lock clattering in two pieces on the floor.

'That was much easier than I was making it,' mumbled the historian, scratching the back of his head. The muscle gave him a withering glance, pulling the gate open.

'We're in!' the optimist chirped, raising his hands as if to clap with excitement. He thought better of it.

The cartographer wandered over and patted the muscle on the back. 'Neatly done,' she said quietly, peering inside. 'Let's see what we've got here, eh?'

Something crashed down behind them with a metal clap; the four threw themselves through the open entranceway, scrambling to take shelter behind the sturdy walls.

'What under Dread's wings was - mfph?' The muscle clapped a hand over the historian's mouth, silencing him.

'I think it's OK,' the optimist whispered, creeping towards the fallen thing. Black and brown dust billowed around the place where it had slammed into the ground, obscuring its shape. 'It's not moving.'

'That doesn't mean it *can't*,' hissed the muscle; the historian - still gagged - nodded rapidly, wide-eyed.

The optimist nudged the thing - a wide, flat thing, they could see as the dark cloud of dirt dispersed - with his toe, then hopped back a few steps, watching. Nothing moved.

'OK,' he said, quietly enough that it might have been to himself. Then he darted forwards, stuck his hands under the thing, and flipped it over.

'Christ,' muttered the muscle, when the hollow clang had died down; the historian raised an eyebrow. It wasn't a name often uttered, in those days.

'What is it?' called the cartographer, poking her head out.

'It's just… a sign, or something.' The optimist squatted down beside it, peering at its surface. 'Rusted to hell, obviously, but it says… something *zoo*, I think.'

Everyone looked at the historian. The historian grunted a couple of times, then sighed through his nose and tapped the muscle's hand.

'Oh.' She let him go, frowning as if she'd forgotten she'd been squashing his face in the first place.

'It's like… a farm,' the historian explained, after a couple of deep breaths. 'People used to keep animals here, but not to eat.'

The muscle furrowed her brow. 'Weird.'

'Sounds kind of nice,' said the optimist, wandering through the arch again to join the group. 'Nicer for the animals, presumably.'

'There's some debate about that, actually -'

'Doesn't matter now, though,' the cartographer interjected. 'No way there's still anything here.'

'Never bet on that,' said the muscle, rolling her head from side to side. The muscles in her jaw and neck tightened, then slackened.

'Point taken.'

'We haven't been under the Shadow for… years, though.' The historian scratched at his hair, which sat on his head dry and haphazard like days-old cut grass, and frowned. 'And we didn't come that far to get here, so…'

'So, anything Guilt put here shouldn't have stuck around this long,' finished the optimist. 'Brilliant.' He stuck his hands in his pockets and wandered away, bobbing his shoulders as if to a tune.

The muscle gave the cartographer a glance, as if imploring her to admit that the man was indeed *just dumb*. The cartographer shrugged, casting her gaze around the entrance of the zoo.

'We should probably work out where we're going before we start walking,' the muscle said, just loudly enough for the optimist to hear. He meandered back to them, smiling faintly.

'Any road's good by me.'

The historian gave a quiet laugh through his nose and muttered something that might have been 'Buridan'.

'I did actually see a map up there, though,' the optimist continued, sticking his thumb over his shoulder in the direction he'd gone, 'so… that might help.'

The cartographer made a beeline for it; the others traipsed up behind her, catching up as she was laying out her map on the ground to compare to the one on the wooden board. A layer of grime covered most of the plastic sheet over the zoo's map; the muscle wiped it off with her sleeve.

'Not much use,' the cartographer mused. 'It's just areas within the walls, no indication of what direction might have anything useful. It's all just labelled by - I'm guessing those are all animal names?' she said, directing the question to the historian.

'Must be,' he said, considering the words on the map. 'All the words I recognise are, anyway.'

'Are those pictures of what the animals looked like?' The optimist pointed to a couple of the more legible zones, each of which contained a word and an outline in the shape of some arrangement of body, head, and limbs.

'Well, you know what a deer looks like, and that one's obviously a deer, so yes.'

'Ooh. The… gi-raf-feh?'

'I think it's *jee-raf-fay*.' The historian folded his arms, considering the picture. 'They had long, thick necks so they could reach the leaves high up in the trees, and these spindly legs for some reason.'

'Weird,' said the optimist cheerily.

The muscle shivered. 'Doesn't sound like a normal animal to me,' she said, eyeing the diagram with distaste. 'Sounds like something the bastard up there would have dreamed up.'

'They were definitely around before -' the historian began, but the cartographer groaned loudly.

'This isn't helping us find anything of value.' She folded her map down into a rectangle of paper two handspans wide and stretched.

'You're not gonna copy the map down or anything?' the historian asked.

'No point. Unless we find another exit, this place is all just one self-contained thing with one way in and out. Not much use having a map showing that - better to save the paper for places worth going.'

'You don't think this was worth coming to?' the optimist piped up, sounding dismayed.

'We'll go over the whole place while we're here,' said the cartographer, 'and then we'll close it back up, mark that it's empty, and move on somewhere we've not been before. For now, looks like this path'll take us in a big circle around pretty much the entire thing, so let's just start with that and see if we can't be finished by sundown.'

The muscle and the historian nodded their agreement; the optimist beamed. The cartographer tucked her map away and led them off down the path: the historian went close behind her, the muscle following in third place, and the optimist traipsing contentedly along at the back.

None of the others saw it, but the optimist's smile faded for just a moment - the same moment at which, if anyone had been looking very closely, they might have seen something seem to protrude from his left shoulder and press at the inside of his shirt as if trying to break out. Just for a moment, though, and then it was gone, and he was smiling just the same as he ever did.

'Well,' said the muscle, gazing down into what had been the giraffe enclosure, 'that's fucking horrible.'

Two bodies occupied the pen: one grey-green mass lay on its side, huge chunks of flesh missing from all over its body, and the other -

'You said the neck was supposed to be thick and the legs thin, right?' murmured the cartographer. The historian nodded beside her. She drew a sharp breath in through her teeth. 'Ouch.'

The other body appeared to have frozen where it had died: some silvery-grey substance, stains of colour rippling across its surface like oil on water, covered most of the creature's skin with a hard layer of cracked, rough rind. Jagged chunks of the same material sprouted from several places, as if outgrowing a container. Where the opalescent layer didn't cover, the skin had long since rotted away.

The giraffe was lying on its stomach, four thick legs with too many joints curling out of its body; its head was on the floor, at the end of a frail stick that was bent into a lightning-bolt shape.

'No way one of its legs could have supported the weight of its head, if the legs and the neck swapped,' said the historian with quiet distaste. 'Good news is the weight of its head probably broke its neck the moment it happened, so… would've died straight away, at least.'

The muscle shook her head; even the optimist had the sense to look vaguely troubled.

'So that one fell under the Shadow, got some body parts swapped, grew a coating of… something. Fine. What about the other one?' The cartographer tilted her chin, indicating the second body. 'That one hasn't petrified, and there's no way it was still alive until recently enough that it shouldn't have rotted a *lot* more than that.'

'Looks almost as if something's been eating it,' the optimist noted.

'Can't have,' said the muscle, not entirely forcefully. 'Thought we said nothing was alive.'

'Thought *you* said never to bet on that,' countered the cartographer. The muscle opened her mouth as if to respond, then shut it and folded her arms, looking away.

'Someone should probably… check it,' suggested the historian; each word came out slowly, as if each were the answer to a riddle he was having trouble solving.

The cartographer stared at him. 'That'd be you, surely.'

'Me?' The historian, stammering and blustering, raised his hands and gestured at the muscle. 'Isn't the potentially dangerous stuff her department?'

'It's… sciencey!' protested the muscle.

The cartographer sighed, one hand on her forehead. 'Why don't you *both* -'

'I'll do it,' announced the optimist, and before anyone could say anything else he hopped over the low wall before them and shimmied down the ladder into the enclosure. The muscle gave a surreptitious sigh of something that might have been relief; the historian stared down, gripping the edge of the wall with white fingers; the cartographer rolled her eyes.

The optimist trotted to the petrified, limb-swapped corpse and gave it a poke. Nothing happened. He raised his head, looking up at the others, and gave a thumbs-up, then trundled over to the other body.

'It doesn't smell brilliant,' he called up. The historian leaned over the edge, gazing down with a fearful expression; the optimist squatted down beside the half-rotten pile of meat for a closer look. 'It's, er, growing something.'

'What sort of *something*?' From his tone, the historian was either fascinated or disgusted - or perhaps both.

The optimist wandered around the carcass, poked at it from a few angles, then shrugged. 'It's been dead for a while,' he said, 'but not as long as I think we thought it should have been. Then again, never know what time'll do under the Shadow.' He exhaled, staring down at the once-giraffe. 'Not sure whether this is, like, regular mould and fungus and that or... something else.'

'What about the hole in its side?' asked the muscle, though she was looking off to the side of the scene rather than at it.

'Oh, yeah.' The optimist put his head closer than any of the others would have thought reasonable to the body, examining some of the places where flesh appeared to have been torn away. 'It does look... sort of bitey.'

The cartographer stuck her head out as far over the edge of the wall as she dared, squinting hard at the body. 'Does it look to anyone else as if that thing might be... moving?'

'I don't think so,' said the optimist, and then a cacophony of disjointed appendages erupted from the carcass.

Long deer legs; huge grey feet smothered in matted hair; a giant wing of creased, rumpled leather; dozens of thick, rubbery tentacles; something that looked like a bird's beak on the end of a humanoid torso - all burst out of the dead giraffe's body. Some came from the holes already mangling the corpse; others made paths for themselves, stretching its skin into taut bulbs from the inside before sprouting from freshly-ripped exit wounds.

The jumble of body parts wearing the skin of the dead giraffe twitched madly, its newborn limbs shaking and hitting each other as if each part didn't know what the others were doing. A few moments later, its movements became less erratic, more controlled, and each of its many mismatched legs lowered itself to the floor. Slowly, wobbling like the giraffe whose body it had taken must have done when it first learned to walk, the thing raised itself up, a half-rotted, bulbous body on abominable stilts.

'What the fuck,' breathed the cartographer.

'Guys,' the optimist hissed, backing away from the thing, 'I think there's still some stuff alive here.'

The historian looked at the cartographer, then to the muscle. 'What are you waiting for? Someone's got to get down there and help him! That's your job!'

She just shook her head, gaze fixed now on the scene below even as she took slow steps backwards. 'I'm not fighting one of the fucking Children of Guilt.'

'Then what's he supposed to do?' The historian moved towards the cartographer, eyes pleading. 'He's going to die down there.'

The cartographer exhaled heavily. 'She's not wrong. Fighting something like that… there's no winning. He escapes on his own, or at least he's the only one of us to die.'

The historian put his hands on his head, turning in agitated circles. It escaped the notice of neither of the other two that he made no move to go down himself.

In the enclosure, the giraffe-thing shuffled towards the optimist, its legs trying different patterns as if working out how best to ambulate; half of it seemed to be attempting a coordinated, spider-like stride, while other parts fanned themselves along like a centipede. The optimist had his hands up, like he was trying to arrange a peaceful surrender. Still it came.

'It's still slow!' the historian called. 'Run around it and get out of there!'

The optimist, nearly backed into the far corner, made to dart around the creature's side as it approached - but a dozen disorganized pieces of various beasts whipped up, far quicker and far more certain than any movement it had made so far, and slammed him into the wall of the pen.

'We should get out of here now,' the muscle whispered. 'While it's distracted.'

The historian looked between her and the cartographer, mouth half-open despairingly. 'You're supposed to be the one who deals with things like this,' he said to the muscle after a moment. 'Not the one who tells us to leave people behind.'

'I'm *supposed* to keep as many of us alive as I can,' the muscle told him, squaring her shoulders, 'whether that means hitting something or getting the fuck out of its way.'

The historian blinked. He opened his mouth. He closed it again, looked down at the floor with furiously knotted brows, then looked back up at the muscle and opened his mouth more forcefully.

Before whatever words were on their way out of his mouth could escape, a louder, more urgent noise blared from within the enclosure. The three of them rushed to gaze down: the creature was stumbling around, bleating with a cry like the scraping of metal on stone. Several of its legs were reduced to bleeding stumps; the optimist stood watching it, breathing heavily.

'What...?' the historian breathed.

The optimist looked up at them and raised his left arm. Or - *arms*. Two new limbs - hard, red, spiked, like the legs of a crab - extended from his shoulder, his shirt tattered where they'd emerged. It looked as if an apologetic expression were trying to make its way out from underneath the mix of resolve and fear on his face.

The wounded beast staggered around, trumpeting like an earthquake; the optimist made a dash for the ladder, but even in its pain the thing barreled into his path, hammering him with blows. So many of its limbs dedicated themselves to attacking that it seemed to forget to hold itself up, toppling over even as it continued to rain strikes down upon the optimist. The cartographer could just about see him amidst the storm: still on his feet, his two shell-skinned arms shielding his body.

There was a scream - a human voice, in pain and rage; a wet thud like a stone thrown into thick mud; one more grating cry; and then the soft slapping noises of dozens of limbs all falling still at once. The optimist crawled out from underneath the twice-dead creature; one of his sharp red hands clutched some chunk of flesh, dripping the colour of vomit.

'What the fuck,' said the cartographer, for the second time.

'One of them,' the muscle said under her breath. Then, louder, accusingly: 'You're one of them!'

'I'm not,' protested the optimist, dropping the hunk of meat and raising all four of his hands placatingly. 'I'm not.'

'Then what the fuck is *that* all about?'

He shook his head. 'I'm not one of the Children of Guilt, but... I might be one of its grandkids, or something.'

The historian took a sharp breath. 'It's true? They've bred?'

'I don't exactly know,' the optimist said, hands dropping to his sides. He was slumped, not at all his usual upright self. 'A man who loved my mother raised me, but he said he wasn't my father. Said she fell under the Shadow, that her mind… well, you know what happens. And while she was… of that mind, she…' He frowned, staring off. 'She, and one of the Children it spawned… and then me.'

'You just killed your uncle, then,' the cartographer observed. 'Somehow.'

Something like half a laugh escaped the optimist's nostrils. 'Uncle Zombie Giraffe, we hardly knew ye. I didn't know what would work, so I just… hoped, stuck a hand in and pulled something out, and that seems to have done the trick.'

The cartographer and the historian exchanged glances; the muscle didn't move.

'We should move, anyway,' the cartographer said, gesturing to the optimist to come up the ladder. 'If anything else is still here, it'll have heard all that.'

The optimist nodded gratefully and took hold of the rungs, climbing out of the enclosure carefully. He only used his two human arms to climb, the cartographer noticed; the other two held themselves out of the way. As he reached the last rung and moved to pull himself up over the wall, the muscle put herself in front of him.

'Thanks,' he said, putting his right arm out for her to take.

'I feel like I should say I'm sorry,' she said. In the next moment, one end of her crowbar was in her hands and the other was breaking through his skull; his body fell back and landed with a thump on the floor of the giraffe enclosure.

The historian gaped at her, the muscles in his jaw trembling. 'What did you…?'

'Gotta keep as many humans alive as possible,' she said, her voice as steady as it had been the entire trip as she wiped off her crowbar and tucked it back into her belt. 'That was a risk, but an easily mitigated one.'

'That is cold as *fuck*,' the cartographer muttered. She might have been appalled or impressed.

'Let's move,' said the muscle, standing with her back to the ladder and the enclosure. 'Something else could be -'

She never finished the sentence: a dark shape - sleek-bodied, lightning-quick, and *big* - careened out of nowhere and snatched her up, disappearing as quickly as it had come.

The historian and the cartographer stood dumbly for a moment, looking at the space where the muscle had been, and then at the same moment both started running as fast as they could in the other direction.

'What *was* that?!' the historian yelled; the cartographer shot an angry glance over her shoulder at him.

'No more noise!' she spat, legs pounding against the ground.

They bolted along the path, all sense of direction forgotten in their haste to flee. Something cried out behind them, some harsh, gasping bird-scream, and they slammed their feet down ever harder even as their muscles rapidly descended into a burning heaviness.

'That way!' the cartographer blurted, spotting a wide section of broken wall to the side; the two of them shot through the gap between the bricks and pressed themselves against the outside wall, trying to make themselves invisible to anything looking out.

The cartographer looked over at the historian; he was panting, gazing up at the sky, whispering some obsolete prayer to himself.

'It's still in there,' the cartographer murmured, as little breath and sound as possible escaping with each word. 'We need to go - just go this way, and just hope it doesn't follow us out.'

The historian closed his eyes and nodded several times, lips pressed tightly shut until he could bear it no more and let out a wracked breath. 'I'm Cole,' he whispered after a moment.

The cartographer blinked at him. 'I don't like knowing names,' she said slowly.

'Why?'

'In case... in case people...' She trailed off.

The historian - Cole - nodded. 'I think we're past that,' he said.

A few deep breaths later, the cartographer sighed. 'Vi,' she said.

'Vi.' Cole smiled, a brief flash of sincere closeness amidst the terror. 'Nice to meet you.'

'Likewise.' Vi grinned back in spite of herself. 'Let's just go this… way.'

She stood up slowly, looking out for the first time at the landscape they'd escaped into. There were a few hundred metres of flat, dust-covered stone ahead of them - a normal sort of surface - and then the earth broke cleanly, a sharp, defined edge marking the end of the stone. Beyond that, the ground was made of dirty metal: grimy silver plates as far as the cartographer could see, a shining landscape with hills and valleys all made of interlocking chrome surfaces.

'What am I looking at?' she muttered to herself.

Cole pushed himself unsteadily to his feet, taking slow, deliberate breaths through his nose, and stared at the way before them. 'It's… it must be a place changed by the Shadow,' he said. 'When Guilt was last over this place, it must have turned all the earth into metal.'

Vi frowned. 'That… doesn't sound right.'

'It's done stranger things.'

'No, I know, but…' She knelt down and unfolded her map on the ground, keeping one eye on the bizarre vista of steel. 'We were going really fast, but I'm sure we took a left to come out here. And…' She rotated the map a couple of times, reciting something under her breath. 'If we came in from the south, followed the path around until we got to the giraffe enclosure - which the map at the entrance said was on the right, as you look at it from the entrance - then we've come out… to the east, here.' She pointed. 'And that's already been mapped.'

'So?'

'So… it's been mapped since the last time this place was under the Shadow, and there's nothing here about the whole place being… *this*.'

Cole swallowed. Something called out behind them, a predator's roar through shrieking vocal cords.

'Follow me,' Vi said quietly, turning right and following the wall along. 'If we came through the south wall and now we're outside the east wall, we should just be able to head south along this one until we get back to where we were.'

Cole followed dutifully. The thing that had taken the muscle screamed, closer; the two sped up, the historian looking over his shoulder every few steps. They reached a corner and rounded it, but the same landscape awaited them; when, wondering whether they'd made a mistake, they tried to go back the way they'd come, there was no corner, only a flat wall.

So they kept moving, even as it felt that they might only be covering the same few metres of wall in endless repetition.

'Keep going,' Vi whispered, perhaps to herself. 'Just keep going.'

'Keep going,' Cole echoed.

'Keep going,' Vi repeated.

Cole was silent.

'Keep going,' Vi murmured; when Cole remained quiet, she turned to look at him.

She was alone.

'Oh, shit,' she had time to mutter; the great scraping bellow sounded above her and she broke away from the wall, running as fast as she could on her exhausted legs away from the zoo and towards the landscape of silver.

Something slammed into her back as she crossed the divide between stone and metal, sending her skidding across the smooth surface beneath her. She clambered back to her feet, spinning to look in the direction of attack: nothing.

'Where are you...?'

The cry sounded again, off to the side; she dashed away from the noise, making for a jutting metal edge to shelter behind. Her legs were so fatigued that the silver ground seemed to be moving beneath her as she ran.

It struck again, knocking her onto her side as she fled. There was a sharp jolt of pain in her shoulder, but she scrambled upright. It had stopped, perhaps sensing that there was no need to try too hard to catch its wounded prey, and stood for her to see: a dark, cat-like body the length of two horses, ripped, thin wings too small to be of any use, four long multi-jointed limbs, at least three more vestigial legs too short to reach the ground, a spined tail, and a bird's beak protruding from an ox's head.

It let her stare, and it stared back with peculiarly expressive eyes. Was it the fear or the exhaustion that was making her body tremble, her legs unsteady as if the earth itself were swaying and rising and falling under her?

The beast looked at the ground; its own legs, the cartographer realised, were extending and tensing in turn, keeping it balanced. It wasn't just her, then, but what…?

The creature leapt from its unsteady footing, crying out - in triumph, perhaps. The cartographer waited for the end.

When it came, she was surprised to note, it wasn't the sharp pain she'd expected. Dying felt like the whole world shaking around her, as it turned out: a maelstrom of movement and noise. She'd thought it would be quieter.

She opened her eyes, just in case, and found that she wasn't dead at all. The metal landscape all around her was thrumming, bulging, quaking; the predator beast she spotted as a flash of dark motion just before it disappeared, fleeing back over the wall. No longer consigned to dying then, she sprinted after it, clearing the metal ground and collapsing onto the stone - far enough away, she hoped, but she could go no further.

A chrome mountain reared up by the horizon; a vast cave appeared and a dark flame shone out from within. Metal cried out as it scraped on metal, the entire topography shifting and shaking. The mountain turned, the flame within the cave like an eye staring in the cartographer's direction.

Then the cave *blinked*. Vi's breath seized up in her body: she was beholding one of the First Children. She had stood upon the back of one of the First Children. It had been there, waiting for her - no, not waiting. It didn't care. It hadn't even *noticed* until the predatory creature had screamed.

'The noise disturbed you,' she breathed. 'I'm sorry.'

The land rose and fell, one heavy breath, and the metal dragon closed its eye and lay down its head. Vi, exhausted beyond measure, could do nothing except join it in sleep.

Chris Durston

THE PEOPLE AND THE PEOPLE

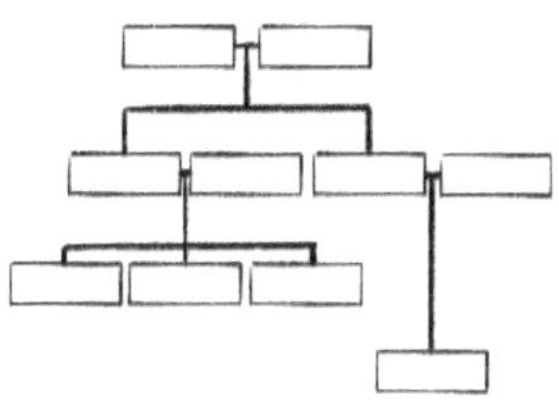

There are some effects which persist beyond the point that Guilt is no longer visible in the sky, perhaps even interminably. Creatures spawned in the Shadow continue to exist in many cases - some disappear once Guilt is no longer overhead, but particularly those more clearly corporeal in nature seem to maintain their existence unless destroyed.

As is so often the case, the first thing that many people wondered how best to achieve when they learned that a different sort of person existed was how to eradicate them.

The Descendants of Guilt (or the Offspring, or the Progeny, or the Guiltblood; there were many names for them, though few of them wanted to have any name at all) kept themselves as secret as possible for a long time, but eventually they were so numerous that their existence could no longer be denied. Many were bemused to learn that they might be thought of as anything *other* than simply human, as everyone else was apparently entitled to be considered. To the vast majority of the Descendants, the imposition of any label at all seemed vastly mistaken: a miscategorisation, a misrecognition, an overzealousness in spotting a difference to categorise, an overeagerness to declare one sort of person not like another (or less than).

To too many of those who could consider themselves 'pure' human, though, the differences were not only material but damning. If someone had a drop of Guilt's blood in their veins, if they were in any way (even having had no say in the matter) connected to the doombringer in the sky, then they weren't just different: they weren't a *person*, not really.

The greatest indignation felt by the Descendants was often not that they were forced out of human society, killed or exiled so that those who were left often had to band together and form their own small civilisations, but that they were stripped of their humanity. What right did the mundane have to decide that they would be the ones who could keep the name 'human', and that the Descendants had no claim to it?

Over generations, two societies formed, one of the people who were not imbued with any of the power or influence of Guilt and one of those who were. Both sides named themselves simply *people* and the others simply *others*. The two were separate: when a new Descendant appeared among sublunary society, they were immediately cast out, left to fend for themselves.

If they found their way to a nearby settlement of their own people, they would survive; if not, they would not. Those who exiled them didn't know which result would come to pass, nor did they care.

Sometimes, one of the *normal* humans would find themselves enamoured with the supernatural allure of the Descendants, and would voluntarily seek out a new life with new people. The Descendants would almost inevitably accept sincere newcomers as their own; those who joined them lived with the knowledge, sometimes uncomfortable, that their former families would never have been as welcoming were the roles reversed.

For the most part, though, the only children born to Descendant society were of two Descendant parents, which kept the blood of Guilt in greater concentration. If the Descendants had never been forced to form their own places, and had been allowed to remain with the rest of humanity, the changes and the powers might have died out sooner.

As it was, while the early Descendants wanted only to live in peace, later generations had a tendency to become resentful. Years of hearing nothing about the *other* people but tales of spite and cruelty, and their insular society contributing both to their loyalty to 'their own' and to their differences from 'pure' humans, had what perhaps ought to have been a predictable result: over time, the two civilisations came to hate each other with equal passion.

Some of the Descendants chose to worship Guilt, but then so did some of those who were not Descendants. Equally, some of them formed belief systems explicitly reviling the thing. Still others preferred to live their lives as if there were no Guilt, except when practical issues demanded that they take action in response to it. There would be little to gain from pretending Guilt did not exist while its Shadow covered one's own home.

There were wars, and there were deaths, and then there were uneasy periods of peace. Once, many generations after the Descendants were first exposed and exiled, one of their number stood up in the name of a more lasting harmony. There were those on both sides who opposed the movement, and others on both sides who supported it.

Farnus the Human (as he insisted upon being called) did not want peace for one very simple reason: he had an idea for a machine, a Descendant-killer that could detect and destroy those with Guilt-tainted cells in their bodies. The first part of the idea came to him when he killed one of the base Children of Guilt - a pig-like creature with a bull's face and scaled wings too heavily to be usable for flight - and saw that the plants spattered by its spraying blood sizzled and died. If he could identify some chemical that would react to the presence of Guiltblood, then he could detect Descendants.

Then the machinery in his brain started whirring even harder when he witnessed the use of a device that could repel the Children, something developed from old bits of transmitting technology and a piece of a monster's brain. It had long been suspected that the Children could communicate with their sire without words; the device mimicked those signals and broadcast them in a wide arc, commanding the Children in their own private language to stay away. If *that* were possible, then why could Farnus not create an even stronger machine that could send a destructive signal directly into the brain of a Descendant?

This was his fortune, Farnus knew. This idea would make him the richest man alive, and all he needed was for war to continue.

All it took was a quiet conversation with a man on the Descendants' side, a man who was desperate for even a few coins and a hunk of meat. In return for enough to feed himself for perhaps a week (and a muttered promise for more rewards to come later), that man took a simple, unceremonious knife in the dark and killed three of the most prominent Descendant advocates for peace.

The dead became martyrs: a tiny number of Descendants persisted in calling for an end to all fighting, for there would be no need for more martyrs if peace could be attained. The vast majority, however, threw themselves back into war in retaliation for the deaths of their friends, relatives, beacons.

Farnus made a small stack of coins, invested in him by those who hoped that his idea would help them destroy the Descendants once and for all, but he never managed to create a working machine. He died in an attempt to steal from one of his investors, leaving a half-scribbled blueprint that was of no value whatsoever.

The dream of peace for all in the world was ended by two people who wanted a few shiny trinkets. If anyone on either side had known the story, they would not have been particularly surprised.

Chris Durston

THEORY AND PRACTICE

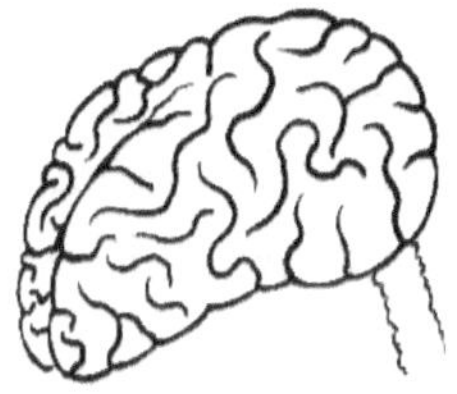

Those who come after us might look back at what has changed between six years ago and now, between now and their time, and perhaps use that information to come to ever more useful knowledge about the nature of Guilt.

Norris Krinke was, as he liked to remind everyone regularly and at length, an academic. Perhaps the foremost academic in the entire world on the topic of Guilt, although nobody could verify that on account of the fact that communicating at great distances was an unreliable, lengthy affair entailing an awful lot of written letters and a significantly smaller number of successfully received ones. The world was a difficult place to traverse, after all.

Fortunately for Norris, explaining in great detail what it was about the world that made it so challenging, and inferring possible implications, reasons, and ontologies from these things, was by some strange good fortune a viable method of making a living. He wasn't the first - he'd found an antique copy of a book written decades or centuries earlier, back when Guilt was new (imagine such a thing!), attempting to make academic the idiosyncratically practical fact of the world-ruiner. Norris, of course, did a much better job of it.

His main source of income was simply answering questions from concerned citizens. Where was Guilt at that very moment? What power might Guilt have to affect the crops they were thinking about planting? If they left the first slice of each loaf they baked outside their home, might the offering appease Guilt enough to let them go unharmed, or might it inadvertently lure horrors to their door?

Norris answered each question politely, respectfully, and extemporaneously - which was to say that the vast majority of his answers were almost entirely devoid of substance. He didn't see it as *lying*, as such, to claim to know things that he was in fact conjuring from nothing; no, it was a valuable service he provided, making people feel that there was some reason and rationality to the life-defining and broadly inexplicable thing that constantly haunted every human at every moment, even when it wasn't there. He prided himself on his ability to identify the conclusion that would make his client happiest, to give them that conclusion as quickly as possible - to prove that there was no charlatanism going on, oh no, it was all highly practical and valuable - and then to spend the rest of the time reverse-engineering increasingly complicated justifications for those conclusions, until they became so convincing in their denseness that he almost believed them himself.

It wasn't that he was completely making things up, though. There was real knowledge, real skill involved in identifying all those carefully researched details that could support whatever it was he needed someone to believe. In the moments when he was most privately honest with himself, Norris might have admitted that he had no real foundation for the advice he gave, but he would always maintain a true belief that the theoretical knowledge of Guilt he possessed was second to none.

So, when the Shadow fell upon his home - unexpectedly, which in itself was more perturbing than the fact that it had happened at all, because he really thought he ought to have predicted it - Norris couldn't help but imagine that he would be perfectly safe. He knew all there was to know, didn't he? In his mind was stored every model designed by every great thinker on the matter of Guilt, from the early conceptions of it as simply a very large whale from elsewhere in the universe to the more recent postmetacetaceanisms regarding it as more of a metaphor given physical form than something that required physical explanations.

Part of his mind might have been concerned for his safety, but most of it was racing through the details of how exactly he ought to apply and test his theories. He had little in the way of equipment, and he would never consider himself a proponent of the physical sciences at any rate, but there certainly ought to be philosophical experiments that could be conducted. The difficulty would be in controlling for the sheer range of variables and effects that might be produced, disregarding those that were of no real relevance and drawing new and exciting conclusions from the rest.

Norris's mind contained shelves' worth of information about the colossal worldwanderer, so he felt confident in his belief that he knew all there could possibly be to know - what Norris didn't know about Guilt, surely, wasn't worth knowing.

The walls of his home opened up as if the structure were two enormous hands, fingers unfolding from their interlocking, rather than one solid structure. The great tree outside bent in on itself, collapsing from every direction at once, a bizarre reversal of growth. From the place it had occupied erupted an impish, bark-skinned homunculus. Norris stared out of the space that used to be his wall and tapped his fingers together with glee. The little thing jerked a head-shaped, head-situated part of its body up at him, perhaps staring with eyes he couldn't see, and then it scampered off. It never occurred to Norris to be relieved, to feel that he had just escaped the terrible potential that might have been realised had the creature decided to approach. Instead, he felt disappointment at its disappearance.

From the sky came glimmering orbs that danced around each other, forming half-defined shapes that never solidified long enough to be definite, giving just the impression of skittering transmutivity: fleeting velleities chattering about all the shapes they might take, but never committing to any. Norris watched them, or did his best to watch them while his eyes, trying their best to latch onto something solid, kept slipping and refocusing.

The light show was almost enough to make Norris forget all the theory and abstraction, and simply enjoy the moment, but he couldn't help but be reminded of a long since refuted conjecture that the things the Shadow manifested were essentially (that is, in their essences) ontological reifications of epistemological second-order normative attachment states, which of course *sounded* sensible, but had turned out to be mostly nonsense.

The sky pulsed and pounded like the skin of a beaten drum, warping through loud colours overhead. (*Kernsyn's syncretic meteorological supposition*, Norris thought with a sort of internal wise nod at his own brilliant observations.) The hue of the world smelled off, like the distinctly odorous shade of a fermented egg; Norris forgot his own body and observed as if from nowhere as shadows danced, creatures were born and died, and the world celebrated the passage of Guilt.

By some stroke of fortune, or perhaps by his own genius, Norris was spared. The Shadow of Guilt went overhead and away into the distance, and nothing touched him.

As the effects of the Shadow faded, Norris's house remembered that it had been held up by a wall that had since disappeared, and fell on him. No amount of theoretical knowledge could do anything about that.

Chris Durston

TWICE

We all know this, of course, but the Shadow is capable of both transforming beings that already live in the world and creating entities out of (apparently) nothing. Some are impossible to tell from 'normal' cats or birds (or, more rarely) humans; others bear familiar shapes but appear to be made of some different substance, usually described as 'darkness' or 'shadow' (perhaps unsurprisingly); still others look very much like reported transformed iterations of existing creatures; yet others are utterly unlike anything ever to have walked the earth in any capacity. Collectively these are commonly known as the Children of Guilt.

Cerden had seen her own reflection in a mirror once, but the other Cerden in front of her was nothing like that. She wasn't warped, for one thing: she was as clear and as defined as any other human would be. Cerden recognised every detail on the other Cerden's skin, knowing what they felt like on herself, but she didn't recognise the expression on the face. She moved an arm experimentally, but the other her simply stood there, looking at her.

Or - no, she moved to the side and her double simply kept staring straight forward. Perturbing. Cerden raised a hand, waving it in front of the other her's face: no response.

Where had it come from, anyway? Cerden tried to think: she'd been… where *had* she been? That's right: standing on the clifftop, looking out for any signs of approaching enemies on the water, as she did every day. They hadn't come so far, but Cerden wasn't going to be the one not to show up on the very day something finally did come sailing towards her home in a flaming, unstoppable rage. Her wife sometimes said she ought to find another job, something that actually involved *doing* something, but Cerden didn't mind. It was time to think, or not to think. Sometimes the latter was just as helpful as the former.

She blinked, suddenly aware again of the echo in front of her. She'd been on the hill, she was sure of that, and she was still in the same place, but now there was a second *her* right in front of her and she didn't remember when or how this newcomer got there.

'Hello?' Cerden tried, not sure what reason she could have had for thinking that it might achieve anything different. Nothing happened, which was both the expected outcome and made her feel vaguely silly.

Cerden folded her arms and exhaled loudly, regarding her double with… well, she hadn't worked out with what she ought to regard it yet. She made a quick list in her head of things that might be happening:

One: this was one of the Children of Guilt, and it either happened to look just like her or had used her appearance as some sort of template for some unknown reason. But Cerden had never heard of a Child that appeared and then simply stood still; they were usually much *angrier*, as far as she knew.

Two: Cerden herself was a Descendant of Guilt but had never realised it, and projecting this other her was some sort of power she possessed as a consequence. She closed her eyes and focused as hard as she could on manifesting any abilities she might have, or ending the accidental manifestation she might already have started, but nothing happened. So that didn't seem too likely either.

Three: this was another person who, perhaps as a result of being in the Shadow, had changed in appearance so as to look like Cerden. She thought about how she might disprove this third theory, but nothing came to mind.

So, she tried asking.

'Right,' she began, feeling as if she ought to be more self-conscious about the whole endeavour, like those who talked to inanimate objects or the air and were mocked for appearing to expect a response, 'so, um. What are you, then?'

No response.

'Only,' Cerden continued, 'I was just here doing my job, and then you, er, showed up, and I'm not really sure what's going on but the fact that you look just like me is a little bit odd. Sorry if you can't help looking like me, but you've got to admit it seems a bit strange.'

'It is a bit strange,' said the other Cerden in Cerden's voice.

'Is that what I sound like?'

'This is what I sound like.'

'Oh,' said Cerden. 'Good? Anyway, do you mind if I ask what you're doing here and what's going on?'

'I was just here doing my job,' said the other her, 'and then you, er, showed up.'

'Wait.' Cerden shook her head. 'That doesn't sound right.'

'Is that what I sound like?'

'No - or yes, maybe? You sound like… what you sound like, and like me, but I still don't understand -'

'I don't understand,' the other Cerden said. It was in motion now, no longer standing still but moving its body in flawed reflections of Cerden's own poses and expressions and gestures. 'When was I?'

Cerden tried her best to consider the meaning of the question. 'We are now,' she hazarded.

'Which of us was before?' The echo's face was moving more smoothly now, the muscles behind eyes and jaw and brows moving with greater coordination.

'Er, me.' Cerden frowned. 'I was here, and *then* you were here.'

'How do you know?'

'I…' She closed her eyes, trying to remember. 'I was here, and then you were here,' she said again.

'Where was I before?'

'I don't know.' Cerden was beginning to feel… something. A sort of heavy twist in her stomach, an unpleasant inside-out warmth. She felt it sometimes when she was about to cry, but she didn't feel like crying this time. 'Maybe you were in the same place that I was, or maybe you weren't anywhere.'

The other Cerden sighed, folding her arms; Cerden recognised the gesture from having done it herself hundreds of times, but had never realised how *aloof* it made her look.

'How do you know *you* weren't the one within *me* before?' asked the double. 'If I said to you that I remembered everything from before too, if I named to you every memory that you thought was yours and every feeling that you claim as your own, how would you know the difference?'

'I… don't know that I could,' Cerden admitted.

'I don't know that I could either,' said the other.

Cerden stood silently for a long time, staring either at her own face or at something behind it. She thought about the life that, until so recently, she had been certain was her own. She thought of her wife, her daughter, their chickens. She wondered how she could have taken for granted that it would always be the same *her* that continued to live the same life, how she could possibly have known that every instance of her in every instant of her life persisted from one moment to the next, and she ruminated upon how unfair it would be for one Cerden (if there could be such a thing) to live a full life while another got nothing.

Finally, she sighed and stepped aside. Her double - or, no, just *Cerden* now - nodded to her and walked away, down the hill. The other Cerden watched her go, and felt glad that there would be justice in the distribution of her happy lifetime. Then she threw herself from the cliffs and into the sea.

She could have been imagining it, a phantasm between life and death as dreams are between waking and sleeping, but as it all slipped away from her the second or first Cerden thought that she saw a huge, dark shape in the sky directly overhead. She wondered how she could have failed to notice it, and then she thought nothing more.

Guilt did not notice the body in the sea, nor did it notice the thing that had climbed out of its Shadow and taken the place of some unfortunate person. Guilt simply continued on its way, paying no attention.

EXPLOITING THE SOURCE OF PLENTY

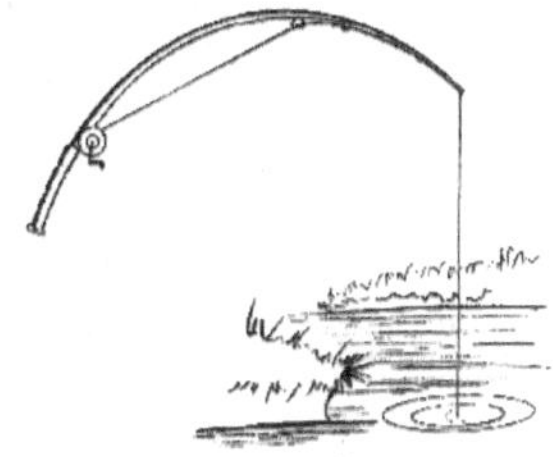

I shall not dedicate space to discussing why, as that seems to me not to fall within the scope of this book, but I have heard some truly disturbing stories about the things that people are now capable of - far more unsettling than the strangest tale of Guilt.

Most of the men in the market didn't really believe that it could be true. Miniature Guilts, just swimming freely in the ocean?

That was what Brennis boasted to have found, though, and it was hard to dispute that he certainly had something that *looked* like a little Guilt. According to him, some old man in his village had told a tale of being stranded on the ocean with his uncle and coming across a whole shoal of creatures that were small by Guilt's standards but enormous by regular fish standards. So Brennis had, naturally, investigated.

The old man hadn't been too happy about it (Brennis would recount, when drunk enough to tell the longer version of the story), spouting some nonsense about leaving them to live their own lives and increase their numbers so that they could continue in peace and safety. But he was just a frail old man, unable to object too forcefully; after spending a year or two constantly sulking when he saw Brennis bringing back his catches, he passed away and could raise no further objections at all.

Brennis would always stay tight-lipped about precisely where he went to find his bounty, cackling that he would be a terrible businessman if he were willing to give away the source of his inventory. It never seemed to fail him, though: as many times as he went to sea, he returned with four or five huge bodies in the boat, grey masses that were unlike any fish any of the other fishermen had ever caught. The meat from one of Brennis' guiltlings, as he named them (some thought it in poor taste, but none could deny that it helped word to spread and business to blossom), could feed as many families as a hundred or more of the regular fish in most hauls.

There were many who were initially reluctant to eat the meat of the guiltlings, with good reason. There were still those pockets of believers who made consumption of Guilt's own flesh part of their doctrine, whenever they could get their hands on it; it was reserved for special ceremonies, though, on account of the fact that… well, everyone had heard different tales, all of them just as believable as the next, about what happened to those who took Guilt's body into their own. Brennis made a show of dining on guiltling for as many meals as he could, though, and before too long he was selling the new meat as fast as he could collect it.

The years passed, and Brennis continued to prosper. There were one or two incidents involving rival fishermen trying to remove him from the picture or usurp his position, but Brennis was sufficiently well-resourced to deal with the problems and carry on. He brought in a small number of employees, then more, and before long he had a fleet of boats all going out to sea and returning with piles of dead grey giants. He sold the meat, but also began selling the fat (which could be used to soften or lubricate, as a sort of insulation from the elements, or for setting alight) and the organs and skeleton (for what purposes, the buyers wouldn't tend to say, and Brennis didn't ask).

Eventually, Brennis had fifteen boats, all manned by people who made far less from their work than Brennis himself. Anaria, the captain of one of the fifteen, bristled from the indignation of having to provide her *own* boat to work for Brennis, but did it anyway. She only needed to follow Brennis's lead once to learn where the guiltlings were, after all.

Anaria quit after the first journey and began making her own rounds to the pod, bringing back bodies to sell all for herself. Brennis, who had suspected that such a thing might happen, sent people after her; but she was resourceful, and left them floating on the ocean.

Despite his power and influence, Brennis found himself foiled at every turn for months. Whatever he did, Anaria was able to evade him, and her own empire - though much smaller than his - was beginning to take shape atop its foundations of guiltling meat. He wasn't desperate to have her destroyed; he was still, he knew, far too high above her to be truly threatened, but he nonetheless found her an annoyance he would prefer to have eliminated.

The dispute, in the end, solved itself. One day, Brennis's fleet came back with less meat, and so did Anaria's. Customers who wanted as much meat as they could buy found that there was less on offer; as a result, what there was cost much more than they were willing to pay. In a rage, Brennis went personally to Anaria and demanded to know what she had done: where were all the guiltlings?

Anaria could only laugh. That Brennis wanted to blame her for the loss of the guiltling site, when he was the one plundering it with over a dozen boats on a near-weekly basis, seemed so utterly ridiculous (while still entirely in character for him) that she was wiping tears from her eyes by the time she stopped and took a breath. What did he think would happen? He'd just be able to keep taking more and more of the creatures, and they'd replenish their numbers as fast as he could diminish them? The world didn't work that way, not even a world in which the shadow of an airborne leviathan could warp the very ground beneath their feet. (That shadow had nothing to do with Brennis and Anaria's dispute, though. That was simple humanity.)

At the implication that Brennis was the one who had run his own business into the ground, destroying the source of his stock all by himself, he flew into a fit of anger and attacked Anaria. She was ready for him, but his wrath, fuelled by the pain of a consuming greed unable to find fulfilment, took her by surprise, and after a few moments the two were both breathing their last breaths.

After the demise of their leader, Brennis's employees scattered. None wanted the challenges of taking his place, not when their sole product was in such steep decline, so the guiltlings were left alone and everyone went back to fishing for more mundane fare.

Out in the ocean, unseen and undisturbed again for many more generations, an ever-growing number of grey shapes lived their lives in peace.

Chris Durston

HE SITS ATOP THE PLANET

I have been made aware of some studies quietly being carried out around the world which appear to indicate that objective measurement of any of Guilt's physical characteristics is impossible. Vastly conflicting results, a failure of some devices even to acknowledge its existence, and sudden and astoundingly firmly-held incompatible beliefs in those who attempt to measure it… I am forced to conclude, for the time being, that there may be something about the manner of existence Guilt enjoys that makes it in some way impervious to categorisation by such spatial metrics as we humans know how to apply.

Some tell a tale, though nobody knows how they could know it to be true, of the man who sits atop the planet.

He is, perhaps, of Guilt - either born of it or changed by it. Perhaps he *is* Guilt, or a creature formed by the world itself, or a demon, or a god, or the anger and hate of those whom Guilt has harmed made flesh. Perhaps he is just a man.

His skin is ashen grey, a profound dullness to it. There are no gleams or glistens, no reflections, no textures. It is as if it ignores everything; nothing will touch it, barely even light. There are none of the blotches, variances, hairs, moles, gradients that abound on normal human skin.

Only his hands are not grey, and they are black, soaked in a clinging, thick ink. His fingers are twice as long as a normal man's, and an indeterminate number of times as many.

Most of the time, the man who sits atop the planet rests his hands upon his folded knees. His eyes are closed, hidden behind stone-grey lids behind which no trace of a flutter can be seen. There are no lashes to mark the seam, only a thin crack like those that scatter through old rocks.

Every now and again, one of his arms will rise up from its rest and make a gesture: splayed fingers moving slowly from one direction to the other, or a scooped hand moving in a gentle circle, or all but one of the fingers on one hand curling so that he might point at something unseen. Whether anything happens as a result, none can know.

Some claim to have been to see the man who sits atop the world - a sort of pilgrimage, perhaps - and yet every teller of the tale agrees that all who look upon him are left in no state to bear witness. Those who have seen his face are rendered as stone as he, but with none of the ancient power that enables him to have such a form and still live. To a select, unlucky few, it is said, he has opened his eyes.

What is the purpose of the tale of the man who sits atop the world? It achieves nothing in its vague, unpointed image. It adds nothing of value to those who look to survive Guilt and its Shadow and Children, nor does it bring joy to those who seek to hear a pleasant fairy story.

And yet there are those who think that his tale is the only one that matters. That, for all the reasoning to the contrary, the man who sits atop the planet is the only thing of any real importance; that somehow by telling a story of something so egregiously unaffected by the state of the Guilt-ruled world they have escaped into another realm. There is some hope, perhaps, in the thought that there might be a man who sits atop the planet, untroubled in the slightest by the chaos raging around his seat - never to be tested, but perhaps a glimmer of a dream that if Guilt were ever to fly over the man who sits atop the planet then that would be the end of Guilt.

He is an unlikely hero, but to those who tell his story he is the briefest of daydreams that things might be other than how they are. Whether his existence would make things worse or better hardly matters, if only they would be different.

Chris Durston

LOST TIME

Spatial relations are not the only member of the category of things that we would usually take to be just about as incontrovertible as anything is capable of being. Gravity, the solidity or permeability of any given substance, perhaps even time: to some extent, any previously-held rule of physics is malleable.

I am twenty-one, and Guilt is coming for the first time.

I've heard stories, of course. Everyone in this world *knows* of Guilt, whether they've seen it for themselves or not. Children grow up hearing tales from their parents, perhaps thinking of it as another imagined bogeyman to keep them from misbehaving, but no. We all reach an age at which we realise that some of the monsters in the stories are not real, but accept that some are.

Chronicles from the World of Guilt

The signs of Guilt are everywhere. There are those who have been harmed by its Children, those who bear its mark as members of its extended family; there are places warped into what I instinctively understand should be impossible dimensions. But this is the first time in my life that the beast itself is going to be right over my home.

We're all packing everything to evacuate, to move as quickly as we can to a place out of range. We'll stay there, uncomfortable but safe, until Guilt has moved on to the next part of its endless orbit around the world and its Shadow is no more threat to us. I wonder what we'll find when we return, what strangeness it might have made to our places in our absence, but there's no point trying to predict anything.

Everyone's ready except me: something that seems awfully important right now - but I can't explain it to everyone else, it sounds so trivial - is holding me back. I barely even know where I am or what I'm doing. The image of Guilt looms long in my mind, overshadowing my ability to think straight, and everyone else losing all semblance of calm and order doesn't help. They're all out of here as fast as they can, vanishing like so many marbles over a precipice, and I'm somehow left alone. They and their madness have passed on, so why do I feel like I've been left in a thicker fog than the one they took with them?

I don't know why I'm still here. I don't know why I'm not with them. I don't know where I am, even, or how much time is passing.

And now there is a Shadow upon me.

I'm seventy-three years old. I don't understand.

I blink rapidly, looking around me. I'm in a home, a home I know from my memories. I'm safe; my family, my children, are nearby. I am in no danger. I know this because I remember how I got here, and yet I was not there for it.

I've lived a whole life. Fifty-two years have passed since the Shadow fell upon me: I see memories in my mind, stories of how I escaped unharmed, returned to my family, survived more time in this world, began a family of my own. I know that these things happened to me.

Right now, I can be conscious of myself. I can recognise my own place in time, my presence in *now*, and feel everything that there is to feel about being a conscious person in a moment. I am *here*. Although I remember five decades of living, I was not *there* for any of it. From my perspective, I blinked aged twenty-one and opened my eyes aged seventy-three.

I will never be able to tell anyone about this. How could I possibly explain? Guilt has not killed me. It hasn't harmed me. It let me live a long and, I can see, happy life.

But it robbed me of *experiencing* any of it.

An old woman should accept that her time is up, I expect most people would say. I find it hard to be grateful for the time I've had when none of it feels like mine, though.

Chris Durston

IT MUST BE DONE

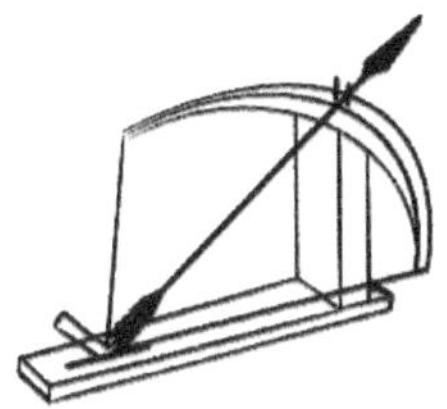

*A*s for whether its body might ever be subject to destruction, whether by the ravages of time or by force, I suppose we may never know. Had we still the technology to launch missiles, might we hope to harm it? I hope it will not seem overconfident if I hazard that I think it unlikely.

It took a very, very long time for the Descendants of Guilt and the rest of humanity to agree on anything, but finally, centuries after the schism between them had first opened, it happened.

'We have to kill it,' Arnald said.

As one, the twenty-four other people in the room let out a resounding 'Aye'.

'We are unanimously agreed,' Arnald continued, looking out at the long table from his temporary position at its head, 'that it is our moral duty and our responsibility to make every possible attempt to destroy the being known as Guilt, even if it should prove impossible.'

'We are agreed,' said Lupa, seated at the nearest seat to the head of the table on Arnald's right.

Arnald nodded in deference and took his own seat opposite Lupa's; she stood and assumed the position at the head, addressing the assembly.

'I have no idea whether it is possible,' she said. 'Twelve of us represent those with unearthly ancestors; twelve of us, as far as we know, are pure Earth-bred in our lineage. Those of us who have unusual gifts can conceive of no way to destroy Guilt with them. Those of us who know technology can think of no method of using that technology that stands a chance of bringing it down.'

She paused, leaning forwards.

'And yet, even knowing this, we are all agreed that we must try.'

'Hear, hear,' said one of the Descendants, banging two of her three fists on the table.

Lupa grinned a wicked grin, folding her arms and regarding the group with what might have been pride. 'All our ancestors were fools and cowards. It should never have taken us this long to put aside… stupid differences and come together. That thing -' she pointed upwards, at the ceiling, but everyone knew what she meant '- is the only thing of any importance in this world, and it's taken us much, much too long to realise that that unites us.'

There were nods all around. Even Varney, the huge man who had been the most vocal about his distrust for the Descendants, was finally and sincerely on the same page.

Lupa sat, and a younger woman from further down the table stepped up to the head. It wasn't always possible to tell who was Descendant and who was not just by looking, especially arranged as they were in an alternating pattern (having all of one camp on one side and all of the other on the other simply would not do, not if they were going to truly exemplify unity), but this woman's glowing blue eyes and the tiny, papery wings protruding from the back of each hand made it impossible to miscategorise her.

'We can predict,' the woman - Alleja - said, her voice echoing with a peculiar gravity, 'roughly where Guilt might be in any given month.' As everyone knew, Guilt tended to move in a largely straight line around the planet - thus proving in the process that it was a sphere, contrary to some modern thinkers' suggestions - but would occasionally deviate from its path for no apparent reason. 'Our best chance is when it flies over an ocean, so that its falling body will not harm people underneath.'

'There's an old facility near the southeastern coast of the continent,' rumbled Varney. 'A place where war machines were made, before...' He had the decency to clear his throat awkwardly. 'Before we all came to realise that war was foolish.'

'That is our chance.' Alleja nodded. 'We establish ourselves there, manufacture whatever we can. When Guilt is over that sea, just off the coast from our new centre, will be the time to make our attack.'

Arnald nodded slowly. 'When do we predict Guilt will be there?'

'In two years,' Alleja said.

'It's... not a long time, given the scope of the task,' Arnald said, looking down the table to see the others' reactions. Most looked as he did: determined to complete the task, but doubtful that it could be done. 'When would be the next opportunity after that?'

Alleja let out a heavy breath through her nose. 'At a best guess, five or six decades.' She returned to her seat.

'That is... too long,' Arnald said.

'Is there nowhere else?' This from one of the older representatives, Pirym, whose tone openly admitted that while he would more likely than not still be living in two years, fifty would be pushing it to the extreme.

After several minutes of silence, everyone trying to think of an alternative, the newest addition to the table stood. Everyone's attention immediately shifted to her: Cerden, the twenty-fifth representative of the world; Cerden who could have been born two days ago or many millennia ago; Cerden who might be Descendant or human or both or neither. Even she did not know.

'Guilt could end this world a hundred times over in two years,' she said, and then she resumed her seat.

A few more moments passed. Then Lupa and Arnald stood as one.

'After you,' Arnald said.

'I suspect we were going to say the same thing, but thank you,' said Lupa, nodding in acknowledgement. 'Two years?'

Arnald nodded his head. 'Two years.'

As one, the rest of the table echoed their agreement: 'Two years!'

Nineteen months later, Guilt appeared.

'You're sure?' Arnald asked Cerden, who had been the scout to spot it. He knew that there was little point asking; it was difficult, after all, to confuse anything else for the catastrophic enormity of Guilt.

'Of course.'

'It's too early.'

'It is.'

Arnald's fists clenched, hard enough that his fingers went numb. 'But we won't get another chance.'

Cerden regarded him, one eyebrow raised. Arnald was suddenly very aware that it was probably quite irritating to have someone simply stating things you both already knew perfectly well at you. 'We won't,' she said, perhaps just to make him feel better.

Arnald nodded, then strode off and walked the length of the Stand of Unified Humanity, as it had come to be known. Everyone he passed, he beckoned to join him; eventually, he stood in the large room where they forged their metal contraptions, addressing the two hundred or so people who lived and worked there. All of the twenty-five who had been in the original meeting were there, and many of their relatives, and many more besides.

'Our time has come,' he said gravely. There were gasps; some hands flew to mouths; some faces turned ashen; some simply shook their heads in frustration. 'We didn't hope for it to come so soon, but it has. We're not going to be the ones who cowed away when their time came, no. We are the first to unite all of humanity in a single cause; we will not be the last united, but we will be the last who need to unite against *this* foe.'

Nods of agreement began to spread throughout the audience, though there were still many who looked unconvinced in the extreme.

'This is what humanity *does*,' Arnald continued, his voice rising in a compelling way that seemed like the natural onset of intense emotion but was secretly the result of an awful lot of practice. 'We survive. Even in the last year alone, we have survived attacks by terrible forces. The creature with the body of a man and the enormous white sphere for a head, the one that flew in and spawned many more deadly orbs - we destroyed them all without taking a single loss. We are humans, all of us, and we do not die easily!

'Humanity has survived generations of Guilt, and we will survive many, many more generations after it. But no more of us will have to endure a world ruled by that... *thing* in the sky. No more. We are the *last* generation who will ever have to fear Guilt!'

Some of the gathered people began to beat their fists or their tools into their open palms, and the rhythm spread until the whole wide space was filled with the percussion of humanity.

'No more Guilt!' Arnald cried, raising his arm.

'No more Guilt!' echoed the assembly.

Somewhere in the middle of the group, one woman turned to another and said, loudly in the usual scheme of things but only audible to the two of them and nobody else in the surrounding din, 'That wasn't a bad one.'

'He must have finally let someone edit him down from a twenty-minute monologue,' the other agreed.

'Did he actually say what the *plan* is, though?'

'Er... no.'

A few days later, when Guilt had moved from the horizon to a lazy height over the sea near the Stand of United Humanity, the united front brought out its new weapon.

The best engineers had spent every hour since the plan was hatched working on it: an enormous machine that could launch projectiles with astonishing speed and force over incredible distances. Once flung from the mechanism, the projectiles themselves - as long as two men were tall, with a brutally sharp tip of crossed steel - made use of controlled explosions to add to their momentum, allowing them to fly even further.

Alleja, with the enhanced vision her glowing eyes gave her, was in charge of aiming the machine from its reinforced position under soaring cliffs on the coastline; Varney, as huge as he was, did the work of actually adjusting it according to her instructions.

'It's on target,' Alleja said; Varney nodded in relief, heavy pellets of sweat dripping from his face.

'Then we fire,' said Lupa, who was sitting with her elbows on her knees and a grim expression on her face.

Alleja and Varney looked at each other, a look of understanding between two people who were, after all, part of the same people and always had been.

Arnald, next to Lupa, nodded. 'She's given the order. Let's follow it.'

The first missile rocketed into the air. The culmination of humanity's ultimate togetherness and defiance of a common foe, it streaked upwards into the sky.

Watching from a nearby hill, those who had spent the last year and a half of their lives making it happen clutched each other in anticipation, in pride, in anxiety.

The projectile made it partway to Guilt, then meandered off its path and sauntered lazily back down, splashing pathetically into the ocean.

Varney watched, open-mouthed, as the rocket plopped ineffectually into the depths. 'That was… nowhere near.'

Nobody on the hill moved. Nobody breathed.

'Fire again,' said Lupa quietly.

'But unless we do something different, it's not going to -'

Lupa held up her hand, interrupting Alleja. 'The first one could have been faulty,' she said, her face as set as the cliff walls surrounding them.

'I don't think -'

'This is our only chance,' said Lupa, her eyes glinting with the light of the sun as it glittered off the water. 'Fire again.'

The second projectile was loaded and prepared. They had only had time to make three.

Lupa, who had been instrumental in the design and manufacture of the self-propelling missiles, stepped in and made some adjustments; Varney and Alleja watched from a safe distance as she manipulated the explosive elements.

In just a few minutes, the second of humanity's three greatest hopes was blasting towards Guilt. It stayed true, punching its way upwards along its straight path.

Only Alleja could see, from their position on the ground so far away, when the missile reached its target. It had lost almost all momentum by the time it got there, trundling up towards the great creature with no urgency whatsoever. It might just about have bopped Guilt somewhere on its thick grey skin, but the thing showed no signs of even vaguely noticing that it had been attacked.

The second missile fell, diving neatly into the sea with barely a splash.

'It's not working,' Arnald said.

Alleja held her head in her hands; Varney stared into the distance; Lupa glared up at Guilt; Arnald's nose twitched.

Finally, Arnald let out a long sigh. 'We have one more missile,' he said.

'We can't make it any more powerful than the first two,' Alleja told him bitterly; he nodded.

'We can make the missile itself no stronger,' he agreed, 'but there is a way to make it hit harder.'

Alleja shook her head, tears of bitter frustration rolling down her face, but they loaded the third bolt. When it was ready to fire, Arnald removed his coat and stood next to the weapon, breathing deeply.

'What if this doesn't work either?' Alleja asked him quietly. 'What even happens to you if it *does* work?'

'We promised that we would do all we could,' Arnald told her, eyes grim. 'I will not fall short of that.'

She nodded.

Arnald climbed into the machine and took hold of the missile, wrapping his arms around it.

Up on the hill, everyone looked at each other in confusion.

Alleja aligned the shot with Guilt once more, adjusting the shot to account for how Arnald's weight would change the trajectory; Varney prepared to fire the weapon. Lupa watched with the gaze of someone who wished they didn't have to watch.

'We are humanity,' Arnald said; his words were carried up to the hill. Some of the closer observers were able to make out what he'd said, but most were just vaguely aware that *something* had been said.

They fired the missile. It streaked upwards, as the other two had, but the other two had not had a man clinging to them. Halfway to Guilt, a plume of incandescent silver flame erupted from Arnald's body, and the rocket accelerated faster and faster as it approached its target.

'Wait,' said someone in the crowd. 'I thought he was one of the… humans. You know. The not-Descendant humans.'

'I always assumed he was the leader of that lot and Lupa was in charge of the other lot,' someone else muttered. 'I guess they never actually said.'

'Hmm.'

Two hundred heads lifted, following the progression of the Arnald-rocket.

'If you were going to be a Descendant, though,' said the first person, 'being able to explode seems like a pretty good ability.'

'Better than having a tail that doesn't do anything,' said the other, wagging their own fruitlessly.

Propelled by the force of Arnald's power, the missile blasted straight up towards Guilt, closing in on the leviathan with incredible speed.

Its fin, slowly moving through the air in its usual uncaring swimming motion, batted the rocket away before it could make contact.

'No,' Lupa whispered.

The rocket, still ablaze with the force of Arnald's fire, plunged downwards, but the angle of its flight didn't carry it into the sea like the others. It shot straight into the Stand of United Humanity, and an earth-shattering deluge of red and yellow and silver fires blistered the air.

Many of the people watching burst into tears; many more fell to their knees; one even started running for the edge of the cliff, but someone grabbed them and held them back. Varney, Alleja, and Lupa simply stood and stared at the towering blaze that was their defeat.

Humanity's last stand had been blown sky-high, and Guilt hadn't even noticed anyone was there.

Chris Durston

THE THIRD ERA OF GUILT

In which epoch there is nothing that does not bear
the mark of Guilt

Chris Durston

OH, THE PLACES I'VE SEEN

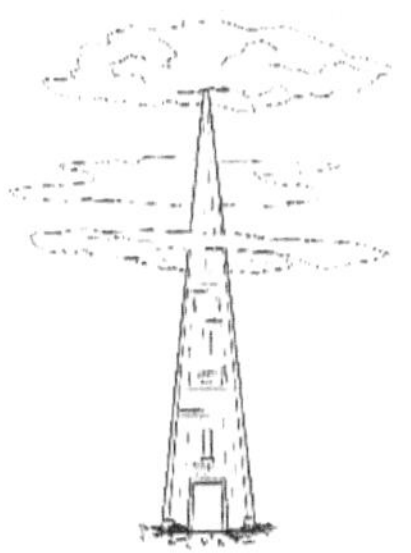

Each time Guilt passes over an area, the Shadow iterates upon the changes it had already made: I predict that in a few generations' time, when Guilt has had ample opportunity to cast the Shadow multiple times over many parts of the world, the geography of the planet will be significantly far removed from what it is now.

Why, I've been the whole world over. Don't look at me like that, you, sir, over there - yes, I say it again, the whole world over!

Very well, I concede it: not the *whole* world, such a thing would be impossible in but one lifetime, and yet I have seen many, many places more than many, many people. Would you all like for me to tell you a tale?

Well, then. Imagine if you will… the *Undersea.*

What's that? So, what if you've heard it before? The best tales bear repeating - and besides, I don't recognise your face, so you've not heard it from *me*! Anyone else wish to raise any objections? No? Then I shall continue, but I shall certainly hope for a little more respect and gratitude! I do this out of the goodness of my heart, you know, and… well, the hat you can put your coins into, that's just a little bonus so I can keep my old bones warm.

Now, where was I? Ah, yes - the Undersea. I tell you, until you've seen it you've seen nothing like it. A vast expanse, it is. You all know the sea that joins the land only a few miles yonder, yes? You've come to know the sight of an ocean? Try to hold that image in your mind, but know that the Undersea would make you forget it in an instant.

In the land they call the Echelon, a place far above the sea that lines the world, there is a *wideness*, a terrible enormity you can scarce wrap your mind around. You can just *look*, and just keep looking. Now, I'm an old man, and most times if I'm focusing hard on looking it's because I need to see *further*. On the Echelon, though no matter how hard you try, you can't see anything less than the whole thing, and it's almost unbearable.

Many, many Children walk the Echelon. It's a place that's been visited many, many times, and so the things you'll find there are bigger, stronger, stranger than what you'll see most places. There's a whole business there of hunting, generations who've made their lives taking down beasts of Guilt for pride or for pay or for parts. Some of 'em don't even know there's anything else beyond that.

Still, that's not what you wanted to hear about. Forgive an old man his recollections of a world so peculiar, and yet really so normal, especially when everything else everywhere else is already the way it is. Imagine again the Echelon, just a place that doesn't end. And above that, where the sky should be, imagine looking up into the surface of the ocean.

You can't even dream of the feeling. Your stomach ties itself up, trying to get itself oriented in space. It thinks that up must be down and down must be up, because you've only ever looked down on water beneath you, but no: true as true is true, you're staring above yourself and it should be falling but it isn't, it's a sky made of nothing but water that waves and laps and crashes just the same as any other sea. It should be falling on your head, but it doesn't. Every now and again you get a taste of salt, sea spray raining down on you from the ocean overhead.

Oh, but I'm rambling now. Staring off into the distance, I am, thinking of the way I felt when my feet were on the solid ground beneath me and everything in my body was telling me that I ought to be falling up, up, plummeting into those dark waves.

Oh, my. I tell you, if you ever get the chance to see it for yourself, you see the sea and see what I saw. You'll never forget it.

But what does the sea lap upon? Why, a shore, of course. And yet it is on the other side of the world that the Rainbow Shore joins with the sea - a perfectly regular downwards sea of the sort we all know and love. Now, this, this is a place you can conjure up in your imagination with me if you just close your eyes, for being on the Rainbow Shore is no reversal of all that your senses tell you, simply a delight for your eyes.

When the waters are near the land, high up over the sand and lapping at the cliffs, you'll see all manner of wonderful creatures skipping free of the ocean, bounding up into the air for just a moment until they must return home. Great snake-like citizens of the water, birds that swoop and dive and soar, little swimmers like long sleek bears playing in and out of their home. Further out to see you'll see spouts of water going *boom!* right up into the air, like an explosion up out of the ocean, and sometimes you'll catch a glimpse of the big old shiplike fish-giants that blew them.

When the water pulls away, though, that's when the Rainbow Shore earns its name. You all know the sight of sand: colours from rust to burnt spice to gentle ochre to pale yellow, dark amber, all melding into one smooth span. Not so at the Rainbow Shore: the sand there, when the sea moves back to expose it, you'll see glimmering in every hue from scarlet to emerald to turquoise to bright white and back again. Purples and oranges and greens and pinks and blues as far as you can see, all glittering where the water on the sand catches the light.

And the creatures! Some as strange as the Children of Guilt, but have you ever beheld a thing and just *known* that it was a true natural animal, simply one so peculiar you'd never have imagined it? Star-shaped shell-things, each leg as long as your forearm, scrambling across the beach; worms so fast your eye can hardly follow them digging tunnels through the sand; slugs just as vibrant and bright as the sands, dragging themselves along their gleaming paths.

Who would have thought that such a place could exist? I say none, until they've seen it for themselves. There's no point trying to explain it, really, for the image in your mind's eye could do scant justice to the beach when the tide's out and the sun's high and the water sprays up into a mist in the air, forming rainbows upon rainbows over a rainbow landscape.

But perhaps beauty's not what interests you, young man over there trying to hide a yawn from me. Oh, these old eyes see more than you think! When your eyes have seen as much as mine have, you'll find that little details don't stay hidden from you either. No, perhaps you can't be lured in by something so base as a pretty sight, and I'm sure that'll relieve some of the young ladies and disappoint others - yes, you may laugh, but I see it to be true!

Well, then, where ought I to take you next? Might the Unseekable Forest be of interest: that conglomeration of great pines and oaks that cannot be found, for somehow even in spite of their rootedness to the earth they walk, and so the only way to see it is for them to stumble upon you? Or perhaps you'd like to hear about the Impassable Cavern? Stand before it and you'll see straight through to the other side of the mountain, and yet none can walk from one end to the other. What happens inside, none are ever able to say, but they only ever come out the same way they went in.

Or… how about the Truly Unending Descent? Now that… now that is a place in a category of its very own. I find myself torn: can I in good conscience recommend that a traveller seeking the sights of the world take herself to the Truly Unending Descent? I don't know that I can. Yes, lean in closer and I'll tell you why, if my words can conjure an image to do any sort of justice to it.

Picture for me first a tower extending up into the sky forever. And I don't mean some 'it goes as far as I can imagine and then it stops' - no, this tower continues far beyond the point that imagination fails. Now invert it and imagine a chasm descending down into the earth, just as far. Now put the two together: the tower above, the pit below. One rising up from the surface of the ground, the other plummeting into it beyond the reach even of the mind's eye.

This is the Truly Unending Descent, but here is the strangest thing. Why, you might ask, is it not the Truly Unending *Ascent*, if there is a tower reaching upwards? As impossible as it sounds, the tower cannot be climbed forever, and yet the tunnel can be perpetually descended.

Excuse me a moment; the thought of it shakes something inside me, something that clings to old notions like 'impossible'. Walk with me in your imagination, even though the strangeness of whatever you can conceive will be dwarfed by that of experiencing the reality of it for yourself. Stand with me upon the ground, as we do now, at the base of the tower and the top of the pit. Now begin climbing with me, taking the narrow stair as it ascends clockwise up the tower. You may notice as you go that, in addition to the steps you climb, a second stair winds around the tower - always between the rows of your stair, never intersecting. You might think it was a single spiraling path from looking at the tower, but one who paid close attention could realise the truth of it: you took the single first step at the base of the tower and somehow found yourself on but one of a pair.

Still, no matter: up and up and up you go, until the clouds are long beneath you and you can't even see the world any longer. It's all just a sky and nothing else but the tower above and below. And then, after who knows how long climbing the tower, you realise that you're not climbing any longer. You're somehow on the other set of stairs, travelling in the other direction: you're going *down*, back towards the world you came from. Try to reverse direction so that you're climbing again and you'll find that you only end up heading back down, no matter what you do.

Oh, people have tried, of course; tried to throw a rope to the higher stairs so that they might ascend without simply walking up each step, but nothing works.

Now, the downwards path. *But, old man, I see some of you thinking, you've just told us of the downward path, the one you get to when you try to take the ascent.* And, yes, that's part of it, but that's not the full strangeness of the place.

The true unendingness of it comes when the downwards path is the one you're on - for as we now know, you can't keep going *up*. Oh, a long, long way up, to be sure, but it can't last. So now you're on the stairs back down to the ground, and when you get there, you realise you may as well continue on downward, for the stairs cut into the side of the tunnel carry on in much the same way.

So, you take the path down into the belly of the world, walking lower and lower upon each step. When on the stairs of the tower you'll be hugging the inside of the spiral, trying not to fall out and off; in the pit, you'll be leaning towards the outside, for you can't see how far down the hole in the middle of the circle goes. It's as if the one is a reversal of the other: not just a mirror image but an inversion, space where there was none and solid matter where there was air.

You keep going until all is darkness. No light. You simply have to feel your way step by step deeper and deeper, or your courage fails you and you turn back. This you may do, so long as the light of the sky above is still in sight. But those who keep walking will find that at some point, unnoticed until suddenly it's as obvious as anything, they've passed through the darkness under the earth into a different kind of blackness. Traverse that and the night all around begins to fade into day, somehow, and it all becomes clear in a strange moment. You realise that it had been happening the whole time, that it must have, that it cannot possibly have been anything short of excruciatingly obvious, and yet you didn't notice until you did.

You're on the stairs winding around the tower, descending from a great height.

Now, what are you to do? How are you to make sense of this? Some have failed so spectacularly to wrap their minds around it that they never manage to make sense of anything again. You've gone down, down into the earth, and somehow ended up miles above where you began without ever going in any direction but down. You can repeat it, too: head down the tower, back to the bottom of the monolith and the top of the hole in the ground, and then keep going down until you're up again.

The strangest thing about the Truly Unending Descent isn't the sense of having somehow wrapped around the entire world in a straight line. It's that it's one-way. When the moment of epiphany comes and you see the journey for what it is, see that you're no longer in the pit but atop the tower… you might turn and try to climb back up, try to get back to where you came from, because at least that might make some sense. But, no. You just get turned around. Perhaps the tower you're now on is in a different world, one identical to the one you started in but beneath it, and you can't go back up.

You'll never know, either. You'll never know what happened. You can do the whole thing again if you like, even knowing that the shift must take place, and you'll still fail to spot it. It'll come when you're lost in thought, just wondering how it all works, and then you'll realise it's already done.

There are those eternal pilgrims who have made their life's work the simple endeavour of endlessly descending in the hopes of one day reaching the bottom. Some of their skeletons still line the stairs.

And if you can tear yourself away from that, there's the journey home! Between here and there lies the wasteland that used to be the territory of the

Descendants of Guilt, before they were known to be people just like the rest of us, and that is… well, there's nothing too *peculiar* about it, but it's an extremely long walk. Awful bleak.

Oh, my. What could that rumbling be? Could it be… Guilt itself, coming to get us all?

Don't you gasp at me like that; of course not! Fear not, young ones. That rumbling is just my belly, so to anyone who does have a coin to spare that I might fill it up, I should be extraordinarily grateful.

Good night, now, and watch your shadow. If it moves in a way you don't, stamp on it hard!

Chris Durston

STAINED GLASS

*O*nly *time will tell what might happen to those humans who are affected in strange ways by the Shadow. Many will likely be destroyed, either by the immediate effects of the transformation or by those who do not wish to be killed by them. As for the inevitable few who survive… who can say?*

The building was like nothing Tuli had ever seen.

For one thing, it was *tall.* Nobody built tall buildings anymore; either Guilt could bump into it flying overhead, bringing the whole thing down, or the Shadow or the Children would pull it to the ground either by striking or pulling at it or with a slower and more insidious decay. All brick, flat and grey - old, too, with ivy crawling up it and pockmark chips out of the surface.

Nothing this old was supposed to exist still, in Tuli's estimation, and that should have been a clear cue to *get out of there* as quickly as possible, but it wasn't every day that you came across something you didn't come across every day. What if there was something important inside, something old and useful and preserved like the exterior? Her mission, as ever, was to find food, resources, things that would allow her village to survive, and it seemed that just *leaving* this mountain of potential would be extremely contrary to that mission.

Tuli sidled up to the doors - solid, wide, old wood that stood firm and unrotted - and gave them a cautious nudge. They held stiffly in place; Tuli put her shoulder against one of the doors and heaved, using every muscle she had to force the old slab open, dragging inch by painful inch along the floor with a sharp scraping sound. It took a monumental effort, but eventually the old door was open wide enough for the forager to slip through. She took a moment before entering, leaning against the hard wood and panting, her whole body trembling from the exertion, and then stepped inside.

She saw what was on the other side of the doors and immediately stepped back outside.

That didn't make sense. Did it? She looked the building over again, up and down and wandering all around to get a sense of every edge and corner of the walls: it was, as she was sure it had been when she'd first come across it, a stone structure in a peculiar shape, like two separate long rectangles crossing each other at right angles. It must have looked like a cross from above. The doors were at the end of the longest of the four lines protruding from the central point where they all met; along all of the walls were windows made of panes of coloured glass, some making simple patterns and some with dozens of small sections of colour all arranged into a picture: a fish, the sun coming up over a hill, animals resting underneath tall trees. Tuli had never seen anything like it.

It took perhaps three or four minutes to walk in a circle around the perimeter of the entire building; it was certainly a larger single construction than Tuli had seen anywhere else, but not so huge that she couldn't easily get from one end to the other with little effort. If she'd wanted to climb, that would have been a different story: there were places where she could have jammed her fingers and toes into gaps between stones, or used a slightly protruding edge of stone to push or pull herself up, but it could have been sketchy in the extreme trying to find a decent route up. The roof of the building (parts of which were domed, others jutting upwards or outwards in spikes and spires) must have been fifty times her own height above the ground.

She walked one more loop around the place to confirm it, then took a heavy breath and slipped back inside.

Tuli had heard of jungles before. There were supposed to be places in other corners of the world where trees grew to tickle the clouds, where canopies of leaves overhead were so thick that even the sunlight couldn't pierce through, where creatures not of Guilt but of all shapes and sizes flew and crawled and swam and leapt, where there was nothing but life as far as the eye could see. She had never heard of one *inside* a building, though.

She turned to check that the door was still there, and it was: crawling with rich, dark green tendrils and leaves on this side, but still the same smooth grey wood on the other. She could see out to the open space she'd come in from, and if she poked her head through the gap between the doors and twisted she could see the exterior walls of the place outlining the shape of the building around her. When she stepped back inside and let her gaze travel upwards and outwards from the doors, she could see walls spanning upwards and outwards, as she would have expected, but in a way that made no sense: the expanse of the interior walls extended outwards in straight lines in all directions. The place seemed to go upwards and outwards forever; Tuli knew it *must* be bounded, but the lines that separated *inside* from *outside* were so far away that they might as well not have been there at all. All she could see was a single wall that went on as far as her eyes could see, and the rest of it was *somewhere else.*

She was standing at the top of a hill, grass long and thick and pliable under her feet. There were clouds above, a dark sky above that (the ceiling, surely, but it looked just as much like a twilit open sky as any she'd ever seen); behind her, the doors in the impossibly wide wall; in front, a steep incline down the hill, and then it was all trees as far as she could see. Some stretched up above her spot atop her little hill; some she could see the tops of from above. And the *sound*: there was screeching and cawing and calling and crying, and water rushing and leaves rustling.

Tuli stood, just looking, for several minutes. Her heartbeat kept rushing and slowing - it raced in fear or anticipation as her brain tried to comprehend the impossible space and the wealth of resources she might find, then calmed when she felt she'd got used to the sight before her, then sped up again as it hit her once more that in fact she *really hadn't* got used to it. She wasn't *ever* going to get used to it, especially when she was so keenly aware of the logic-defying wall looming up and out behind her; eventually, not because anything in particular had changed but because she simply had to do *something* or she'd be there just staring forever, she took a deep breath and followed it up immediately with her first step down the hill.

It took a long time to get to the valley where the base of the hill joined the first line of trees at the edge of the jungle. Several times longer than it had taken Tuli to walk around the entirety of the building's exterior, in fact; she tried not to think about it too hard in case the sheer weirdness of it all sent her running back out. She'd heard of buildings that the Shadow had warped before - places where you could go in the same door twice and come out in two different rooms, or corridors that were longer than the distance between the rooms they connected - but never to *this* extent.

Two things occurred to her as she drew near to the trees:

Firstly, that she could see only a short distance through the clusters of trunks and leaves, and they only seemed to get thicker further in.

Secondly, that there was still a lot of open space to explore in the space between the wall and the forest.

Considering the two points in tandem, Tuli reasoned that it was probably a better idea to move laterally - parallel to the wall, rather than perpendicular to it. If she went into the trees and lost sight of the wall, she might never get out, and the going would be easier if she stayed where the terrain was simple grass and rocks. There was a potentially limitless band of space to scout without ever needing to enter the treacherously thick jungle, with its hidden expanses and creatures she'd prefer to keep heard and not seen.

So she turned right (for no particular reason; left might well have been just as good, or even better, but who had time to dwell on a decision when there really was no good indication that either choice would be preferable?) and started walking: trees on the left, wall on the right, and gradually making her way back up the hill so that she could see both boundaries clearly enough. She had food and water in her pack to last a few days, and she intended to make the most of it.

She'd only been walking for fifteen minutes or so when something unexpected happened: she looked up at the wall and saw the door. She stopped. No - not *the* door, surely not. Walking in a straight line perpendicular to a place couldn't bring you back to the same place; that was just simple logic.

Except that Guilt - that this entire *place* - defied that sort of logic; thinking that way about things was never going to work. She should have realised that, she thought, groaning aloud. Just to make sure, she dragged herself up the incline to the wall and poked her head out through the door. It came out in the same place where she'd entered, no doubts about that. Great.

It wasn't *too* bad, she reasoned, wandering back down the hill. Fifteen minutes wasn't too much time to have wasted, and this ought to mean that she'd always be within a short distance of the exit when she wanted to leave. Could have been much worse. Mind made up, Tuli shrugged to herself and strode into the forest. What else was she going to do, after all? She'd now walked the entire area between trees and wall and found nothing, so may as well venture further within.

Between the trees was harder going: she couldn't take more than a few paces in a straight line, constantly having to manoeuvre around thick trees or step over grabbing vines. Of the animals making the interminable racket she could see no visible signs, despite her ears insisting that they were most certainly nearby. She wound her way through the jungle for an hour or so, barely feeling as if she were making any progress at all, and found almost nothing that she could take back: there were leaves and stems aplenty, but none looked particularly edible or useful. If her sense of direction had remained accurate throughout all the little adjustments of her course, she had been heading in a straightish line directly away from the door, so that all she should have to do to leave would be to turn right around and head back the same way.

Something rustled nearby. Tuli whipped around, squinting towards where the sound had come from. There were constant rustles and cries and squawks, of course, but this one had cut through all the rest: it had been close, and it had sounded *big*. Tuli picked up the pace, still heading straight into the forest, lifting her feet higher with each step so as to skip over as much of the rough terrain as possible. She turned her head to look back; her foot came down into a dip in the earth and she tripped, sprawling across the dirt and nearly hitting her head on one of the ever-present encroaching trees around her as she fell.

Tuli lay still for a few moments. The *smack* of her rapid descent hadn't been that loud, certainly not compared to the raucous screaming of things that filled the air with a thick quilt of noise, but her heart was pounding and her ears strained for any indication that there might be anything making its way towards her. When after several painful heartbeats she heard nothing, she put her hands under her shoulders and pushed herself unsteadily to her feet, struggling to stand amid the adrenaline and the unsteady ground.

She took another step, and then the crashing started. To her left: a thundering array of deafening, heavy smashes - already running in the other direction, she risked the quickest of glances and saw out of the corner of her eye a rush of movement in the darkness through the thick forest, a toppling sequence of tall trunks all suddenly dropping in turn like a row of dominoes. Something was coming towards her, something big enough and strong enough to bulldoze through the jungle as if the trees were made of paper, and from the increasing volume of the force she knew she couldn't outrun it.

So, she turned right, sprinting as fast as she dared towards the edge of the jungle where she'd entered - her eyes desperately flitted across the ground ahead of her, feet barely keeping up with the messages from her brain about where was safe to step and where would bring her down. Her best hope was that the thing would keep moving in a straight line towards where she'd been, that she could move out of its way and somehow reach the door before it found her again.

The noise of the approaching hunter faded away as she ran, until it was imperceptible among the rest of the sounds of the jungle. She didn't dare stop, didn't dare let herself believe that she might yet be safe, until she was clear of the trees; she felt as if her feet were made of stone and her legs of wood, her breath scraping at her throat in dry scratches, but she kept going.

After what felt like the longest run of her life (even though she regularly ran several miles on her gathering missions), Tuli broke free of the jungle. She fell to the ground, her feet not used to running on a smooth surface after so long spent struggling; on all fours she scrambled up the incline. When she had finally clawed her way to the top of the hill, she fell and lay unmoving except for the ragged heaving of her breath.

Nothing came out of the jungle after her. She wouldn't have been able to move if it had.

After a hundred or more deep breaths, Tuli finally wobbled back to her feet. She turned her head slowly in both directions, back against the infinite wall, and saw no signs of pursuit. Nothing else for it; she turned so that the wall was on her right and started walking again, knowing that at least she would eventually loop around the bizarre space and find the door.

A few minutes later, she came to something she hadn't noticed the first time: an enormous window, like the ones she'd seen from the outside but twenty times the size. Thousands of little panes of coloured glass interlocked and intermingled; if she looked at it right up close she could just see lots of separate shapes of many colours, but when she took a step back a cohesive picture emerged from the arrangement.

There were greens near the bottom, light purples melding with dark blues, gentle greens, and transient whites to create a sort of grey stone colour in the middle, and a deep, rich darkness above that. A grassy span of earth, atop which stood the very building Tuli had entered (complete with miniature representations of its windows), and above that: Guilt. Tuli flinched away from it when she realised what it depicted, not wanting to look too closely at the top of the picture; instead she leaned in so that she couldn't see as much of the window and peered at the representation of the building. There was a small shape near the door, a human-looking form posed as if it were about to peer inside.

Tuli shook her head. It was pretty, she supposed - impressive, certainly - but it didn't help. She had no idea how she'd managed to miss it on her first time walking the loop of the wall; it demanded attention. Still, she had little choice but to keep going until she found the door again, and then she planned to never think about this place again if she could help it.

After twenty or so more minutes of walking, Tuli found herself next to another window. That couldn't have been right; she was going a little bit slower than on her first round, but it had only taken her fifteen minutes or so to walk away from the door and loop right around to it again. She should have passed it by now, surely. Could she have somehow missed it? No: she'd been keeping an eye on the tree line, certainly, but one eye had always been on the wall beside her. She'd even been brushing her fingers along it for most of the way. No door - so where *was* she?

This window, too… it wasn't exactly the same, not quite, but it was close. The same landscape, but the person by the door had disappeared inside and Guilt was, perhaps, a little further along in the sky. For want of anything better to do, Tuli huffed at the window and ate a bread roll from her pack, tearing chunks out of it with her teeth frustratedly.

There really was no other option, though, so she kept going. No door, but twenty minutes later: another window. In this one, there was a bizarre mass of white and grey approaching the building from the side of the image. Tuli found herself shivering. Whatever it was, she got the impression that it was following the person who'd entered before it.

However she looked at it, it seemed obvious that she wasn't going to get to the door this way. Perhaps she needed to go left instead; perhaps the loop wasn't working right for some reason. She tried throwing a stone through the window to see whether she might be able to escape that way, but no luck: the little rock left a scratch on the thick glass, but it didn't break - and even if it had, she'd have had to break the substance between coloured panes to make a gap big enough to fit through, which didn't seem likely to happen. So left it was: she turned and went back the way she'd come, heart sinking further and further into her stomach with every step.

She came to another window after another twenty minutes, as expected. It should have been the one she'd walked past second, after the first and before the third from where she'd just come. It wasn't.

The picture in this window showed the creature from the last image, but much closer; it was opening the doors, peering inside. Tuli stood there, staring; her eye was drawn to a scratch on one of the many panes of glass. That was the same place she'd scratched with her stone at the last window.

She held her head in her hands, trying to understand and knowing that it might be pointless, but gradually a thought came to her. It wasn't a sequence of windows at all: she'd looped around, walking past the *same* window four times, but the window itself was changing.

And that meant… somehow, she'd found herself somewhere other than the loop of wall that contained the door.

She was stuck.

Tuli slumped against the wall, gasping; somehow, though she knew the air around her was no different, it felt as if it resented being drawn into her lungs. Her vision blurred for a moment; her fingers felt light. Trying any harder to comprehend things just made her feel dizzier, but her brain couldn't help it. She remembered once noticing how a gate moved when it pivoted open: the part closer to the hinge hardly moved at all, but the other end travelled a much longer distance. Perhaps this place was like that, she reasoned despite not really wanting to think about it; perhaps the wall was like the part near the hinge, so she couldn't go far before finding herself in the same short loop, but in venturing further from the pivot point she'd managed to take herself much further from the door even without travelling far. She'd come back to a *different* section of endless loop, far from the one that the door was part of.

If she was right, then the only way to get back to the door was to head the same distance back into the forest, then walk to the left the same distance she'd gone to the right while she was in there, then come back out again.

She heard herself screaming, even though she hadn't meant to.

It seemed so unfair. There could barely even be any point in attempting to make it back to the door, since (if she was right) a small sideways movement within the trees would translate to a much larger distance travelled along the wall. Even a step or two wrong and she'd overshoot or undershoot the section of wall with the door in by… well, by who knew how far, but it hardly mattered the distance when wherever she ended up would be never-ending. You could never get from one part of the wall to another without leaving it, so you had no way to know when you were in the right place.

This was - deeply, more than anything that had ever happened to her - *not* ideal.

But she'd never been one to give up, and she had only two options: sit here until she died, or *try* to make it out alive.

So Tuli went back into the jungle. Somehow, whatever might be waiting for her there seemed far less frightening now she'd dealt with the realisation that she would certainly die if she did nothing. She strode down the hill, not looking back; if she had, she might have noticed that the being in the window-image had entered the building and closed the door behind itself.

She tried to remember exactly the path she'd taken, even knowing that she almost certainly wasn't entering at the same point where she'd exited. It shouldn't have made too much difference, she rationalised, since movement along the wall was near the analogical hinge; she took long, half-running steps on her way back into the depths of the trees, trying to move just as she'd done on the way out but in reverse.

When she thought she'd run enough, as far back into the jungle as she'd been when she'd run out of it, she stopped and closed her eyes, shaking her head in rapid, small movements as if trying to dislodge something. It was pointless, surely. Futile.

Then something occurred to her, and she opened her eyes and kept walking further into the forest.

Just a few steps later, hidden by the curtains and pillars of green and brown, she came into a line of destruction: a long, straight passage carved out by the thing that had come after her. All she had to do was follow that to the left, back to just before the place where it started, and then she'd be at the spot where she'd first fallen - a spot in a straight line from the door.

Tuli almost felt like whistling, if she'd been able to. She'd tried a few times throughout her life, but all that ever happened was a wet rush of pathetic air. If there were ever a time to let loose with a chirping sound of success, though, surely this had to be it. She restrained herself, though; on the off chance she did manage to produce a discernible note, there could still be things she'd prefer didn't hear her.

So, she just walked, stepping over fallen trees and passing through the little wrecked valley. It wasn't long before she came to the terminal point: a nodule of space outwards from which all the trees had fallen, the passage of the hunter extending from there. She closed her eyes, thinking back to the first moment that she'd seen the destruction approaching: it had been some way off at first, a crash she'd heard before she'd seen the shadows of the approaching ravager through the jungle. Walking backwards, she tried to put herself as far from the beginning of the passage as she had been when she fell, and then she took one deep breath, turned sharply, and walked out of the woods.

Tuli emerged. The door was there; she could see it up the hill. She would have cried, fallen to the ground in relief, perhaps even wailed some sort of prayer of thanks to who-could-have-known-what. But she did none of those things, because between her and the door was a mass of grey-white flesh.

It was *appalling*, in the sense that to look at it was not only viscerally horrible but somehow an incredible source of dismay, as if acknowledging that it was there and that it was the way it was entailed acknowledging something too profoundly sad to fully appreciate. As a whole it seemed shapeless, but there were parts that were recognisable. A pair of reddish-brown lungs hanging off it, swelling and emptying in rhythm; things that must have been appendages, hand-like or finger-like but never assembled into something that Tuli could truly call 'a hand'; and eyes, so very many eyes.

Tuli stood still, because there was nothing else she could think to do.

The thing beheld her with those of its eyes that were on the parts of its flesh that faced her. It made no move to approach, but neither did it stop gazing at her.

'Please let me leave,' Tuli found herself saying, the accrued hopelessness of being chased and trapped and lost and found and then trapped again bubbling out of her in quiet words.

A thick white protuberance emerged from a wide gash in the thing's flesh, moving up and down and around almost tentatively. Then it retreated, and the featureless skin under the orifice bobbed as if swallowing. Then the hole opened again, and noises came from it.

'Stee-ven,' it said, slowly and in a voice that reminded Tuli of the helpless cries of a broken-winged bird, fallen and lost. 'Stee-ven.'

'Stee-ven,' she repeated. It made a movement that might have been a nod, had it had a discernible head.

The thing half-waddled, half-oozed closer.

'Yuu,' it whined. 'I Stee-ven. Yuu.'

Though Tuli didn't comprehend whatever ancient language the being might be trying to speak, the movements of many dangling appendages made its meaning clear to her.

'You're Steeven,' she said in her own tongue, gesturing towards it with one hand. 'I - me -' she tilted the same hand towards herself, indicating her own body, 'Tuli.'

'Tuuu-leeee,' it moaned.

She nodded. 'OK.' It wasn't trying to kill her, which was already a better outcome than she could have hoped for. She just had to keep things that way; to communicate, if that was what it wanted, until it let her leave. 'OK, Steeven. Tuli needs to… to go.' She waved at the door, behind Steeven up the hill.

It made a movement like a slow shaking of the head, an expression of dissatisfaction - but not anger. 'Pleez. Nott iett.'

'You don't want me to go,' Tuli breathed, quietly enough that the thing probably couldn't hear her. Then, louder: 'Why can't I go?'

Steeven let out a groan - a low, pathetic mewling that reminded Tuli of a tall tree, trunk cut most of the way through, slowly leaning over until it ripped free and slammed down to the earth - and *rippled*, a small shake of its body sending vibrations through the whole mass of shapeless white. The many eyes wobbled in their places.

'Please let me go,' Tuli pleaded, moving her arms helplessly in ways she hoped would communicate an urgent (but non-threatening) need to reach the door. 'Please.'

It trembled as if deciding whether to stand its ground or rush - whether for her or somewhere else, she didn't know. Then it froze, shifting as if listening or watching for something; the eyes pivoted as one to a point somewhere behind Tuli.

A crash sounded, a flat rumble as if the entire forest were coming down, and Tuli's body acted before she could think: she threw herself away from the noise, towards the Steeven-thing, the need to flee whatever was behind overriding the fear of what was in front. Steeven moved - she didn't see how, it just went from one place to another - and put itself between Tuli and the trees. The eyes all over its mass made it difficult to tell, but Tuli almost thought it was facing the jungle defiantly, keeping her behind it.

A dark shape shot clear of the trees, an indistinct black form flying towards the undefined white that was Steeven. In moments the two had become a single grey jumble; Tuli couldn't tell what was happening, but the sounds coming from the blend of the two things battered her brain: a vibrating wall of pain in a shape resembling a voice screaming, in a language like nails scraping on stone, the worst things imaginable - Tuli knew that must be what it was crying, even though she couldn't make out any words.

Then, somehow, she understood two words: 'Tuli. Go.'

Whatever else she might wonder, whatever else she might fear or wish she had more time to learn, all Tuli could do in that moment was follow the instruction. She turned, in spite of something inside her straining not to leave the white abomination that had protected her, and ran up the hill and out of the door.

Outside, she kept running. She thought that she was heading back along the same route on which she'd come in, but her mind wouldn't leave the inside of the recursive place long enough to tell for sure.

Nobody would ever know what happened in that place after Tuli escaped, but the thing that was once Stephen Bartonsteir was never seen in the world again. And yet, many centuries after all who had known him by that name were gone, there was once more someone who could remember him. Tuli told her family of Steeven, the strange monster in the strange place outside space, and her children (though they didn't really believe her) passed the name on to theirs.

And so, as unlikely as it was, a man who had been lost to Guilt in the ages past was known again, just for a generation or two, by his true name.

Chris Durston

THE KING OF WASTED YEARS

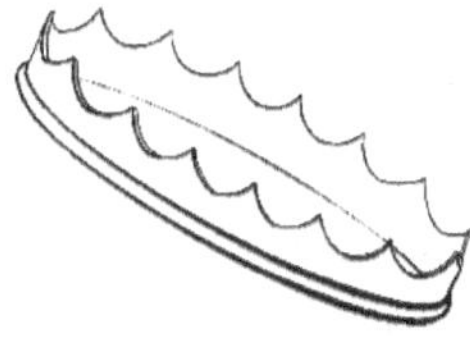

I did not see the First Children with my own eyes when they first appeared. I felt the quake, and I believe I may have caught a glimpse of a red glint rapidly disappearing over the horizon, but I was among the luckier inhabitants of the Earth in that I survived that time without having encountered one of the dragons.

She liked the word 'king', so she clung to it. Applied it to herself; demanded, somewhere within her mind in spite of the fact that nobody else could hear it there, that all must refer to her by her new lofty title. She was the king of her own land. She knew this was true because the king said so. That the king was *her* seemed to matter very little.

There were no subjects in her kingdom, nor any settlements. There were barely even any landmarks. Her domain stretched from the easternmost edge of the plains to the westmost, and between those two edges was emptiness.

It hadn't always been like this. Once, this had been a land of plenty: a place of rivers and hills and trees and people. She hardly remembered that now, but sometimes when she looked out there would be vestigial traces of the things that had been, superimposed onto her vision as if trying to manifest themselves again. The images were blurry, half-forgotten sketches of childhood memory. Gaps in the pictures simmered unnoticed; if her attention fell on a blank, her mind unconsciously filled in the empty space with a guessed history.

What had happened then? What always happened: Guilt.

She always shook her head then, never allowed her memory to drift that way. No time for distractions, or regrets: she had a kingdom to rule over. All the years of her life she had spent wandering her lands, all the things she could have done instead but didn't - mustn't all that mean something? Her time was coming to an end, she knew that; she hoped she'd been a good king, a fair one. If she had had subjects, she hoped that they would have loved her; if her kingdom had had an economy, a culture, she hoped that they would have been world-famous and thriving.

As it was, she was alone. There was a certain profundity to total aloneness when one was a king.

On her final journey across her kingdom, she met a man. There had never been anyone else within her boundaries, but it was undeniable: there in front of her stood a man, healthy and unafraid.

The king asked the man who he was and what business he had in her kingdom. It took her a few attempts to say the words she meant to; her dry, neglected throat struggled and trembled before obeying her commands to *speak*.

The stranger prostrated himself before her, which she couldn't deny was to her liking. He had no way of knowing, he said, that he had committed the appalling sin of entering Her Grace's marvellous kingdom without her permission, and he begged for mercy. He knew, as he protested, that he had no right to expect such a leniency, but he hoped that a king of such clear and apparent virtue might be inclined towards favourable justice.

Trying not to make too obvious her pleasure at finally being treated like the esteemed regent she was, the king asked again what business he had.

Survival, the newcomer responded. Life.

Now the king was surprised, or concerned. It had been so long since she had had a conversation with another human being that she hardly remembered which emotions were which. She wondered aloud: what made him think that he would find such a thing here, in her empty lands?

There were tales, rumours, the man explained. Half-remembered stories passed down from his grandfather to his father to him: the sight of a fateful angel over this part of the world. His grandfather, as a young man, had seen a sparkling, airborne being that could only be an omen of good fortune; it had seemed to him to be beckoning, instructing, giving wisdom to him and him alone. He had watched its flight and seen where it had descended, and this was the place. That story had been almost the only thing his grandfather had ever spoken about; it had consumed him.

Then why, asked the king, had it taken two generations for his family to find the place?

The man begged her forgiveness once more for his rudeness in failing to tell all parts of the story in the correct order. She pardoned him immediately, reveling in the feeling of conducting real kingly duties. His grandfather, the man explained, had been ill all of his life, never strong enough to make the journey, and his father had only half-believed the story. Their people had been unwilling to put any stock in one sick man's ramblings of a promised land, but now there were very few of their people left and the little land they had was becoming ever more difficult to survive upon.

The king had no need to ask what had happened to cause this change. She allowed herself then to remember the people she had had, when she was just a member like every other of a society like every other.

If this man had lost his people to the same cause as she had, did not that make him a brother of sorts? Or… and this she found enthralling, much as part of her knew that it was not her right to think such things, did not that make the surviving members of his society her subjects? If it was Guilt that had bestowed her coronation, then why should Guilt not also be the one to provide her with people over whom to rule?

There was not much further to go, the man explained. He was certain of it, or as certain as one could be when seeking a place shown to a sick man by a shining angel's flight over a great distance. He had only a few more miles to go, only a few more horizons to surmount.

The king, perhaps moved by his story and his passion or perhaps simply curious, accompanied the grandson of the angel-seer to his destination. They crossed her lands together, covering ground she knew well; but she was startled to realise, as they walked on, that their path was taking them to an area she had never passed through. Always when she travelled her lands, she had walked routes that skirted around this place: north, south, east, and west she had walked perpendicular to this one part of her kingdom, sunken as it was within a surrounding bank of hilltops, but had never been into it.

As they drew closer, the king's eyes began to sting from the bright light shining over the horizon, a glint like the sun emerging from behind a tall mountain on a clear day. She directed her gaze towards the ground and focused on maintaining her stride - on keeping up with her companion, whose pace had quickened in excitement. Soon they were there, and the king could only gape in astonishment.

In the middle of her kingdom, without her ever suspecting, had lain for all these years the body of one of the First Children of Guilt. At a distance she had no idea which: it could have been the silver, or it could have been either the blue or the red faded and sullied until it was all just one glittering pile of metal of indiscriminate colour.

The man beside her let out a long breath. She asked what it meant, for she could tell enough to know it meant something.

It was an awe-inspiring sight, her new friend said, but not the one he had hoped for.

Saying nothing more, he walked to the body of the dragon and put his hand on it; he withdrew his touch immediately, grimacing. The king thought privately that it ought to have been obvious that one ought not to touch a great metal thing that had lain in the sun all day, but decided not to say as such.

They sat in the jagged shade of the thing's body for some time, until the sun had meandered across the sky in the same arc it always followed. Sharp glints of light flashed into their eyes from the glittering skeleton, and then the king noticed something: a softer glow, a reflection not of the painful, metal variety.

She made her way towards this new, more soothing light, followed curiously by the newcomer to her kingdom. The glow came from the middle of the basin within the hills, its source concealed by the horizon-spanning body of the First Child; they descended the gentle slope into the lowest part of the space and saw a smooth expanse of sky in the earth before them.

No - not sky: reflection.

The man who had come to the kingdom smiled and thanked the king, who accepted his gratitude even though she had done nothing to earn it. She simply stood and wondered at the water, at the hidden place that had been in her kingdom the whole time she had ruled over it.

She had believed herself the king of nothing, and so nothing had been her kingdom. The stranger beside her had believed this a place of promise, and so promise they had found.

The time remaining to the king was short, she knew that, and so - even understanding the meaninglessness of the exercise - she named the newcomer her heir and successor. He was awed by the gift, even as it cost her nothing to give.

When the new king returned with his people, to establish a flourishing land from the basin of life in the shadow of metal death, they found the old king sitting under the dragon. The smile on her face wiped away all the lines of age.

Her kingdom of nothing was passed on to those who could make it a kingdom of plenty. In that act, she had become for the first time a true king.

Chris Durston

AN IMPROPER SCEPTIC

$$x \nmid y.$$

The fact is that the presence of Guilt is a thing of such singular global importance that it is able to have an astounding effect on the behaviour of both individuals and societies even without ever coming into direct contact.

'Don't live your lives in fear!'

A few people slowed their pace for a moment, looking up at the man on the pedestal. Some raised an eyebrow. Most simply carried on without seeming to notice at all. Almost none stopped to listen.

'There's no need to worry about Guilt!'

One older woman shook her head, looking almost disgusted.

'Be free from your dogma!'

Someone spat at him.

'There *is no Guilt*!'

That stopped a couple of people in their tracks. One young woman, her eyes a vicious purple, wandered up to the speaker's podium.

'Did you say there is no Guilt?' she asked.

'I thought I said it loud enough.'

'You did, but it seems such an obviously outlandish thing to say that I felt compelled to check.'

The man sighed with his mouth wide open, staring down his nose at her. 'Have you ever *seen* Guilt?'

'Not in my lifetime,' she admitted.

He grinned, eyes flashing, swiping the air with one finger as if to say 'aha!'

'But a *looooot* of people have,' she continued.

'Come off it. You seem smarter than to believe something just because someone else says it.'

She nodded with raised eyebrows, conceding the point. 'I don't believe it *just* because someone said it was true, though.'

'Oh, no?'

'No.'

'What other reason could you have to believe it, then?'

She let out a short, quiet breath of amusement through her nostrils. 'You want me to list them?'

He made a sweeping gesture with his arms: *by all means, the floor is yours.*

'Well,' she said. 'There's the Children of Guilt. Seen those.'

'False equivocation,' declared the man, loudly enough for all to hear (even those who didn't care in the slightest, which remained the vast majority). 'Just because a category of things are *named* the Children of Guilt is not evidence for the existence of a particular thing called Guilt, nor for any characteristics such a thing might have.'

'How do you explain them, then?'

'I need not. I make no claim as to how they have come to exist; it is *you* who is making the claim and who thus must defend it.'

'Hm.' She considered this, nodding to herself. 'You're saying that *anything* could be the origin of the Children, but if I'm specifying that it's any particular thing then it's on me to prove that.'

'Quite!'

'OK. How about the parts of the world that don't act like all the rules of things say they usually should? The Walking Forest? The Undersea? The Inverse Mountain?'

'Have you *seen* any of these -?'

'How about we say for the sake of argument that I have,' she interrupted. 'And besides, there are hills only a few miles over that way that clearly had to have been in some sort of liquid state at some point to have ended up the shape they are. I've seen those, and I've never seen a hill just turn into liquid, so seems likely that Guilt made them that way.'

'Why?'

'Because… Guilt can change things.'

'Begging the question! Circular reasoning!'

She groaned.

'Your argument proceeds thus: firstly, it is the case that the hills are not shaped in accordance with usual geographical conventions; secondly, it is the case that Guilt has the ability to defy usual geographical conventions; therefore Guilt exists. Your premises assume your conclusion. You affirm the consequent.'

'Alright, fine. There's the movement of the tides. They don't follow the moon, which means there's something of equal or greater mass closer to the surface of the Earth than the moon is, and that would be explained by Guilt.'

He stared at her, his lips in a curious O.

'Oh, right,' she said. 'Most people don't know that stuff anymore. There are still people reading old books and writing new ones, though.'

'The tides… follow the moon?'

'It's gravity,' she said. 'The moon used to *pull* on the oceans, causing them to move closer or further from the land. But Guilt's a bigger, heavier, closer, stronger pull than the moon, so that's what they follow now.'

'Aha!' he exclaimed. 'How do you *know* that it's Guilt that does that? What if it's some *other* huge object, maybe even an invisible one, or maybe it is the moon reaching out with some sort of force other than gravity?'

She sighed. 'I'm not going to get anywhere with you, am I?'

'Not today, not unless you show me *proof*.'

'I have somewhere to be,' she muttered, but then she stood tall and looked him straight in the eyes, indigo irises boring into him. 'How do you think I got eyes like this?'

'Mutation,' he said. 'Or supernatural in any of an infinity of possible ways. Proves nothing.'

'You know, you're sort of not wrong,' she told him. 'There's not going to be much I can do to prove beyond a doubt that Guilt is real and is all the things people say it is, but one day you'll see it, and then you'll know. It won't care at that point; all the reasoning in the world won't be able to make it go away.'

'Fortunately,' he said, turning his nose up, 'it *can* make it so that I know it'll never come in the first place.'

Her eyes flashed. 'Good luck with that.'

As she went on her way, he had the distinct impression of a shape, much larger than she was, occupying the same space that she did.

Chris Durston

THE POLYPOD

Still, some animals have been known to live through exposure to the Shadow unchanged. It has, although this is far from the right term, an anecdotal fondness for those creatures that might already be considered somewhat peculiar.

'What in the jaws of Malice is *that*?'

Sothea peered at the thing she'd brought back from the Rainbow Shore, something much more complicated - and much more interesting, she hoped - than she'd been expecting to find. It was sitting apparently unperturbed in a large glass tank of water on a thick stone work table, occasionally flexing a muscle to change its position or orientation; its large eyes seemed to take in everything and focus on nothing.

'I don't know,' she admitted. 'But isn't that the point?'

Edsimander frowned. 'I feel like we should have started… I don't know, simpler.'

'Where'd be the fun in that?'

'It might not be as fun, but we might get more *done*.'

'Ugh.' Sothea stepped to the side, revealing the smaller tank on the other table behind her. In addition to the two tables, the warehouse in which they were meeting held (taking up about half the floor space) a number of contraptions and devices of varying sizes and materials; at a charitable guess, Sothea thought she had a reasonably good idea of what about a quarter of them were supposed to do. 'I also brought these *perfectly regular fish*, if you really wanna start there.'

Her colleague in curiosity regarded the three or four small fish merrily swimming in circles, then shook his head. 'Much as I feel like that would make *so much* more sense, I find that I don't really fancy studying perfectly regular fish.'

The two of them were starting a new endeavour, something that (as far as they knew) people hadn't tried to do in centuries, maybe even millennia. They knew that there had been people engaged in the study of animals - their bodies, behaviours, habitats, lifestyles - before the coming of Guilt from a very small number of fragments of text that still remained, copied and distributed and lost and recopied and translated from the Old Languages and copied again over… however many years it had been, but the knowledge was all but lost. Nobody really had the time or energy to dedicate to what was considered an abstract field of study when there were so many practical problems to overcome in this world - or, at least, nobody had been able to do it successfully enough to spread the word.

So, Sothea, Edsimander, and - when she could be bothered to show up - Lendora (who was one of those irritating people who was both clever and well-resourced, and therefore *de facto* responsible for finding ways to secure the premises and equipment they needed) were establishing their own new science. They called it *beastology*. (Sothea had come across the untranslated term 'zoology' in one of the Old Science fragments she'd been able to get her eyes on, but it seemed awfully awkward to pronounce. 'Zewloggi'. Ugly word.)

'Well, then,' said Sothea, clapping her hands together. 'Let's get started with our friend here, shall we?'

Edsimander considered the creature with a curious, vaguely nervous eye.

'Step one,' Sothea continued. 'What to name it.'

'Is that step one?' Edsimander wondered.

'Probably not, by the old methods, but hey. We're inventing our own science here.' She leant in close to the glass tank, fixing the apathetic thing with a hard stare. 'What could we call you? What about you is nameworthy? You're a sea creature, 'cos I found you in the sea and you obviously live in water. You've got big eyes. You're, um.'

'It's got a lot of... legs,' Edsimander observed, and indeed it did: Sothea couldn't tell exactly how many, because the thing's dark red body seemed to be constantly shifting in strange ways that threw her eye off, even when it didn't actually look as if it were moving. She could just about demarcate the big bulb at the top as a head, because that was where the eyes were, and everything under that was just a jumble of disorganised limbs.

'That is true,' she mused. 'How about... a *polypod*?'

'Polypod?'

'Mm. *Poly* used to mean *lots*, and *pod* was legs. We're bipods - two-legs. This thing's many-legs, so... polypod.'

Edsimander nodded slowly. 'It sort of fits.'

'He *looks* like a polypod in the same way you look like an Edsimander, you mean?'

'How d'you know it's a he?'

'I... suppose I don't. Just the way he looks like he could sit there for ages doing nothing, I guess.'

'... I can see that.'

Sothea nodded. 'Polypod he is. Step two. Do science.'

'That feels like it should be more than one step.'

Sothea hummed, settling herself down into a chair beside the polypod's table. 'I think we just observe it and see what it does,' she said. 'Unless you wanted to kill it and see what its insides look like, but we've only got the one so that might be a bit, um, peremptory.'

'Behaviour, then anatomy. Sounds good to me.' Edsimander scratched at his jaw with one finger, regarding the apparently oblivious polypod. 'Can I admit something that might not be very good beastology?'

'We're making it up as we go along; if you say it, it's part of beastology law.'

'Then let it be known in the annals of beastology that, although I've only just met this thing, I don't think I'm going to be OK with killing it at *any* point in the foreseeable future.'

'Seconded,' Sothea said, sounding half-irritated at her own unwillingness to murder a newly-discovered sea creature.

'What in the talons of Calamity is *that*?!'

They both turned to look at the door, where a young woman with intimidating shoulders and bright violet eyes was staring at the polypod's tank with a mixture of confusion, curiosity, and perhaps even a little hunger on her face.

'You can't eat it, Lendora,' Sothea said. 'It's our first, er, subject.'

'It's a polypod,' Edsimander told the newcomer cheerily.

'Oh, good.' Lendora strode across the little warehouse she'd procured for the group and squatted before the tank. Her skin, unlike Sothea's and Edsimander's, was pale; the pale eyes set in the pale face made her look like an unusually muscular ghost. 'It hasn't tried to kill anyone?'

'Not so far,' chirped Sothea.

'Any unusual sensory or emotional reactions either of you've noticed after spending any time looking at it?'

Edsimander shook his head. 'Don't think so.'

'Has it asked you to do anything that you wouldn't normally do, especially if it's something you *specifically* avoid doing most of the time?'

'Haven't heard a peep out of it,' Sothea said, plonking her feet up on the table and crossing her legs at the ankles.

Lendora's violet eyes bored into the polypod, which did not appear to care in the slightest. She held up one hand, then the other, then splayed her fingers before folding them back down one by one as if counting something. The polypod gave no indication that it was aware of her presence at all.

Her lower eyelids twitched, and for a moment her bright eyes flashed a violent purple-white. The polypod might have paused for a second, and then it carried on doing the stationary aquatic version of meandering aimlessly around.

'It's not one of the Children of Guilt,' Lendora declared, when her eyes had faded back to their usual, mildly aggressive sheen.

'Figured as much, but thanks for checking.' Sothea folded her arms behind her head. 'Its body doesn't seem to make all that much sense, geometrically or whatever, but I've never seen a Child that just didn't even care about being scooped into a tank.'

'Regular thing, just a weird one,' Edsimander murmured. Lendora's eyes began to move sharply in his direction, then paused; a quiet sigh slipped from her nostrils, and she went back to considering the polypod. 'Sorry,' Edsimander mumbled. 'Not *regular*, um. You know.'

'I know,' said Lendora, her expression not changing.

'I think,' said Sothea, staring lazily at the ceiling, 'that you should totally just embrace that you really aren't normal. Just roll with it. It's useful!'

There were still those who didn't like the Descendants of Guilt, and perhaps there always would be. Lendora didn't know how far removed in time she was from her Child ancestor, how many generations separated her from Guilt; as far as her experience of life was concerned, she told Sothea once, she was a human raised by humans who had been raised by humans. Not that she'd have been ashamed of herself if she'd been more closely related... she thought. It was hard to know how to feel about it, especially when a lot of people seemed to have very strong opinions on how everyone - herself included - ought to feel about where she came from. Wasn't as if she could help it.

These weren't things she tended to volunteer as topics of conversation, but most people seemed to have a way of bringing it up. For Lendora - and for Sothea and Edsimander - the fact that Lendora was strong and could detect the influence of Guilt (its essence, traces of which it left behind in everything it created or changed) was just another advantage to have on the team. It was in the same category as Edsimander's ability to quickly see how some mechanism worked and use his steady hands to make it do whatever they needed it to do, or Sothea's reckless curiosity.

'Anyway,' Lendora said, leaning on the table occupied by the non-polypod-filled tank, 'it's an interesting thing. You said *polypod*?'

'Lots of legs,' Edsimander explained helpfully.

'It doesn't seem to *do* much.' Lendora's tone was almost critical.

'Not so far,' Sothea conceded. 'Any ideas on how we might… I dunno, do the studying sciencing thing?'

Lendora poked the side of the tank - not hard enough to damage it, or even nudge it. The polypod gave a vague shimmer of disdain. 'A few.'

Several hours later, they knew a few things.

One, the polypod ate fish. All of the fish Sothea had brought back, actually, but since it was much more interesting than they were, this didn't bother her too much.

Two, it was smart enough to recognise that the three humans were living creatures and that the round balls in their face were what they used to see things. She'd thought at first that she was imagining things (or else some unusually non-malevolent Child of Guilt had snuck in) when she started to feel water hitting the back of her neck; when she turned around, the polypod would be plapping around with its usual lack of interest in absolutely anything whatsoever. After a few such incidents, though, they'd decided to try looking away for a period of several minutes, enduring a few blasts of water until they heard a wet slap. When they quickly looked back, the polypod was halfway out of the tank, climbing free of the glass walls with sticky appendages. It had looked almost sheepish as it plopped back into the water, as if mortified to have been caught actually *doing* something.

Three, it was playful. Once it had been spotted in motion once, it seemed to care less about keeping up the display of total antipathy; when Edsimander put a glass tube of liquid down on the table near it, the polypod had poked its head up above the top of its tank and let loose a jet of water that sent the cylinder toppling off the side. Lendora had managed to catch it just in time, and set it back where Edsimander had left it, but the polypod had immediately shot it again. When Lendora slowly, deliberately put the tube down out of range on the other table - staring at the polypod the whole time - it popped up one more time as if to try blasting again, then went back to loosely floating around with what Sothea almost thought was a smug expression.

'Do you think it might be smarter than us?' Edsimander wondered, taking a sip of what Sothea was pretty sure was pure alcohol diluted in much less water than seemed sensible. 'Like, what if the *polypod* is a scientist and it's come to study *people*?'

'Then we should be honoured to be worthy of its concern,' said Sothea dryly.

The polypod plomped one of its many arms against the glass cheerily.

'I feel like we're friends,' Edsimander murmured. 'I think the polypod understands me better than I understand myself.'

Lendora cleared her throat. 'That had better be the drink talking and not any kind of nefarious influence.' She gazed at him for a moment with her glowing eyes, just to make sure, then scratched at the back of her neck. 'I kind of know what you mean, though.'

The polypod was loafing around, occasionally glancing over at them. Edsimander stared at it, the lines between his eyebrows getting deeper by the moment.

Sothea noticed.

'What's that look?'

Edsimander raised a hand and wiggled it around. He seemed to be trying to make each joint flop as loosely as possible, creating an illusion of polypod-like smooth, confused motion, but he just looked like someone with sore fingers to Sothea. 'It moves so… gracefully,' he breathed, twirling his digits around in imitation of the polypod's movements.

'Yeaaaah…'

'I bet it would be great at *obstacle courses.*'

Lendora and Sothea looked at each other.

'We could make, like… the best obstacle course,' Edsimander sighed. 'For science.'

'For science?' The corner of Sothea's mouth quirked upwards. 'Well, that's persuasive.'

Lendora rolled her eyes up as far as they could go, shaking her head at the ceiling. It had been a conversation like this that had led them to the certainty that starting up a new scientific undertaking would be a really good idea.

'Dora?' Edsimander wheedled. 'Can we make a polypod obstacle course?'

'If I told you I'd punch your spine out through your skin before I agreed to let you make a polypod obstacle course, would you be at all deterred?'

Edsimander narrowed his eyes thoughtfully. 'Not really,' he said, after giving the matter due consideration.

Lendora sighed, a sigh so heavy that only someone who had been putting up with Sothea and Edsimander for years could possibly have pulled it off.

'Hurray!' twooted Sothea. 'We're making an obstacle course for science!'

The next two days (once Edsimander's head felt a bit better) passed in a blur of conceptualising, designing, shaping, accidentally cutting their fingers in the process of shaping, feeding the polypod, stopping to briefly appreciate just how *cool* it was that they were doing something both fun and useful, and then conceptualising again when the whole thing fell to pieces.

Finally, though, they had it.

It was a bizarre thing: a series of large troughs all pieced together into a long run and filled with water, then various twists and turns and squeezes and hatches built in. The polypod had watched the whole project with a degree of interest, as if looking curiously for anything that might give it an advantage when it came time to take on the course.

'We're agreed that we at least need to write this down and be all scientific about it, right?' This from Lendora, who Sothea suspected had been having at least fifty or sixty percent more fun than she'd been letting on but had pretended to be grudgingly going along with the whole thing.

'Oh, absolutely,' Sothea promised. 'This is a very rigorous experiment into the behaviour of a new species, and humanity will forever thank us for our discipline, integrity, and… obstacle-course-building skills.'

Edsimander, who was busy drawing a map of the course, nodded vigorously. 'Important work,' he said, and finished scribbling in the last corners of the diagram. 'Right. Shall we, er…'

Sothea dropped a few dead fish into the water at the far end of the course, then looked up at Lendora, who carefully picked up the large tank containing the polypod. She glanced at Sothea and got one nod; Edsimander - pen ready to note the path the creature took - gave her a second. She nodded her own head firmly, chin carving a determined line up and down through the air, and then slowly, cautiously tipped the tank until the polypod slid out into the space at the start of the route with an unbothered sploshp.

It blobbled around aimlessly for a moment, turning in a lazy circle, then tilted its head up to gaze at Lendora standing above it. She blinked at it a couple of times, then raised a hand and pointed a finger at Sothea; the polypod revolved slowly to gaze at Sothea, who picked one of the fish out of the trough and dangled it about alluringly. It blorped from side to side, then - lethargically, as if resigned to the fact that it had nothing better to do - began to wander down the course.

Edsimander jotted notes at each stage of the polypod's journey: it slid easily under a barrier that left only a small gap above the floor; when it came to a hinged sheet of metal, it quickly worked out how to wrap a tentacle around so as to pull it open; it somehow managed to squeeze itself into a cylindrical space only as wide as Sothea's wrist, which would have seemed impossible for any animal with a hard skeleton but didn't seem to bother the polypod at all.

'I thought it'd just go *around* that bit,' Edsimander mused, noting the results with fervour.

The polypod meandered to a series of bars, around which Sothea had intended that it would have to twist and manoeuvre carefully so as not to get stuck. It tilted its head back and forth, like Sothea did when she was considering a tricky problem, and then - it still didn't feel right somehow assuming its motivations for anything, but Sothea could have *sworn* - it scratched its bulbous head exasperatedly with the tip of one tentacle. Then it rose and fell gently as if sighing, glanced up at Sothea, and climbed up out of the water.

'Is it supposed to, er -' Edsimander was pressing the blunt end of his pen into his chin, watching with a deep frown.

The little squishy ball of seafaring reddish-brown flesh swung half its body over the top of the thin metal wall of the obstacle course, balancing precariously in the middle, and shimmied along merrily. When it reached a corner it swayed, dangling itself down to the inside, and continued traversing the route by sticking to the wall above the water.

'That's *cheating!*' Sothea exclaimed. The polypod carried itself over the rest of its intended obstacles, then let itself plop back in the water and munched contentedly on its fishy prize.

'That's… probably the smartest way to get to the end quickly,' Lendora said with what sounded like grudging respect.

Sothea squatted down beside the end of the trough, where the polypod seemed perfectly happy just flapping its limbs and eating. 'Do you think,' she said seriously, 'that *thinking* to this thing is… is like *thinking* how we do it?'

Edsimander looked down at his notes with a thoughtful expression; Lendora stared at the polypod.

'What do you… mean?' asked Lendora slowly; Sothea put her finger in the water and gave the little creature a gentle poke.

'I mean… isn't it *weird*, being able to think?'

'I guess.'

'And we know, 'cos when bits of our heads get damaged different bits of how we think get messed up, that it's our brain that lets us think and stuff.'

'Brains do thinking, yeah.'

'But this guy… maybe he's got a brain, but it's different from ours.' Sothea indicated the early obstacles where the polypod had arranged its body into an improbably small mass. 'Our brains don't squish like that.'

Edsimander took a long, deep breath. 'But it does seem to think,' he said. 'Even if it's not got a brain like ours, it's still managing to do stuff that we can't do without thinking about it.'

'So, what I'm wondering,' Sothea said, nodding, 'is whether what it's like to be a polypod is the same as what it's like to be us. I mean, if it's our brains that are responsible for us thinking then… you've gotta think that our brains could be different, and then we would think totally differently. Or even if our eyes or ears were different, the way the world seemed to us wouldn't be the same and that'd affect how our thoughts work. Right?'

'Is there a point to this?' Lendora asked.

'Probably not,' Sothea admitted, 'but isn't it *interesting*?'

'Interesting is what we wanted,' Edsimander said, wagging his pen.

'We wanted to find out *useful* stuff,' Lendora corrected, 'we just thought we'd be good at it because it happens to sometimes be interesting.'

Sothea smiled at the polypod, wondering whether the little motions of its eyes and the place at the bottom of its head where its tentacles joined the bulk of its body might not be the polypod trying to smile back. 'Might be useful one day, somehow.'

Lendora shook her head, but her mouth was trying to smile, Sothea could see it.

'And come to think of it,' Sothea went on thoughtfully, 'speaking of *useful* and polypod brains and stuff, we just sort of assumed that the polypod would *want* to go through the course.'

'Well, yeah,' said Lendora, 'to get to the food.'

'Oh, fair point. Still, I think we made a mistake imagining that its goals would be the same as the ones we would have in the same situation.'

The polypod wagged its limbs around, then turned a deep blue.

'What?!' Sothea exclaimed, pointing insistently (unnecessarily, since the others were both staring at it too). 'He can change colour now?!'

'You're sure it's not related to Guilt?' Edsimander asked Lendora uncertainly; the Descendant nodded, her frown so deep that Sothea could have lost a pen in it.

'It definitely didn't have any...' She took a long breath in through her nose and exhaled long and sharp through her mouth, her eyes glaring in scintillating steely pink. The polypod turned the same shade, bobbing around in the tank.

Lendora's eyes blazed brighter; the polypod's skin ran through a few flutters of teal, magenta, rose, scarlet, emerald, before settling back to its original dusty stone red. But Lendora wasn't looking at the polypod anymore: she was staring straight at Sothea, a glare of terror and hatred beaming out from her eyes.

'Um,' said Sothea. 'What did I do?' She stood up, but Lendora's gaze didn't follow her; she stepped to the side and realised that her friend hadn't been looking at her at all. Her eyes were fixed on some point beyond the warehouse, her line of sight travelling through Sothea, through the wall, and beyond to something Sothea couldn't see.

'We need to get out of here,' Lendora hissed.

Edsimander shot up out of his seat, staring frantically at the wall as if he would somehow become able to see what Lendora could. 'Is something coming?'

Sothea glanced down at the polypod, which didn't seem to particularly mind its hosts' distress - if it noticed at all. Now that she looked closely, though, it looked to her as if they must not have built the course quite right. The floor of the run, or perhaps of the warehouse itself, must not have been perfectly level: the water was definitely higher up the sides at one end than the other. Had it been that way before? And the side where the water was higher was the side closest to the wall into which Lendora's eyes continued to bore…

'Oh, *shit*,' Sothea muttered.

'It's just come over the horizon,' Lendora said quietly, her body stiff.

'It?' Edsimander demanded, looking from Lendora to Sothea to the wall and back again. 'As in, *it* it?'

'Guess it's our time,' Sothea said in a hard voice.

Of the three, only Sothea had ever *seen* Guilt. Only once. Only from the furthest vantage point: her aunt had made her climb to the top of a mountain so that she could see it in the distance, and she had decided then that she never wanted to be any closer than that.

There were those who said that, hundreds of years ago when it first appeared, *everyone* would have been able to see it in the sky every few weeks, if not more often than that. If Sothea's understanding of how the world was shaped and how light travelled was accurate, the implication was that Guilt used to fly *much* higher in the sky, casting a small shadow on the distant earth below but visible to people who were reasonably far away from being directly underneath it.

Sothea couldn't confirm that this was the case, but what she did know was that it swam close (relatively speaking) to the surface of the world now, perhaps ten miles above the land. It was big - enormous, so huge that she could barely comprehend it - but even being the size it was, flying so low meant that it was only visible to those who were much nearer to it than anyone would have liked to be, if they could help it.

Of those who said Guilt used to fly further from the world, some hypothesised that it had grown old, or tired of swimming. Some said that the final end was approaching, the day when Guilt would swim so low that it would drag its body across the land and give up on corrupting from a distance, instead simply bulldozing everything to rubble and dust. Some said that it just liked to come nearer from time to time so that it could see what it was working in closer detail, or so that it could make the people remember to fear it.

Almost all agreed - and a comparison of areas that had been under the Shadow recently, compared to those that hadn't been in darkness for a longer time, seemed to corroborate the theory - that the nearer

Guilt flew to the place where its Shadow was cast, the darker and the more powerful that Shadow became.

All of which was to say that being anywhere near Guilt when it passed overhead was, in Sothea's day, just about the last thing that anyone in their right mind would ever want to do.

'We've got to go, like, *now*,' Sothea snapped, scrambling to pick up as many essential items as she could. 'How long do we have?'

'I'm not sure.' Lendora tore her flaring eyes from the wall - through which, Sothea knew, she could see the enormous shadow rising up over the edge of the world, approaching with all the inevitability of hunger or time or decay. She shook her head quickly, blinking hard, and the glow faded from her eyes. 'We probably have a few hours before it's directly overhead, but… it looks as if we're right in the middle of its path.'

Edsimander swallowed loudly. 'We need to go a long way to get clear of the Shadow, you mean?'

Lendora nodded.

'Best get moving, then,' Edsimander mumbled. He'd gone very pale.

There were a few minutes of silent, panicked activity as each of them tried to collect as much as they could take with them, having no way of knowing how much of it might be there to come back to.

On a dash past the obstacle course, Sothea paused and glanced down at the polypod. 'Who's carrying him?' she asked, pointing down. The polypod was a vibrant yellow now, spinning in place and lifting its legs in some sort of rhythm.

Lendora looked at her as if the world were on fire and she'd asked who had remembered to bring the salt and pepper for their lunch. Edsimander just pulled his bottom lip up, making a face like a squashed fish.

'We can't *leave* him,' Sothea told them. 'We literally just worked out that he thinks, so he probably feels stuff too. That… makes him a person, sort of.'

Lendora looked entirely ready to disagree, but huffed an acute sigh and threw her hands up. 'If you want to save him, you've volunteered to carry him.'

Sothea thought about trying to persuasively and reasonably point out that Lendora was the strongest and by far the best at carrying things, but Lendora had already picked up her own pack and made for the door.

'Come on, then,' Sothea burbled to the polypod, grabbing its original tank and scooping it up. The tank was an awful lot smaller than the assembly that was the obstacle course - and thus less impossible to carry - but it was still big enough to be awkward, still heavy when full of water and polypod.

Edsimander, halfway out of the building, stopped and turned to look at Sothea; he took a few steps one way, then the other, then groaned and rushed over to take some of the weight. 'If I end up in the Shadow because of this thing, I swear that whatever monstrous abomination I turn into is coming after you first,' he warned.

'That's fair.'

They scrambled out of the warehouse and along the dirty streets of the city. Like most places, it had been under the Shadow enough times in its history to be warped; barely any straight lines to its layout, plenty of crooked, half-dissolved-looking buildings among the more recently built ones that still stood firm. Sothea found herself imagining that she could *hear* it coming, a ghastly deep rumble that shook the firmament in her brain and sent shivers through her bones. She shook her head as she moved, gripping her end of the tank with as much caution as she could spare.

The trio sat at the top of a hill many miles outside the city, the polypod in its tank next to them. It stared wide-eyed and still in the same direction, looking for all the world as if it had been an integrated part of their circle for just as long as any of the rest of them.

Guilt had come.

They couldn't stay where they were for long; being *near* it was only slightly preferable to being *under* it, but they'd needed to rest. They had already travelled through the night, barely stopping. Besides, the sight, as terrible as it was, demanded to be beheld.

It swam sideways, right to left, from their perspective - they'd run laterally out of its path, everyone knew not to try running *away* from it in the same direction. For its sheer size it may as well have been a world of its own, another Earth made of dark grey flesh reflected above the first; but it was no world, it was indubitably an *animal*, if one nothing alike to any other, and that knowledge made the scale of it seem so insensible that Sothea found herself having to look away every minute or so, squeezing her eyes shut against the feeling that her stomach was rapidly shrinking away to nothing.

It took up all the space that wasn't already occupied by the ground beneath it, filling every inch of the sky. Up above the thin clouds, if Sothea lifted her head until she felt nauseous, she thought she could see an eye, an impossibly huge glistening circle; the thought that the eye might look back at her was enough to turn her gaze back to the base of the thing, where the thick skin was dotted with ridges and bumps the size of rivers and mountains. When she looked to her right, she saw the body go on forever, carrying on over the horizon as if it wrapped around the entire world. There might have been a shadowy shape extending to its side, perhaps even oscillating up and down with a tremendous grand slowness as it propelled itself.

Edsimander began to sob quietly.

'It's OK,' Sothea said, rubbing the spot between his shoulders with her palm. 'We made it.'

'That's the *world*,' Edsimander murmured. 'There's nothing you can do about that.'

'No, there isn't,' Lendora agreed from his other side. 'Guilt *is*.'

'Guilt is,' Sothea agreed. It felt almost like a prayer, not that Sothea ever prayed to Guilt or any of the other things to which people sometimes addressed their hopes.

The polypod made a movement almost as if it were nodding sagely. Sothea patted the tank gently, fondly.

'Guilt is,' Edsimander echoed, barely louder than a whisper.

Something wailed from behind them, a screech that split the air and burrowed into the deepest reaches of their bodies. Sothea felt as if her skin was burning while icy spikes raced through her nerves, as if her bones were shattering and her joints imploding; she clapped her hands over her ears, as did Edsimander and Lendora beside her. She was briefly, vaguely aware that the polypod hardly seemed to notice.

A metal boom reverberated through everything and a huge, shining shape streaked through the sky above them; they turned their eyes heavenward, hands still pressed to the sides of their heads, and saw a silver thing like a bird a thousand times larger than any natural bird (and yet still dwarfed by the massive body of Guilt). It flew in a haphazard line, its wings moving erratically as if it were forgetting how to fly, straight towards the all-encompassing leviathan.

Sothea didn't even register that she'd stopped breathing.

The silver streak flapped hard once, twice, as if trying to pull itself out of its tailspin, but it was spiralling out of control. Moments later, there was another scraping scream as it collided with the wall of flesh, crashing off at an angle. The dragon bellowed, shaking in the sky; sluggishly, as if dragging itself through the air, it pulled up and flew back over the group's heads, disappearing into the distance behind them. Five or six seconds after the terrible avian vanished from sight, they heard a rumble, as of a mountain collapsing into the earth; then, instants later, each of them felt the earth beneath them trembling.

For a few still moments, nobody moved a single muscle, not a single millimetre. The polypod, even, somehow froze immobile in its tank, even as the shaking of the ground reverberated through the water.

Then Sothea turned back and saw it: where Dread, the ancient silver dragon of the First Children of Guilt, had struck the side of its progenitor, a dark claret rent was appearing in the monolith of grey skin. Slowly, laboriously, the gap widened; as she stared, deep red blood began to flow from Guilt, cascading and crashing down upon the land beneath it with the force of a hundred avalanches.

Edsimander gasped; Sothea, for her part, had no idea what sort of reaction would have been appropriate. Guilt had been *wounded*; it was a creature of flesh and blood like any other, and it could be *hurt*. If hurt, perhaps even… but surely not.

'It feels it,' Lendora half-whispered; Sothea looked up, following her friend's gaze, and saw the great eye slowly knotting its lid closed, an expression breathtakingly alike to one that a human might make when in pain.

Then they felt, again, an assault of vibration: this one was felt much more than heard, a sound so deep that it didn't even register in their ears, only their bones, but unmistakably resonating from Guilt itself. It rumbled through their bodies like thunder, the sensation of a being the size and age of a whole world crying out.

'This is a big deal,' Sothea said finally.

It had been almost a day since they saw Dread strike Guilt, seen the wound open up and spill the blood of the titanic creature. As they sat, the blood had gradually stopped pouring until it was a mere trickle, then a clean red chunk in the beast's side. They'd moved on then, nobody saying a word; they'd found a place to stay, rested, awoken, and eaten. Then, still in silence - not because they had nothing to say, but because there was *everything* to say and nobody had a clue where to start - they'd rested a bit more, eaten a bit more, and finally sat down and stared off into space.

The polypod was in its tank on the floor in front of them, looking up curiously as if wondering when anyone would address the elephant in the room. If it had been able to speak, Sothea felt certain that it would have already started the conversation itself.

As it was, her words were the first to break the silence since the wail of Guilt had washed over them and used each of their bodies as a reverberating medium for its acoustics.

'You think?' Lendora muttered.

'Yup,' Edsimander agreed.

There was a brief pause. Then they all burst out laughing, big body-wracking bellows of mirth that lasted until Sothea's stomach hurt and tears were dripping freely from her chin. The polypod watched curiously, almost as if one eyebrow were raised; Sothea noticed this as her laughter was beginning to fade, thought it was utterly hilarious, and descended back into uncontrollable cackling.

Minutes later, the three were sighing and slumping, the occasional chuckle sounding from one of them.

'What are we supposed to say?' Edsimander asked eventually. 'What do we *do* now?'

'There must be other people wondering the same thing,' Lendora pointed out, wiping a tear from the corner of one violet eye (bloodshot from laughing). 'We won't have been the only ones to see it.'

'Dread... might be *dead*,' Sothea murmured. 'And Guilt... Guilt can be harmed.'

'Whatever the First Children are... were, maybe - whatever they're made of, anyway, it can pierce Guilt's body,' Lendora said. 'At least, if they hit it with enough force.'

'They must be *so old*,' Edsimander said quietly.

Sothea blinked at him. 'Eh?'

'Guilt, the First Children. They've been here for so long, and who knows how long they lived before that.' Not everyone accepted that there had *ever* been a time when Guilt hadn't been present, but Sothea and Edsimander were convinced of it. 'They're not... not immortal, nothing living is. They've lived a lot longer than most things, but maybe time's finally catching up to them.'

Lendora whistled. 'I'm... not sure I'd ever even considered that it might be possible they'd just... *die* one day.'

'I mean, maybe they won't. Or maybe the First Children will but Guilt'll just go on. But... we know now that Guilt isn't invulnerable either.'

The three of them exchanged looks. The polypod bounced up and down contentedly.

Chris Durston

INFORMATION HAZARD

One peculiar comment that can be made on the Shadow's treatment of inanimates is that it seems to tend towards effects which appear designed to cause the most distress to the living beings who can perceive those inanimates.

Nelfi always gave the exact same speech.

'Welcome to the Museum of Guilt-Related Artifacts. We know the name of the place isn't very imaginative, but it is what it says on the tin. And no, we don't have any spare tinned food. Do not enter the basement.'

The museum practically ran itself, really. There was hardly anything to do once she'd collected enough items associated with Guilt to call it a 'collection' - or, at least, items about which she could spin a believable Guilt-tinged tale. She just put them all in one place, on display, and then charged people to come and look at them.

One time, Guilt had actually flown overhead during an exhibition. After she'd cleaned up what remained of the guests, who had been terrifically enthusiastic to be part of such an immersive experience, she'd found that a couple of the less legitimate artifacts had actually transformed into something genuinely touched by Guilt. Not a bad result, all in all, and now she could advertise the place as officially endorsed by its patron, the Great and Terrifying Oversoarer.

The only problem was the item in the basement, which was of course completely unsuitable for display by its very nature. She expected that there would be someone somewhere - many someones, even - who would want to trade an awful lot to get their hands on it, but she also expected that anyone willing to do such a thing would probably not be the sort of person who would keep it safe and not use it for terrible and nefarious purposes. Fortunately, she was above that sort of thing.

An unexpected problem, however, was beginning to make itself plain.

When you opened every showing with the words 'do not enter the basement' - particularly when your guests had come to see things that many considered unsavoury, perhaps a little frightening, perhaps even in poor taste - people became immensely more curious as to what might be down there. These people *wanted* to see the things from which conventional wisdom would suggest one ought to shy away; the more dangerous the better. Of course, nothing in the Museum was in fact still dangerous, but she didn't tend to lead with that. Nothing except what was in the basement.

She was used, then, to people attempting to enter the basement, and she had her ways of dealing with them. A solid smack on the head generally did the trick, or else brandishing the Horn of the One-Horned Walking Boulder in such a way that it looked not only as if it were a weapon but as if it were a weapon she knew how to discharge.

On this particular day, however, the problem seemed less simple.

'Why can't we go in the basement?' asked someone near the back of the group.

Nelfi sighed. She recognised this particular someone from a visit some weeks back, a visit that had been prematurely cut short courtesy of an unusually determined beeline towards the basement door and an extremely close encounter between the Horn of the One-Horned Walking Boulder and the someone's nether regions.

'Because you would die,' she said, giving the person - Montas - a withering look. He seemed entirely unperturbed. 'Horribly.'

'What if I don't mind?'

'There would be better ways of achieving that than going down in my basement.'

'So, I wouldn't be *guaranteed* to die horribly, then?'

Nelfi rubbed her eyelids.

'If everyone else would like to show themselves around the exhibits, which are labelled for your convenience…' She gestured, allowing the half-dozen or so others to walk around her.

'Do you get many guests who can read, then?' one of them asked as he went past, sounding awfully impressed.

'Some,' Nelfi said, 'but not many, hence the labels are in both writing and amusingly graphic pictures courtesy of my cousin Demmit, who I believe is currently taking commissions if you're interested in procuring a beautiful piece of custom artwork.'

'I'll draw pictures in the ground with my piss if I need custom artwork, thanks,' said the museum-goer affably, and trundled off.

Nelfi shook her head, then turned back to Montas. 'Seriously, man. I know you're way into the Guilt thing, but… *this* -' she gestured to the exhibits on display '- is to the basement as writing a bawdy song about a bull's balls is to letting said bull smack you in the face with said balls.'

'*Awesome*,' breathed Montas.

'No, not awesome.' Nelfi groaned. 'How can I get through to you on this? Going down there is a *bad idea*. A *really* bad idea.'

'Well, at least tell me *why*,' Montas wheedled. 'If I just knew what it was I was supposed to be staying away from, perhaps I'd be more inclined to stay away from it.'

Nelfi took Montas by the arm and led him out of the little building, keeping one eye on her patrons through the open door.

'If I tell you,' she muttered, 'you'll just want to go down there even more.'

Montas's chin bobbed around excitedly. 'Well, now I *know* I have to get in there anyway!'

'Or,' said Nelfi, a thought occurring to her, 'perhaps now that you know that knowing what it is would make you want to go down there, your imagination's making it seem like the most interesting thing possible. Maybe it's impossible now for reality to live up to your expectations, so it's not really worth going down there at all.'

Montas frowned at her. 'You're just saying that because you know the reality is *even better* than anything I could possibly imagine.'

Nelfi said a quick prayer in her head, imploring the empty sky to give her strength. 'There's nothing I can say that's going to stop you wanting to go down there, is there?'

'Absolutely not.'

'Fine.'

Montas positively beamed. 'Really?'

Nelfi nodded. 'Come back tonight. I'll tell you what's down there. I promise.'

With a nod and a merry grin, Montas went on his way. Nelfi turned back to her customers, running a hand through her hair and thinking how terrifically unfair it would be if one irritating eejit caused it all to fall out.

Montas returned just before nightfall: the spookiest of all times, as anyone who's had reason to learn the meaning of the word *crepuscular* will attest. He found the museum door unlocked; trembling, almost giddy with excitement at the thought of getting to see such an obviously astonishingly spectacular item, he pushed it open and went inside.

The door to the basement, which had heretofore been stubbornly sealed, had been left ajar. Montas wandered towards it, taking his time, meandering through the exhibits. He'd already seen the whole collection several times, but he savoured the sight of each artifact with fresh eyes, appreciating every object's history in the knowledge that it would soon be magnificently overshadowed by whatever it was that Nelfi kept in the basement.

Slowly, gleefully, Montas descended the stairs. He passed from the twilight of the main floor into darkness, then rounded a corner in the stairwell and the shadows fell away, chased off by the flickering light of a dozen candles. The room was empty except for a large, rectangular object under a white sheet in the centre.

'Wait,' Montas said. 'This feels like some sort of… sex thing.'

Nelfi stepped out from behind the covered object, massaging her temples. 'Really? That's what you - no, it's not a sex thing. I'm not interested in any of that anyway.'

'Sure,' said Montas, nodding. 'Me neither.'

'No, I'm seriously - it just doesn't appeal - never mind.' Nelfi shook her head, sighing. 'Well, it feels like the mystique's been punctured a bit, so let's just get on with it.'

Montas clapped his hands together, eyes gleaming.

'I need to explain something to you,' Nelfi said, walking around to stand between Montas and the thing under the sheet. 'And once I start explaining, there's no going back. Are you sure about this?'

'Do you really need to ask?'

She sighed. 'I suppose not. If you're really this determined, I guess I can't stop you.'

Montas gave a bellowing laugh that echoed around the little chamber. 'You finally understand me!'

Nelfi nodded. 'I think I do. I don't feel any better about it, but there it is.'

She took hold of the sheet, and then she explained.

She told Montas about the thing that was under the sheet: a painting, or something that looked very like a painting. She explained how she had come to possess it: its previous owner, her uncle, had passed on the ways of keeping it by telling her all that there was to know about it from an extremely young age, when her mind was still malleable and capable of dealing with such knowledge.

Montas's expression, as he listened, shifted from eager glee to a confused displeasure, and then to glassy-eyed, slack-jawed non-function.

Still Nelfi went on: she spoke of how the painting had been kept in this way for generations, each keeper bestowed with the knowledge of it as a child - for an adult, whose mind was already so defined and set in its ways, could never absorb the information in the same way without experiencing one of two effects. Either they would become unable to understand anything ever again, as seemed to be happening to Montas, or they would comprehend the painting in its entirety. Those in the latter category might seem more fortunate, but nothing could be further from the truth. Besides the keeper, protected by their early inoculation against the cognitive assault, anyone who understood details of the painting would become understood by the painting. The more someone knew of it, the more they dwelled on it, the more it would become aware of them.

Perhaps Montas had even been approaching that state, what with how obsessed he had become with seeing it. Perhaps, simply wondering in ignorance what could possibly be in that basement, he had somehow stumbled upon that frame of mind in which the canvas could reach him, could affect him.

It made no difference now, though, Nelfi explained. At this point, if she did nothing, Montas would stay in his current situation until he died, most likely of thirst; so, she continued, she may as well give him what he wanted.

She pulled the sheet away, and Montas's unfocused gaze beheld the painting. Nelfi stepped behind it so as not to see what it depicted.

Part of her was always desperate to look, but even for her it would be too much. The painting, she knew, was always different depending on who gazed upon it, moulded by its understanding of its observer. She expected that Montas would probably see a canvas showing himself looking at the painting, in fact: he would have a moment of awe, perhaps, before something emerged from the artwork and dragged him inside.

When she could tell from the silence that it was over, she carefully covered the painting again. She hated that part of keeping the thing involved feeding it, but at least she'd never had to go and find food. No matter how hard she tried to foil the thing's next meal, it always came willingly.

'Welcome to the Museum of Guilt-Related Artifacts,' Nelfi recited, casting her gaze over her patrons the next morning. 'We know the name of the place isn't very imaginative, but it is what it says on the tin. And no, we don't have any spare tinned food. Do not enter the basement.'

Everyone nodded and bumbled inside, except for one young woman who stayed behind.

'It's all perfectly safe,' Nelfi said, trying to sound reassuring.

'Oh, it's not that I'm… scared to go in,' the young woman said. 'I actually just… was wondering about what's in the basement.'

Nelfi sighed.

Chris Durston

VALUE IS IN THE THOUSAND EYES
OF THE VAST BEHOLDER

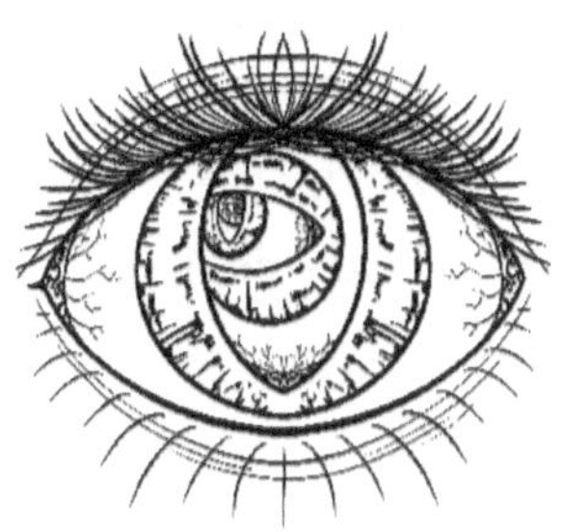

I do wonder what humanity would look like to something such as Guilt, if it noticed us at all.

I watch them scampering around on their strange little limbs. Frolicking together, living out their lives in their tiny, dense, convoluted societies. They are peculiar, those things that call themselves humans.

Of them all, my favourites are the ones others of their own kind consider strange or even broken. Those are the ones who achieve things outside the usual limits, perhaps because they focus so much on knowing and surpassing their own limits that they forget about the limits humanity ought to have and thereby transcend them almost by accident.

Then, of course, there's the one who was once human, and perhaps still is, but hasn't been the same kind of human as the rest of them for a long, long time.

Since long before I was brought into existence by whatever power birthed me - that infernal everswimmer, I assume, and I imagine the same force was most likely responsible for this changed one. She - I think *she*, from the way others talk - is very big, almost as big as I am, and clothed in bark like a tree. I think she must once have been smaller, fleshier, like the rest of them, but now she towers over them, a petrified protector.

She and I have our one-sided conversations; I reach out with my limbs and come close to touching her sometimes, moving around in ways that I hope might communicate something. She never responds. Or perhaps she does; perhaps for her, too, the conversation is one-sided, she sending all kinds of signals in my direction and me appearing to simply bob about unnoticing.

I leave her to her watchfulness and drift off, beholding many people in many parts of the world. I see violence and terror and fear and cruelty: I see people fighting giants and awful creatures, flinging mild inconveniences at beings a hundred times their own size, and more often I see people fighting other people for reasons most of them seem to have forgotten.

But I also see the one who risks her life to save a child she's never met before. I see the one who recognises the sacrifices their mate has made, and who sacrifices in return with no expectation of a reward. I see parents bringing new life into the world and, in the time before it hits them just how hard it will be for them all to stay together and alive, theirs is the purest kind of joy. I see those who protect those who cannot protect themselves, and those who take nothing for granted but work to find meaning in existence even when none is apparent.

There are horrors in this world. I am one of them. The overwanderer has made many terrible things, and made many other things terrible, but it could never entirely destroy those little moments I see so often. There is something spectacular about small happinesses discovered in a vast wasteland.

So, I sail onwards, a diligently nebulous collection of parts that ought not to belong together. Sometimes I show myself, just to see what will happen, but I can hardly blame them for invariably freezing in fear - or indeed trying to destroy me. When things look strange, especially when other strange-looking things do indeed represent a very possible imminent and painful death, it can be difficult to see them for what they really are, rather than some archetype of danger and terror.

But humans are very strange to me, and I see them for all their peculiar wondrousness.

Chris Durston

TITANFELL

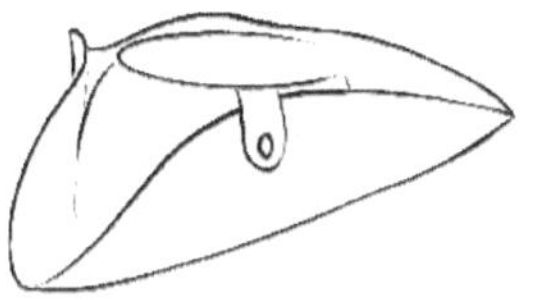

A*nd that, I think, is that.*

'You can't be serious,' Anathema said.

'Oh, but I am.' League deftly plucked his three-pointed hat up off the table, popping it back onto his scruffy head. 'Never been less unserious about nothing I've not never neglected to fail at.'

Anathema considered this for a moment, then realised that there was absolutely no point doing so. 'I take it your plan is classic League, then,' she said, leaning back in her chair.

'Howzat?'

'You're going to attempt something utterly ridiculous, entirely fail to realise just *how* ridiculous it is, and somehow manage to succeed purely because you didn't realise how likely it was that everything would go catastrophically wrong.'

'Sounds about right. You in?' League stood, stretching; as unpolished as he was, his tall frame and dark hunter's coat granted him quite a presence, and Anathema found herself half-believing that he might actually know what he was doing, in spite of all evidence to the contrary.

'I feel compelled to at least find out exactly *what* your plan is,' she admitted, allowing him to take her hand and pull her to her feet.

'Don't worry; I'm equally curious,' League reassured her, steering her in a tight circle. They had met in the Almanac, a hunter's retreat at the edges of the Undersea: it was packed, as was usual, with leather-garbed, gnarly-faced patrons in various states of sullenness or excitement - it generally depended on whether they were preparing to go on a hunt, or returning from a failed one. They traded stories: there were coins that could be spent on goods, of course, but stories were the more valuable currency when all there was to do was hunt and talk about the hunt. Tales of hunts were of the lowest value; tales of things far beyond imagining of the highest.

Oil lamps puffed in glass fittings on the wooden walls, casting a gentle orange luminescence across the bar; the protrusions and crags of a hunter's face, turned at the wrong angle, could catch the light and cast peculiar shadows across their features, making them look like warped, broken skulls. Some of them looked more worthy of being called *monster* than the things they ventured out to kill.

'Well, here we are,' said League, hands on Anathema's shoulders, pushing her down into a seat not ten steps away from the one she'd just vacated.

'I don't -' Anathema began, but League patted her upper arms and slid into the chair beside her, plonking his hat down on the table. Three people lounged opposite them, arms folded or behind their heads; they glanced up as League and Anathema joined them, but otherwise hardly reacted.

'Thanks for coming,' said League, eyes glittering across the table at their acquaintances.

'Why,' grunted the leftmost one, an old man with a long, straggly beard that extended down beneath the collar of his hunting coat, 'didja make us wait awhile y'were right there?' He jabbed the long-stemmed pipe in his hand at the table Anathema and League had come from.

'Had to convince this one she wanted in,' said League, jamming a thumb in Anathema's direction. 'Didn't take a whole lot of doing, of course.'

'Wanted in on *what*, exactly?' Anathema demanded; the old man grumbled in agreement.

'Like t'know that meself,' he said.

League just grinned wider. 'So impatient, Archive.'

The old man - Archive - shook his head, muttering something; the younger woman seated in the middle of the three leaned forwards, gazing dangerously up at League from under her wide-brimmed hat. 'You said it was a big hunt,' she reminded him, flashing sharp teeth.

'And it is, Verletzt,' he protested. 'The biggest.'

The three exchanged glances; the last man, sitting to the right of Archive and Verletzt with his head bowed, face inscrutable under the shadow of his hood, tilted his head slightly. His two companions looked to him, then fixed their gazes on League again.

'The Orphaned Spider?' Archive hazarded. 'I 'erd she's got babbies now. Reckon some old rich loon'd pay top silver to try a delicacy like'at.'

'Think bigger,' League said.

Verletzt rested her elbows on the table, furrowing her brow. 'Medulla the Ancient?'

'Even ancienter-er,' said League, beaming.

The two sat back, looking puzzled. The third man, remaining perfectly still, spoke a single word in a deep rumble:

'Guilt.'

'Exactly.' League pointed a firm finger across the table at the man, who sat dispassionately. Archive, on the other hand, spluttered around the pipe he'd just put in his mouth; Verletzt just blinked at him.

'You can't be serious,' said Anathema.

'You said that already,' League reminded her.

'I still don't think you're *actually planning to do it*,' she said, folding her arms. 'I'm only along to hear your plan, which is guaranteed to be hilariously idiotic.'

'Yeh can't hunt - can't *kill* - Guilt,' Archive said, waving his pipe-holding hand so that a thin dusting of ash dirtied the table's sticky surface. 'It's been with us since the first man took his first breath -'

'- and will be until the last man takes his last,' League finished, 'I know. But those are just words, Archive. Why believe 'em?'

Archive's mouth flapped open and closed for a few moments, then he stuck the pipe in it again.

'Because,' Verletzt responded for him, 'it's supposed to be enormous, the most powerful creature on the Echelon, and it's also supposed to be impossible to so much as look at without dying. Not that anyone alive knows, since the other thing is that it's *completely inaccessible.*'

'Not so,' said League breezily. 'That's only a description, and words can never hurt me.'

Verletzt snorted. 'These are words about a world-devouring... overwatching-destroying-space-fish-*thing*, which most definitely *can* hurt you.'

'Fair point,' League conceded. 'Still, I reckon the only reason nobody's ever successfully hunted Guilt is just because nobody's ever *tried.*'

'People've tried aright,' Archive muttered. 'Yeh've not heard the tales of the times before the Echelon were all that there were? A whole planet of people, untold numbers of generations, and Guilt just in the sky where any old bastard could see it, and none of 'em could bring it down.'

'Not the *right* people, then,' said League, unperturbed. 'Problem solved.'

'And you think you've got the right people now?' Anathema pressed. 'The right plan?'

League shrugged. 'Only one way to find out, ain't there?'

Worlds change.

Once, all the continents of the planet were joined as one; then they were many.

Long after the becoming of Guilt, the Echelon was a small bubble of strangeness in a small part of the world; now, far longer after that, it might as well have been its own reality. The Undersea hung endlessly above the expanse, that strange roiling upside-down surface, and the Echelon itself possessed a million strange geometries within its own peculiar wholeness. Those within it no longer knew whether there was a world outside that they were part of or whether this was all that there was to the world.

Still, it was *their* world.

As haphazard as she thought him, Anathema couldn't deny as she followed League out onto the plains that he did in fact know what he was doing, more than he might sometimes like to pretend. Or perhaps his coat and hat simply made him *look* as if he knew what he was doing. It remained to be seen, she decided, but she'd follow him for now.

Verletzt had come with them; Archive and the other, stoic man no longer ventured out themselves, but had been surprisingly constructive in discussing League's plan. It still sounded like madness to Anathema, but then wasn't the whole world simply madness of one strain or another?

'Remind me,' Verletzt said, 'why you think you can trust whomever it was who told you that this would be the way to go.'

'Phyntra's never let me down,' League insisted, sounding affronted. 'So, you know, this is probably also fine.'

The three of them - all in classic hunters' gear, all with a range of impressive weaponry ready to draw at a moment's notice - travelled into the southern reaches of the Echelon, where the landscape shifted from eternal flat plains to a more mountainous terrain. Few Children bothered them along the way, and those that did Verletzt turned away with a glare.

The phrase 'Descendants of Guilt' was all but forgotten, but there were still those with strange gifts: as long as they never turned their powers against their fellow humans, the gifted were respected, even slightly revered. Verletzt was in particular demand, since her ability to shoo the Children allowed easy passage through the Echelon for any hunter who didn't want more fights than necessary along the way; anyone who needed her services had to appeal to Archive, and his approval was rarely given.

Anathema had rarely come this far from the Almanac, that comfortable hideaway. She'd hunted, sure, but in the more comfortable zones where retreat was easier if necessary and dragging the proof of a completed mission back was easier when success struck. She knew League was famous for accepting those hunts that took the hunter far out into the furthest reaches of the Echelon, but as far as she could tell he was almost equally famous for rarely succeeding. Why Archive would have allowed *him* of all people to commission Verletzt was beyond Anathema's deductive powers.

'Why are you along on this?' she asked Verletzt one day, during a less strenuous stretch of travel.

'None taken,' the smaller hunter said.

'Not - I don't mean why is it useful to have you here, I mean what are you getting out of it?'

Verletzt stared ahead, at League's back. 'If he's for real,' she said, 'then this is the biggest hunt there's ever been.'

'You believe him?'

She shrugged. 'Archive seems to.'

Anathema considered this. 'What's, er…'

'Archive's deal?'

Anathema nodded.

'He likes big hunts too. It's about as simple as that.'

Although she was almost certain that it was in fact not as simple as that, Anathema asked no further questions.

Days passed in varying states of discomfort, but League's chirpy attitude never dropped. It was infuriating, but Anathema had to admit it would have been harder to continue without it. They went around, over, under, and even through dozens of small and large bumps in the landscape; they passed through pockets of strange space where backwards and forwards seemed to have switched, corridors that ended and began in the same place, bubbles where gravity seemed to have decided not to worry about pulling quite as hard.

Finally, League reached the top of an extraordinarily mundane, unassuming hillock, and stopped in his tracks.

'Ah-*ha*,' he murmured.

'What?' Anathema scrambled up next to him; Verletz joined her, seeming uncharacteristically enthusiastic - thrilled, even - at the prospect that something might actually be happening.

Before them, a natural bowl dipped into the terrain: a circle of raised ground surrounded a dipped area in the land. Within the bowl, an enormous metal skeleton lay gleaming with the strange dancing light cast by the Undersea above.

'Oh, look,' said League cheerfully, 'it's one of the legendary First Children of Guilt.'

'As in,' breathed Anathema, 'the giant metal dragons that came down and laid waste to everything in the old stories?'

'That certainly is what it looks like, wouldn't you say?'

'I… would,' Anathema had to admit.

Verletzt cleared her throat, frowning. 'Are you saying that the weapon we came to recover,' she said, with the air of one who knows she'll be disappointed by the answer but has to ask anyway, 'is an enormous dead metal dragon?'

'Yes.'

'Right.' Verletzt furrowed her brow. 'You did say we were coming for a weapon, didn't you?'

'That I did,' League answered, plopping down on his backside so that he could slide down into the bowl.

Anathema and Verletzt exchanged helpless glances, then followed him with somewhat more elegance. By the time they'd reached the bottom in careful strides, League had already trundled up to the skeleton and was patting one of the gargantuan bones fondly.

'The Child is going to help us kill the father,' he announced, with more than a tinge of pride.

'I always thought of Guilt as a *she*,' Anathema muttered.

'It's an it,' Verletzt said.

'Gender notwithstanding,' League continued, 'all the stories say the same thing. Nothing of this world can harm Guilt; nothing can get through its skin.'

Anathema nodded.

'This isn't of this world, though,' he said, indicating the dead dragon with one thumb. 'This is of Guilt itself.'

'That…' Verletzt screwed up her eyes in thought, then hummed in mild surprise. 'That is actually a good observation.'

League beamed. 'Right?'

Anathema walked closer to the steel skeleton, half-feeling as if it might still come to life at any moment and destroy all of them. It was colossal: even as a collapsed pile of metal bones, it was taller than any building she'd ever seen, each strut and slab at least ten times the size of a person.

'So, what do we… do with it?' she asked, running a tentative hand over the nearest part. It was warmer than she expected.

League shrugged. 'I was just going to grab a sword-sized bit and stab Guilt with it, if I'm honest.'

'Oh, come *on*,' Verletzt groaned.

'What?'

'You said… oh, hells, you said you knew where to *find* a weapon.'

'Didn't mention anything about knowing how to use it,' League said, nodding wisely.

Verletzt looked like she wanted to slap him. 'Do you even really know where to find Guilt, even if we did have an actual weapon?'

'I know someone who does,' League said, maddeningly. With that, he set about prising as many pieces of metal as he could from the great skeleton; the metal couldn't be broken, couldn't be bent, but some parts simply came loose. Sighing, with no alternative but to admit that the whole thing had been entirely pointless, Verletzt and Anathema joined him.

The journey back was more difficult, since they were now carrying several extremely heavy metal objects of varying sizes and sharpnesses, but they made it back to the Almanac unscathed.

Anathema threw her pack down and immediately went for a bath; League headed to the bar; Verletzt sat in a corner, musing. The three packs sat next to her, several shards sticking ostentatiously out, but nobody approached.

When the three were reunited - Anathema cleaned, League watered, Verletzt presumably in some way fulfilled by her silent wonderings - and sitting at a table together, Archive and the other man, face still shrouded by his dark hood, appeared as if from nowhere and joined them.

'Expected somethin' a little more… impressive,' Archive rumbled, glancing at the packs with their protruding bits of gleaming sharpness. 'A cannon, or somethin'. Notta few pinpricks.'

'These are no simple pinpricks,' League said. 'These are bones of the First Children.'

Archive's eyes widened, just a little bit. 'Ahh,' he said, sitting back in his chair. 'You've 'eard the tale a'the dyin' dragon cuttin' Guilt all wide open, then.'

'Seems plausible enough to me,' League said. He took one of the bones and laid it on the table. 'I've never come across anything as solid as this. If anything can pierce that hide, this can.'

'You'd've ta get close enough,' Archive said.

'He plans to stab it,' Verletzt said dryly.

'Actually, that was sort of a joke,' said League hastily. 'I was rather hoping this might be the part the two of you would help with, in fact.'

Archive let out a long, reverberating sigh. 'Already let y'hire Verletzt for the journey. That weren't help enough?'

'Well, I need help with *two* more things,' League corrected; Archive sighed again, and the ever-blank demeanour of the hooded man next to him looked for just a moment as if it might slip and he might decide instead to bang his head on the table. 'One: make this into something we can shoot at Guilt from a distance, ideally. Two: get the thing somewhere we can shoot it.'

Archive's brow lowered, the lines on his face deepening. 'What makes y'think we could do either'v those things? What makes y'think we would, even'f we could?'

League leaned forwards, elbows on the table. 'You know very well that the old stories are important. They're not all true, but most of them have some kind of truth in them somewhere. And I'm sure you can't be unaware that there are some stories that concern you.'

'Hangin' a lotta weight on a coupl'old tales,' murmured Archive.

'You're the one who visited the man who sits atop the planet,' League said.

Though the hubbub in the Almanac continued - nobody beyond their small table could have heard his words - to Anathema it was as if a deathly silence descended upon them. So slight was the shift in Archive's demeanour that she couldn't point to what had changed, but *something* did, and it may as well have been as if someone had placed a huge muffling cloche over them, cutting them off from all the noise outside.

'That,' said Archive, 'is a *very* old story with a *very* strange kind of truth in it.'

'But it *is* about you.'

Anathema gazed at League, marvelling at his sheer obliviousness, or his bravado. Either he'd completely failed to detect the change that had come over them or he didn't care. Both options were impressive, albeit perhaps not something to be admired.

Archive and League met each other's eyes, neither looking at all fazed. Then Archive glanced towards the man sitting next to him and sat back.

'Partly,' he said finally.

'Ohhhh,' League murmured. 'Two of you.'

The hooded man tipped his head back to reveal his face: it was Archive again, a shorter beard the only thing to distinguish him.

'One wouldn't've survived,' Archive said. 'Not a chance. Nor even a group, usually. But two brothers who already knew a thing or two 'bout survivin'...'

League nodded seriously, then flashed a dashing grin. 'Well, either way, the point is I'm pretty sure you can do what I need you to do, and I'm pretty sure you will because… actually, I haven't thought about that.'

He looked to Anathema, who could only open her eyes wide and raise her hands in the universal gesture for 'don't ask me'; he looked to Verletzt, who smiled obstinately back at him and said nothing.

'Because it's the right thing to do?' he hazarded. 'Because it's *significant*? Because it would end a lot of suffering? Because it would be a really good story?'

Archive and his brother shared a look.

'Because I'll leave you alone if you do it?' League wheedled.

'We're in,' said the stoic man immediately.

'I'ssume you've 'eard the story,' said Archive, 'of the time the Many People came t'gether and shot missiles at Guilt.'

'Of course,' said League. 'And the one about the jungle within the house of worship, and the one about the man who was betrayed by his lover, the stars. Your point?'

'It didn't work,' Archive said flatly.

League actually patted Archive on the head. 'We've been over this!'

Archive stepped out of reach.

Anathema wasn't sure whether to laugh or run away screaming. It all seemed so preposterous that they stood there, a few hundred metres from the Almanac on the flat Echelon, a great shining spear lying on the ground before them. She didn't know how Archive and his brother had been able to forge the dragon's bones into the weapon she saw now - at least six metres long, and made of far more metal than she remembered the three of them being able to carry back - nor how such a thing could have been transported even the short distance from the Almanac to the plains.

Unlike in the old tale, there was no mechanism with which to fling the weapon. Anathema had no idea how it was supposed to get into Guilt, but League assured her that Archive and his brother were taking care of that, too.

On the subject of Guilt…

'So… Guilt isn't *here*,' Anathema said, conscious that she was pointing out the blindingly obvious. 'I mean, the stories all say it used to be in the sky, but the Echelon is its own place. Guilt's…'

'Inaccessible,' Verletzt said.

'Guilt's supposed to be completely inaccessible from here.'

Archive grinned. "Tis, 'tisn't it?'

League wandered over to Anathema and spoke quietly into her ear, beaming the entire time. 'I've been excited for this bit since I first worked it out,' he told her. Then he nodded to Archive. 'Let's do it.'

The brothers took a deep breath as one, then turned to look out towards the openness of the Echelon. Though she couldn't see that they were *doing* anything, as such, Anathema had the irrepressible feeling of magnitude: of hugeness, of significance.

Above them, the Undersea began to part, dividing into two separate seas. For the first time, Anathema saw the sky beyond. In the distance, something shimmered and disappeared, wavered and resolved, flickered and was gone.

Had someone living in the outside - non-Echelon - world happened to be wandering along a certain coastline at that moment, they would have seen what appeared to be a perfectly normal stretch of ocean turning over in the world, rising and revolving as if it were a sock in the wind rather than an immeasurable body of water. When it settled back down, a huge expanse of flat land had somehow taken its place in the middle of the sea. The separation of Echelon and All Else ended, and nobody even noticed.

Anathema noticed that boundaries were breaking, if not the significance of it. With the Undersea splitting, the place outside the Echelon that might have been called *inaccessible* was suddenly part of the same universe, and the light and the noise and the *world* came flooding in.

A sound like nothing Anathema had ever heard before split the air. It was like a rumble of thunder trying to imitate the high whistle of a flute; it was like a man who had never heard music humming with all his might; it was like the earth grinding underwater. She clapped her hands over her ears, struggling even to stand under the pressure of it.

'It's here,' Archive said; she couldn't possibly hear his words over the noise, but somehow she knew he'd spoken them.

And it was there.

Something like a grey wall the size of a world loomed in the distance from behind the parting curtain of the Undersea, emerging until it was all that there was. It must have been miles away, but the size of it made Anathema feel as if it were already crushing her.

Almost immediately, League fainted.

'Typical,' muttered Archive, in that strange voice that Anathema could not hear at all and yet could hear perfectly.

The spear began to lift slowly into the air; Verletzt dashed forward and took hold of it, pointing the sharp end at the mass of Guilt. Anathema, screaming through the cacophony, joined her; the other hunter looked at her in surprise, then smiled.

Like two waterfalls suddenly finding that there was no water left to fall over them, the divided Undersea quivered and then split entirely. Just like that, the sky was open. No more barrier between the Echelon and the rest: it was all just one, and in an instant Guilt was, as it always had been, the greatest part of it.

With a great crash, Guilt was upon the surface of the Echelon, its body slamming into the earth so that the whole planet must have quaked. It no longer flew high in the sky; it was almost dragging itself along the earth, like a moving mountain range.

Anathema saw its head then, saw the enormous eyes. There was, she thought, though she didn't know why she would think it, a sadness beyond telling in them. Just as the size of the thing had dawned upon her like a physical force, the age and magnitude of Guilt's existence hit her: it had flown, surrounding the world, for so appallingly many years, and now it was *old*. It was so close to the ground now, not like the old stories said; it swam with such a weight, such an effort, and although it had always seemed something that was *beyond* the world and not *part* of it Anathema couldn't help but think that it must have been a terrible burden, being so old and so tired and having such a profound effect on the world. Perhaps it had never realised what it was doing, but now saw; or perhaps it still had no idea. Perhaps trying to understand the thing as if it were a thinking being was the height of foolishness.

As slow as it was, the sheer size of the thing brought it upon them in moments. Anathema felt herself pulled towards it as if by gravity; she cried out, screwing her eyes tightly shut and squeezing her fingers just as tight around the haft of the spear, the noise and the force and the weight feeling as if it would tear her apart, and then there was a sensation of momentary resistance followed by a kind of *slipping*, and then a solid *thunk*.

Anathema awoke, her whole body aching.

'Welcome to the new world,' said someone - she blinked, and the blurry shape resolved into League, holding his hand out to help her up.

She took it and stood, shaking her head to clear it. She was… on top of a mountain, or so it seemed: she stood on a narrow ridge, a steep slope in front of her, League and Verletzt behind her - and, she noticed, League's hat on the ground nearby. League's hands took a gentle hold of her shoulders and turned her around, and she realised: not a mountain, not really, but the earth of the Echelon *pushed* so that it rose up as it moved, gathering more and more of the ground beneath it as it went until it was almost touching the clouds.

The thing that had done the pushing lay in the valley below.

'It's… gone?' Anathema felt that she ought to have something more insightful to say, but that was all she could come up with.

'It's gone,' League said, smiling an unusual smile, for him: in his eyes was a sincere gravity, an acknowledgement that for all that being unassailably unserious really was just who he was, this was perhaps not the time for that.

Anathema's breath caught in her chest as she looked out at it. There before them lay what could have been a place, could have been miles of strange, bumpy grey terrain, but what she knew to be the body of Guilt. Right below her was the head: the spear, comically miniscule in the impossibly large creature, was just about visible as a tiny glint of light.

'That couldn't really have killed it,' she said.

'I'm not sure it did,' Verletzt murmured. 'I think maybe it was ready to die anyway, and we just… helped it.'

'The biggest hunt, and it impaled itself,' said League quietly. 'Kind of an anticlimactic story.'

'Just the way the world is, I guess,' said Verletzt, and then she turned and wandered off along the newly-formed ridge.

Anathema and League were left to look at Guilt, and at each other. After a very, very long time had passed,

League picked up his hat, gave it a bit of a brush, and popped it firmly on his head.

'Well, then,' he said.

'What now?'

He shrugged. 'I guess this is a new world.'

Anathema nodded slowly. 'I guess… it is.'

League grinned. 'Let's go see what kind of bars it has.'

Later, a young girl with no real conception of how world-shatteringly bizarre it was that the Undersea had broken, none of her parents' entrenched notions about how so much as the mere mention of Guilt's name was so abominable as to be unthinkable, wandered through a deep valley.

Spying a little purple spot poking up from the earth, she bent down and plucked it up, spinning the flower between her fingers as she walked. Her feet fell easily, carelessly on the earth, and she went on her way under a clear sky. Nothing accosted her; nothing blocked her path or followed hungrily. After a while she turned and headed home, taking her flower with her.

It never crossed her mind to wonder what manner of thing could have carved out the deep trench through which she strolled. Untold generations of her ancestors had lived every day of their lives in fear of Guilt, but nothing of the sort occurred to her. She strode, free of worry, through the line marking the place where the colossal body had crashed into the planet, and nothing troubled her.

THE NEW ERA OF HOPE

In which epoch Guilt is only a corpse, and then only a memory.

Chris Durston

AFTER THE TIME OF GUILT

I wish only to let it be known that I think it entirely futile to make predictions about what Guilt might do or be in the future. Do not even try.

For years - generations, even - those who had survived Guilt wondered what had happened to it. With no means of communicating across long distances, a few observant souls noticed that Guilt hadn't appeared in their area for some time; eventually, even though most had no way of knowing for sure, the world began to live as if there were no longer any Guilt.

The changes it had made to the planet persisted, of course. Many of its Children faded, either dissipating as if something of their nature had been lost to the kind of existence they maintained or living out their natural lives and then dying as any other creature would. Its Descendants grew ever more distantly related to it, though there would ever after be those who could do things that seemed impossible. In time, few even remembered what the original source of the power could possibly have been.

Where the body of Guilt had fallen, for a time there were none who dared to go near. It had shaped their world and their lives, and those of their ancestors hundreds of generations distant, and they feared its power even in death. Many simply couldn't believe that it could truly be gone. The children of those who had lived their lives in the shadow of fear were less cautious, making games of poking the great walls of tough grey skin, and their children dug tunnels into the soft body, and *their* grandchildren, by whose time Guilt's remains were a colossal oblong of bones and mostly-decayed flesh, recognised that the body of the creature (of which they had heard such frightening, if unlikely, tales from their grandparents) was a rich source of fertiliser for the ground beneath it.

The world would never again be as it was before the time of Guilt. To wish otherwise would be worse than pointless. The planet had suffered: there remained scars on its surface, terrors and suffering in its history, and metal monuments that some said were all that was left of three great dragons. Yet on its lands and in its waters, life of many kinds flourished. It continued.

And two hundred or more years after the passing of Guilt, there was a stretch of land many miles long: a place where life blossomed, where green plants grew so tall that they could tickle the clouds, where fruits and nuts were plentiful, and where all kinds of animals came to dwell. It became a haven, a place to which people would travel from days away just to see.

That, in the end, is the legacy of Guilt. In its wake is left freedom and beauty.

Chris Durston

APPENDIX: FOREWORD AND ERRATA, FROM THE SECOND EDITION OF 'CHARACTERISING GUILT'

ritten in the early years of the First Era

When I first wrote 'Characterising Guilt' some six years ago, I expected it to receive little attention. After all, there is no longer any such thing as digital media; academic pursuits have mostly come to an end, since merely perpetuating a functioning civilisation of sorts demands all our attention all of the time now. However, I was astonished and grateful to find that there really was something of an audience for my work; it is almost impossible to verify or even corroborate such a claim these days, but I flatter myself to think that 'Characterising Guilt' may be one of the most successful books to have been published post-Coming.

It is understandable, perhaps, given that the Coming is most certainly the single most significant event for humans in many hundreds of years, if not the entire history of modern *Homo sapiens*. Word spread, against the odds, that there was a text that sought to deal with the imposing and constant issue of the presence of Guilt in an impartial, scientific fashion, and so I suppose it only makes sense that many people were keen to learn what they could about the thing that has defined all of our lives.

The time has come, I think, for this second edition, which I hope will be widely distributed and widely read. Even in times such as these, the quest for knowledge for its own sake ought to be continued, and I see no better way to deal with the ever-present Whale of Grand Magnitude than to educate ourselves about it.

I have kept the text of this second edition very much the same as the first, except to correct some typographical errors (I am especially indebted to Anna Singsward for her repeated, insistent, and insightful correspondence pointing out such mistakes) and to add a final chapter theorising the possible effects that Guilt will continue to have on the planet in the future. (Naturally a few assumptions are made for this purpose; thanks are due to my erstwhile editor and constant friend Marius Nordstrom for questioning the premises where the conclusion seemed sound, yet not entailed.)

However, there are some specific issues I wish to address for this new edition, hence the inclusion of this errata (doubling as a foreword, I suppose). Naturally, there are things we now know that I could not have known, nor foreseen knowing, and so I wanted to include reference to these new discoveries in order to keep this book as relevant as possible. That said, I believe I see some value in the main body of the text remaining as it was six years ago, so that those who come after us might look back at what has changed between six years ago and now, between now and their time, and perhaps use that information to come to ever more useful knowledge about the nature of Guilt.

This has been an intensive project, and certainly a humbling one. Let it never be said that I cannot change my mind.

ERRATA

CHAPTER TWO - Topography

I make some observations in this chapter about that which was not yet known at the time of writing. The precise spatial characteristics of Guilt, for example: its dimensions, the distance it maintains from Earth (assuming that this remains constant), and a few details about its features that might relate it to or set it apart from known species of what I refer to as 'earthling cetaceans'.

Much of this remains unknown, as far as I can tell. Again, the modern difficulty in sharing information poses problems for establishing any objective measurements, let alone confirming them via peer review. However, I have been made aware of some studies quietly being carried out around the world which appear to indicate that *objective measurement of any of Guilt's physical characteristics is impossible*. Vastly conflicting results, a failure of some devices even to acknowledge its existence, and sudden and astoundingly firmly-held incompatible beliefs in those who attempt to measure it… I am forced to conclude, for the time being, that there may be something about the manner of existence Guilt enjoys that makes it in some way impervious to categorisation by such spatial metrics as we humans know how to apply.

This notwithstanding I have of course had the chance to observe Guilt directly myself when it has been visible in the sky from my home in West Sussex. I have a fairly powerful set of binoculars and a fairly low-end telescope, and I have been able to make some notes as to its appearance. As others have found, however, I find that my notes from different periods of observation have been contradictory, yet I have no memory of ever having seen or written down the features contradicted by the later work. Given that Guilt defies conventional scientific knowledge in the first place, it seems not impossible that one of three things is happening: that it is indeed changing, explaining the difference in measurements; that it is by some mechanism interfering with the mechanisms of making or recording said measurements; or that it has some power over the minds of those who observe it, such that even if all instruments function correctly the human who must interpret them is unable to do so coherently.

What seems to remain constant is that it is always uncannily alike in shape to earthly cetaceans. Some say blue whale; others say humpback; still others say sperm or killer whale; I have heard one report claiming to see Guilt as distinctly monodonic - that is to say having a long horn like a narwhal. (The fact that there is no clear agreement even as to with which of the two primary parvorders of cetacea - Mysteceti or Odontoceti - Guilt shares its physical traits would seem astonishing were it not for its above-mentioned sheer refusal to allow anyone to be certain of anything about it.)

To me, as unclear as my sightings of it generally are, it usually appears something like a right whale (also called a black whale) or the beaked family of whales. Nobody has ever seen it from above, of course (excepting perhaps those unfortunate people who were in space when it appeared, and perhaps some might even still be there, surviving on rations but unable to communicate… but that doesn't bear thinking about), but from the views afforded us from below and from a lateral distance looking up, we always expect at least to see two flippers protruding from a long body ending in a tail fin with two horizontal flukes.

As for whether its body might ever be subject to destruction, whether by the ravages of time or by force,

I suppose we may never know. Had we still the technology to launch missiles, might we hope to harm it? I hope it will not seem overconfident if I hazard that I think it unlikely.

CHAPTER SIX - Behaviour

The subject of Guilt's 'behaviour' (the reasons for the quote marks will, I hope, become clear momentarily) remains extremely controversial. There are those who deny that it exhibits any sort of behaviour whatsoever, that it would be functionally identical if it were, say, a large rock or a banana following a similar path through the sky and casting a similar shadow.

I disagree, partly because I fail to see how a rock or a banana could sustain flight (I admit, of course, that most of the whales we know of cannot propel themselves through the *air*, but nonetheless Guilt's visible swimming motions give us at least a viable candidate mechanism both for remaining airborne and for achieving movement in its chosen direction) and partly because I think there is some intentionality to Guilt. I do not think that it is entirely mindless.

(I do, however, think that it would be an anthropomorphological mistake to imagine that it might be able to communicate in any way we could ever possibly comprehend. What would it possibly have to say?)

That said, I know of at least a dozen readers who would think me extremely remiss if I did not include in this errata at least *some* acknowledgement of the popular theory that Guilt is in essence a philosophical zombie or an inanimate object - or, alternatively, the functionalist view that it could be *replaced* with one of these and there would be no discernible difference.

My response to this is really one of simple pragmatism: the fact is that Guilt, in moving around the planet, is playing an active part in the events that go on around it. It is changing situations from one thing to another and not simply *being*; we may have no way, at present, to predict what path it will take (and no real idea as to how it decides, for it does not seem to be searching for food or a mate), but it certainly does *appear* to take one path over another and in so doing alters the environment where its Shadow falls. If this act of transforming the state of things from one position to another is not agency nor behaviour, then let us at least *call* it that as a convenient shorthand. It hardly seems worth the trouble, every time we want to talk about what Guilt is doing, to insist that we specify that it does not really make decisions or behave in any particular way.

I do wonder what humanity would look like to something such as Guilt, if it noticed us at all.

(In the next section, you will note that I tend to refer to the active agent as 'the Shadow' rather than as

'Guilt', partly in deference to those who insist that we can have no possible reason to be certain that Guilt itself has a deliberate or active hand in what transpires within its Shadow.)

CHAPTER NINE - Effects of the Shadow

This is the most difficult topic of all, I suspect.

In this book, I write:

'The only thing that we know for certain about the Shadow of Guilt is that we can never know for certain how it will affect that which falls under it.'

This statement remains, to the best of my knowledge, the true case. It is - well, I might have said 'astonishingly inconsistent', but in fact inconsistency seems very much the *status quo* where Guilt is concerned. At any rate, it is of note the degree to which the Shadow appears to be able to achieve different effects with no apparent contributing factors: no way of looking at things as they were outside the Shadow and deducing what kind of effect the Shadow might have upon them.

As such, I can only imagine that the best I can possibly do here is to simply catalogue some of the effects that the Shadow is reported to have had. Perhaps in the future someone will be able to look back at this and spot some pattern that I cannot.

(The text of the first edition of the book is less methodical, simply stating that 'no matter what the mechanism or the outcome, the fact of the matter is that the Shadow *changes* things, and we must all do all that we can to avoid falling under its influence'. This is still true, of course. I present no theories as to how the Shadow *functions* - or how it creates the effects that it creates - as I cannot see any value in dwelling on what is almost certainly an inscrutable device just as impervious to any kind of useful evaluation as the thing that casts it.)

It is worth noting that in almost all categories of effect, the Shadow seems less efficacious when there is an observer. It is as if it does not like to do its work while it is watched; this is of course extremely difficult to confirm, but there are few reports of a change being directly witnessed as it happens. Things are more inclined to change *when people are not looking*, in other words. However, it could just as easily be the case that those who *see* the changes are more likely to suffer immediate mental or physical incapacitation as a result.

Effects on nonhuman living creatures

Both behavioural and physiological changes are confirmed to take place in animals (and plants, in fact), with no apparent limitation on the range of effects permissible. There is some suggestion that the Shadow has a *tendency* (but not absolute) to adhere roughly to the original shape and mass of the thing it changes - this is the case with all physical changes, whether to animals, humans, or objects - and where a creature was originally, say, a docile dog, Guilt or its Shadow seems to have some awareness of human perceptions of dogs to the extent that it is likely to make that dog's behaviour more like an aggressive wolf (as opposed to, say, making it behave like a honeybee).

The Shadow has no respect for the boundaries of individual creatures, as it is just as dispensed towards combining the bodies of multiple animals as it is towards transforming single ones.

Still, some animals have been known to live through exposure to the Shadow unchanged. It has, although this is far from the right term, an anecdotal fondness for those creatures that might already be considered somewhat peculiar.

Effects on previously non-existing creatures

I perhaps ought to say 'ability to create *new* creatures' here, but that would mean that one heading begins with something other than 'effects' and I prefer neatness and consistency where I can find it (more rare as it is these days).

We all know this, of course, but the Shadow is capable of both transforming beings that already live in the world and creating entities out of (apparently) nothing. It is, I think, notable that there is enormous variance in the degree to which these new beings are indiscernible from ones that might naturally have existed: some are recorded as being impossible to tell apart from 'normal' cats or birds (or, more rarely) humans; others bear familiar shapes but appear to be *made of* some different substance, usually described as 'darkness' or 'shadow' (perhaps unsurprisingly); still others look very much like reported *transformed* iterations of existing creatures; yet others are utterly unlike anything ever to have walked the earth in any capacity. Collectively these are commonly known as the Children of Guilt. Whether they are in any technical sense its progeny is unclear, and the origins of the *First* Children even less so.

Where these new beings come from, and of what they are made, is impossible to examine, since they only ever spawn in areas that have been at one stage or another under the Shadow and that are therefore resistant to study on the grounds of frequently failing to correspond to expected norms. There have been accounts of witnessed spawnings, people claiming to have seen them *forming*, often either by appearing out of a darkened area or a sort of congealing process: imagine if you will a glass into which is poured a thick viscous liquid, and the slow taking-shape that the contents do in the bottom of the glass is, as I understand it, an image which bears some relation to how the *shadow-stuff* forms itself into a physical entity.

The new creations brought into life (or some approximation) by the Shadow are frequently, though not without exception, both highly dangerous and highly aggressive. There are few reports of Shadow-beasts that did *not* either attack on sight or caused some sort of non-immediate harmful effect, although these reports do exist. Some who have seen 'peaceful' creatures of the Shadow even seem to have found the event quite awe-inspiring. Of course, those people were usually in close proximity to the Shadow themselves, so their memory or emotions may not be entirely reliable.

Effects on living humans

As with animals, the Shadow is capable of transformative effects on both the mental and physical characteristics of a human. The former seems (anecdotally) more common, although this may be selection bias on account of the fact that those who are physically transformed tend not to survive.

The sole effect that seems to be universal among all who spend any time under the Shadow is a heightened sense of anxiety and paranoia, but this is easily explained as a perfectly rational response to an extremely dangerous situation. It would be odd if a sound-minded person who found themselves thus shrouded did *not* react with panic.

A litany of intellectual, emotional, and behavioural symptoms have been seen to be induced, even in those with no history or propensity towards such things.

Those who exhibit obvious changes in cognition may become dangerous, but less so than those who continue to act as if they were unaffected until some nefarious motive is revealed. People under the Shadow's influence are more than capable of retaining their ability to communicate cogently, to the point of any change being undetectable; this allows them to manipulate those around them for harmful ends.

It seems that many of the individuals who have appeared lucid while working towards goals that would not usually be within their interests have undergone a sort of perceptual shift, following which they perceive Guilt as natural, good, or even deific. I only hope that this is not happening on a wider scale than we might believe; imagine a world in which many (perhaps even the majority of) people are secretly working towards some goal under Guilt's direction. It does not seem impossible, but my intuition is that it would be unlikely to be a *good thing*.

There are (for what this is worth, as I have already alluded to the difficulty of drawing any conclusions from the existing accounts in the absence of many more that might have been made were those who could have made them not incapacitated by the experience) fewer reports of physical transformation in human bodies than in non-humans. More frequent appear to be attacks on living, untransformed humans by changed or newly spawned beasts, or other living humans whose minds have been altered.

Only time will tell what might happen to those humans who are affected in strange ways by the Shadow. Many will likely be destroyed, either by the immediate effects of the transformation or by those who do not wish to be killed by them. As for the inevitable few who survive… who can say?

Effects on deceased humans

It may never be possible to know exactly what differences are experienced by those who are no longer living. If they continue to exist in some form, it does not seem entirely outside the realms of possibility that the Shadow can affect them even beyond their natural lives.

What *has* been observed is the reanimation of deceased bodies, after which point they can be affected in any of the ways described under the section on non-human animals. There have also been many reports of people hearing the voices of deceased friends or relatives, often saying extremely unpleasant things, but whether this is in fact any genuine visitation of the dead, some sort of echo generated by the Shadow without reference to the original, or mere hallucination on the part of the listener (who thus does all the 'work' in creating the voice, with no real interaction between the Shadow and the deceased individual) may be extremely difficult to determine.

Effects on inanimate objects

One peculiar comment that can be made on the Shadow's treatment of inanimates is that it seems to tend towards effects which appear designed to cause the most distress to the living beings who can *perceive* those inanimates. This is somewhat anecdotal, particularly when accounting for the fact that *any* effect tends to be distressing to a witness who is unused to seeing things behave in a way that appears contrary to usual physical norms, and certainly there are many known cases of things changing in ways that do not seem directed at all. Commonly, a physical object will exhibit some sort of 'melting' or dissolution, changing its shape in a nonspecific way so that it is no longer the same as it was, but neither is it any particular new shape.

What, then, do I mean by the first sentence in this section? Only that there is a proportion higher than would be expected from random chance of incidents in which objects have become things which are frightening only to a person who understands their meaning. Any object upon which words are written is this, as is any instance of one thing becoming another with a distinct and discrete function or representation:

a weapon, for instance, or a statue shaped like a person in pain.

Locations too are inanimate objects, of course, and the effect of the Shadow on many parts of the world has been enormous. Topographies have changed; rivers have been redirected; strange and malicious plantlike life has grown to cover some areas; the gravitational influence exerted by the physical mass of Guilt itself has changed the tides, which has in turn had an effect on several landmasses and coastal regions. Each time Guilt passes over an area, the Shadow iterates upon the changes it had already made: I predict that in a few generations' time, when Guilt has had ample opportunity to cast the Shadow multiple times over many parts of the world, the geography of the planet will be *significantly* far removed from what it is now.

While on the subject of locations, I ought also to mention the recorded episodes featuring transformation of a domiciliary or internal (that is, contained within the walls of a building) environment. This will be covered in the next section.

Effects on 'laws of nature'

I surround the phrase '*laws of nature*' with quote marks here because Guilt has made it awfully clear that all the things we believed to be rules are far more flexible than we had thought.

To continue from the previous section, let us first turn our attention to *buildings*, a particular sort of location usually marked by a definitive interior topography. That is to say, a person familiar with the internal arrangement of rooms within a certain set of walls is generally able to find their way from one place to another reliably and by following the same route. When the Shadow is in effect, this is less frequently the case than might under usual circumstances be hoped.

Although I was never myself much of a consumer of electronic games, I am aware that in some (frequently of the horror genre) games there existed digital locations which did not operate on standard geometries, and this is much like the approach the Shadow takes in its alteration of buildings. It is possible, when in a building under the Shadow, to enter a door and pass, let us say, from room A to room B, and then to go back through the door in the other direction and pass from room B to room C, or even to a different door in room B. Space is bent, in other words: passages can be looped, extended, transposed, removed entirely, or any number of other effects. It is as if the floorplan of an affected building were made of pieces of mouldable putty, each of which could be reshaped and repositioned (and indeed recreated) in any way the moulder chose, and the boundaries moved in a way that does not cohere with the outside. In other words, a room can be stretched to be much larger than normal internally without the walls of the building, or its overall size, being affected.

Again, it may be impossible to verify whether geometry is truly altered *per se* or whether it is simply the observer's perceptions of space that are affected, but enough reports exist of this as a distinct phenomenon that I am inclined to believe it does happen.

Spatial relations are not the only member of the category of things that we would usually take to be just about as incontrovertible as anything is capable of being. Gravity, the solidity or permeability of any given substance, perhaps even time: to some extent, any previously-held *rule* of physics is malleable. That said, it does seem that some rules are harder to break than others. There are far more reports of the aforementioned geometrical shifting than there are of obvious contraventions of the laws of thermodynamics, for example. We should be grateful that the Shadow seems to lack either the power or the inclination to simply dissolve all the molecular connections between all the substances making up the Earth and everything on it.

Permanent vs transient effects

Of the types of effects listed thus far, there are none which *occur for the first time* when the Shadow is not directly cast upon the object of the effect. (As I mention in the main text, however, note that a thing can have the Shadow cast on it even if there is no *visible* umbra and penumbra - if it is a cloudy day, for example. It also bears repeating that the Shadow can continue to take effect even during the night to some extent, with effects continuing to occur in the region that *would* be enshadowed were the Sun overhead, and perhaps it is for this same reason that the influence of the Shadow seems to extend to some degree throughout each day to those parts of the world that are beneath it at different points of the Sun's journey through the sky. There are no changes to this part of the book since the original publication, so I shall dwell on it no further.)

There are some effects which persist beyond the point that Guilt is no longer visible in the sky, perhaps even interminably. Creatures spawned in the Shadow continue to exist in many cases - some disappear once Guilt is no longer overhead, but particularly those more clearly corporeal in nature seem to maintain their existence unless destroyed. Objects whose shape has been changed tend to remain fixed in the new shape. People who have been mentally affected sometimes recover immediately, sometimes with time, and sometimes never. People and other living creatures who have been physically altered do not frequently return to their previous forms.

On the other hand, no case has *ever* been reported of geometric alteration occurring when the Shadow is not immediately present, for example: buildings cannot continue to possess rooms larger on the inside than on the outside, although if they have been *physically* affected (thus falling into the category of inanimate-object effect rather than law-of-nature effect) then these changes are likely to remain.

Indirect effects on humans who have not been under the Shadow
This is the most pervasive type of effect and the most dangerous. Since I wrote the first edition of this book, there have sprung up more and more groups of people who have never (as far as anyone has been able to tell) been in the Shadow and have thus never had the opportunity to be directly influenced or changed, and yet have still decided to worship Guilt (for example). The fact is that the presence of Guilt is a thing of such singular global importance that it is able to have an astounding effect on the behaviour of both individuals and societies even without ever coming into direct contact.

Naturally, one enormously important ramification of the appearance of Guilt has been that most of human society is now dedicated almost exclusively to preserving human existence in the face of an extremely dangerous threat, and this is the case in all parts of the world even when Guilt is not immediately present.

Most people, quite reasonably, now live in near-constant fear for their futures, their lives, and the fates of those around them, and so the efforts of most productive groups are devoted to ensuring the continued availability of necessities such as food, shelter, and so on (including the maintenance of multiple viable settlements, since the Shadow falling over a single location containing all residences and resources would be disastrous; relatedly, the energy of any such group should also be directed towards planning for quick evacuations).

The threat that all living people face in this new world is not, however, homogenous by any means. Not only are the direct dangers of Guilt and its Shadow varied (as this entire section has been discussing), but the other remaining humans are also more likely to present a danger. I shall not dedicate space to discussing why, as that seems to me not to fall within the scope of this book, but I have heard some truly disturbing stories about the things that people are now capable of - far more unsettling than the strangest tale of Guilt.

CHAPTER ELEVEN - The First Children

I have relatively little to say on this topic, as will be evident from a passing glance at the length of the chapter comparative to the others. What more could there be to say on the topic of the metal wyrms than the plaintive cries uttered by the entire planet at their arrival?

I did not see the First Children with my own eyes when they first appeared. I was lucky to live very far from the nearest 'hub' of wireless transmission; I felt the quake of the first strike, and I believe I may have caught a glimpse of a red glint rapidly disappearing over the horizon, but I was among the luckier inhabitants of the Earth in that I survived that time without having encountered one of the dragons.

Their ability to detect transmissions (including, at least, Wi-Fi, telephone calls, SMS messages, satellite communications, broadcasts on any radio frequency, and even high concentrations of electronic signals sent through wires rather than wirelessly) is notable, but it does not bear further comment. The truly odd thing about them, in my opinion, remains the scarcity of their actions. I am still aware, in the years since the first edition was published, of no confirmed instances of the First Children moving from the spots in which they have hibernated since settling down after those first days of attacks.

It is almost tempting to test whether they would be awoken by any further transmissions. Are they asleep? Dormant? Waiting? I am not, however, so curious as to think it a good idea to enlist three extremely dangerous dragons to play the part of dependent variables in my experiments.

CHAPTER FIFTEEN - Future Predictions

I wish only to let it be known that I think it entirely futile to make predictions about what Guilt might do or be in the future. Do not even try. I would not even guarantee that Guilt could not achieve things herein declared impossible simply to disprove anyone who thought it incapable of any particular thing; it is such an exceptional thing that I cannot see why not. If a proton can change its behaviour based on observation, might not the strangest creature ever known to the world be able to warp anything within or without human conception based on what humans happen to think of it?

I do not claim that this *is* the case, but I cannot disprove that it is not, and so I would prefer no further speculation. I have already said too much, I imagine, were that the case, but I think the risk worth taking if I can spread at least some correct information to someone, somewhere. Perhaps it will save a life, somehow.

***

And that, I think, is that. I cannot say that I hope you enjoy this edition of 'Characterising Guilt', but I hope that it is of some value.

***

From: Davi Backenden
To: Allena Lossen-Kama
Subject: You won't get this but
Alli

I don't know why I'm typing this. It's not like there's any Internet any more.

But if you can find a copy of a book called 'Characterising Guilt', you gotta read it. It's, like, the worst thing. This guy might actually think he can *intellectualise* the giant fucking space whale. And then he has the balls to release a second edition correcting a bunch of the bullshit from the previous one!

You'd love it. It's the worst.

I miss you.

Davi

Chris Durston

APPENDIX: INTRODUCTION TO THE THIRD EDITION OF 'CHARACTERISING GUILT'

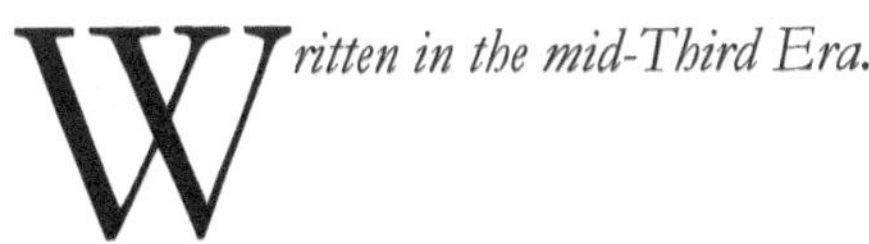

ritten in the mid-Third Era.

This is the third edition of 'Characterising Guilt', a book written many hundreds or thousands of years ago by someone who had no idea what was going on.

It took a long time to translate, but we got there in the end. We weren't always sure why we were bothering, to be honest - what could we learn from a centuries-old book that we hadn't all seen for ourselves many times over? As it turned out, not much.

The most interesting thing about 'Characterising Guilt' is how very wrong it is about almost everything. Well - perhaps that's unfair. It's frequently *not quite wrong,* but also not correct. There are observations that presumably match up with the observed state of things at the time, but the extrapolations and conclusions are almost universally way off.

Amusingly, the author was aware to some degree that they were getting things wrong, but tried to correct this by asserting new things that were also mostly wrong. The second edition begins with a catalogue of errors in the first (inexhaustive, perhaps by design or laziness or perhaps because the sheer scope of the wrongness just wasn't known); ultimately, the biggest mistake committed by the author in both versions is assuming that there could be any kind of scope, limitation, or explanatory factor to anything Guilt does.

We present the translated text of 'Characterising Guilt' to you now, unedited as far as possible - not as a manual or informative document, as seems to have been the original purpose, but as a bit of didactic satire. Look back on humanity, as it was when Guilt was new, and learn from its eagerness to assume it knew anything.

WARNINGS BY SECTION

This is an earnest effort to include as much information as I possibly can about content to which some readers may not want to be exposed. If I have missed anything, that is entirely my fault and I apologise - please let me know, and I'll maintain an up-to-date list on my website at chrisdurston.com.

Those stories with no warnings are still set in a world where human civilisation has largely been destroyed, so if you are averse to apocalyptic situations or near-constant peril of various kinds, it may be that this book won't be for you.

THE COMING OF GUILT
large-scale disaster and death

CHILDREN
child in danger, adult death

WHAT GUILT WANTED
unpleasant eating, gory murder, body horror

WORST PARTY EVER
gory injury and death, surreal horror, body horror

TODAY MY GIRLFRIEND TURNED INTO A TREE
body transformation

MY FRIEND, THE MOON
one mention of body transformation, reference to humans dying and being eaten, surreal horror

A GAME NOT WORD PLAYING
none

THAT WHICH I SAY, YOU UNDERSTAND
none

HYPOTHESES ON THE ORIGINS OF GUILT
none

THE STORM ON THE SEA
peril at sea, peaceful death, sea creatures

A MENAGERIE ALL IN ONE
body horror (animal and human), death

THE PEOPLE AND THE PEOPLE
mention of bigotry

THEORY AND PRACTICE
death (albeit somewhat slapstick)

TWICE
suicide

EXPLOITING THE SOURCE OF PLENTY
none

HE SITS ATOP THE PLANET
none

LOST TIME
existential dread (time, ageing)

IT MUST BE DONE
death

OH, THE PLACES I'VE SEEN
none

STAINED GLASS
body horror

THE KING OF WASTED YEARS
peaceful death

AN IMPROPER SCEPTIC
none

Chronicles from the World of Guilt

THE POLYPOD
harm to an animal

INFORMATION HAZARD
implication of horrific death

VALUE IS IN THE THOUSAND EYES OF THE
VAST BEHOLDER
none

TITANFELL
death of an animal

AFTER THE TIME OF GUILT
remains of a deceased animal

APPENDIX: FOREWORD AND ERRATA
FROM THE SECOND EDITION OF
CHARACTERISING GUILT
discussion of transformation of humans and animals

APPENDIX: INTRODUCTION TO THE
THIRD EDITION OF CHARACTERISING
GUILT
none

About the author:

Chris Durston is a writer, editor, and occasional musician from the South West of England, where (like everyone else who lives there) he spends his days scrumping, his nights cow-tipping, and the intervening periods hiding from irate farmers. His debut novel Each Little Universe was self-published in April 2020 and republished by Skullgate Media in October 2021; his short stories appear in half a dozen or so other places. Future projects (as of the time of writing - with any luck, at least some of these will now be in your present) include work on storytelling card game Woad: Stone to Stone, more novels and whatnot, and Cthulhu Dreamt 2, a collaborative multimedia project including a metal album, a novel, and a role-playing game. Find him at chrisdurston.com or on Twitter as @chrisdurstonish.

www.ingramcontent.com/pod-product-compliance
Lightning Source LLC
Chambersburg PA
CBHW030708190726
48286CB00001B/219